Yes, Captain

Book 1.5 Rule of Three

Ann Grech

Blurb

A cruise ship captain with an unbreakable rule. A dancer who tempts him to toss the rulebook overboard...

Will Preston lives by one edict: don't date staff.

But the new dancer onboard has the silver fox sailing into unchartered waters. Young, sexy, and with a penchant for lipstick and heels, the man pushes all Will's buttons.

It's not just the tropical sun that's heating things up; their chemistry is sizzling.

Will's been burned before. Can he throw caution to the wind and chart a new course with Eddie by his side? Or will an interfering crew-member steer them into stormy seas?

Yes, Captain is a stand-alone, steamy age-gap MM romance set on a cruise ship in the South Pacific, with a flirty dancer who loves pole dancing and his shy captain. Yes, Captain was previously published as Dance With Me. This re-release includes over 30,000 words of never-before-seen bonus content.

To my amazing hubby.
I can't wait to spend another holiday in paradise
with you and the kiddos.

ACKNOWLEDGEMENTS

This story was inspired by a trip we took on the Carnival Spirit a few years ago. It was ten days in absolute paradise sailing around the most perfect of tropical islands. Lifou was my favourite, and I was glad to share it with Will and Eddie.

Thank you to the team of stars who help me with my books—Becky Johnston and the team at Hot Tree Editing you manage to turn my mess of a manuscript into polished perfection. Linda Russell and the team from Foreword PR, your patience and good humour when I am pulling my hair out because I can't find the right cover images and God help me figuring out the titles! Tracy Reeds from Be My Book Boyfriend for all your help and keeping me on track. I appreciate it, honey. Clarise Tan from CT Cover Creations, you create magic from my haphazard ideas. Thank you!

Thank you also to my beautiful friends and inspiration providers, Viva Gold, LJ Harris, JJ Harper, Angelique Jurd, Tracy McKay and Megs Pritchard. Thank you for your advice, motivation and most of all, your friendship. I'm grateful every day for you being in my life.

To my hubby and kiddos, I couldn't do this without your support. You're with me for all the highs and lows. I love you all to the moon and back.

Last and most certainly not least, thank you to you, the readers and bloggers, for your unending love and support. Sharing, reviews, general shout outs and, importantly, reading our words means the world to every author.

Ann xx

ONE

Eddie

Twelve Years Ago

Eddie cried quietly in the room he shared with his two brothers. He was the middle child of five, an older brother and sister and a younger set of each too. But none of them suffered like he did. His brothers were stocky while he was slim and almost delicate. Even his sisters were made of a stouter build than Eddie. And the bullies took every opportunity to remind him of that. Eddie reached up from under his bed, feeling around until his fingertips touched the blanket off his bed that he liked to sleep with. The texture of it—silky and soft—made him feel safe and warm. He pulled the blanket down and rolled as best as he could, wrapping himself up tightly in the confined space between the bottom bunk and the floor.

Eddie tried to block out the pain. It wouldn't do to tell his parents this time. The last time had made things worse. Now it wasn't only the constant taunts that hurt, but the bruises too. And they were getting worse.

Duncan had nearly popped his shoulder out this time, twisting his arm behind him and pulling his elbow up. His shoulder had screamed in pain, but Eddie had bitten on his tongue until he'd tasted blood, not uttering a sound while his muscles and probably bones, too, teetered on the edge of snapping. Eddie wished he could say he didn't know what it was for, but he did. The last time it was because he'd been giggling with Jess, picking out which of the boys in the class above them were cute. Duncan's older brother, the blond god and sports superstar, was both their number one pick. Eddie had whispered that he'd love for him to be Eddie's first kiss. Jess had agreed, biting her lip and blushing. She'd pashed her friend Julie once before, but never a boy.

They thought they were quiet, sitting on the floor in the library huddled between the stacks, the big hardback books propped up on their knees like a shield. But Duncan's side-kick, Harry, had overheard them. He must have been in the row behind because if either one of them had seen him, they both would have scampered away. The two boys were the schoolyard bullies, and Eddie and Jess tried their hardest to hide from them.

It hadn't worked this time though. They'd waited until after school when the grounds were almost deserted, save for the few students who did art and dance classes.

Duncan's brother had set his mates on Jess, following her after her photography lessons. The four of them had kissed and groped her until she'd begged them to let her go, her terrified cries echoing through the deserted buildings. She'd been surrounded, pushed from one to the other, her knees grazed and her palms bleeding from being shoved down onto the ground. Eddie had happened on them as he'd been walking to his dance lessons, wandering through the near-empty school grounds. One of the boys had taken a step closer, bending down and pinning her shoulders to the concrete. Eddie had reacted purely on instinct, dropping his duffel and launching himself at them. He'd tried to fight them off, kicking and punching the much bigger boys. That was until Duncan and Harry had dragged him off their older brothers and their mates, pushed him face first into the dirt, and kicked him until it hurt to breathe. He didn't know what had spooked them or why they'd stopped before they'd killed either one of them, but they had. Whatever it was, it had sent the boys skulking away, leaving Eddie and Jess scared and bleeding on the ground.

Jess didn't come to school the next day or the day after that. Her mum had called his and explained that Jess was going to start at a different school in a few weeks after her bruises had healed. It was the first time they would be separated for longer than a couple of days since they'd met in primary school. He'd wanted to move away from the secondary school too, but his mum and dad didn't have the money to get him into the exclusive private one. He'd offered to give up his dance lessons—all of them—for the chance to get him out of there, but his parents hadn't agreed. Instead, they'd gone to the school and made a big deal out of what had happened. When Eddie wanted to sink into the shadows, they'd dragged him into the spotlight, insisting on meeting with both Duncan and Harry's parents and making the bigger boys apologize to him.

That was the reason why he'd been pinned up against the brick wall, and his arm twisted until it nearly popped out of its socket. He'd already missed a few dance lessons. Now he was probably going to miss the concert too. He couldn't dance if his shoulder was buggered.

He knew his parents were worried about him, but their attempts to be helpful were only making things worse. They'd asked his big sister, Maggie, to keep an eye out for him during school. She was three grades above him and took her responsibilities seriously too. She'd want him to hang around with her group of friends so she could mother him. It wasn't bad enough that he was a loner now and the tiny kid—skinny with soft features and a grace that years of dance lessons had drummed into him. Now he had to hang around with his sister too. As if he needed anything else to get picked on for. Duncan and Harry were already relentless enough.

Eddie cried harder, biting down on the blanket to muffle the noise when he heard footsteps in the room and the door close. A big hand closed over his arm and rubbed gently. "You all right, lad?" his dad asked softly, his voice warm and soothing like hot cocoa.

"Leave me alone," Eddie whispered, sniffling and trying to wipe away the tears that refused to stop falling.

"Nah," he huffed. "Come to check up on you." Eddie hissed but didn't struggle when his dad gently tugged on his sore arm, shuffling him out from under the bed.

"What's wrong with your arm?"

"It just hurts a bit." Eddie cried harder when his dad cradled him in his arms right there on the floor.

His dad sighed. "I'm sorry, son. If we could do anything more, your mum and I would."

"Please don't." Eddie gasped in terror. "They'll do it again."

"Same boys, huh?" His dad growled, tensing beside Eddie.

"I'm sorry," Eddie whispered. He squeezed his eyes tightly closed as he trembled against his dad's broad form. "I wish I wasn't like this."

His dad reared back like he'd been slapped. "Like what, son? You're smart and fun, and you're an incredible dancer. You light up the stage when you perform."

"They keep calling me a faggot. I'm skinny and weak. I'm not like you or Jack or Noah. I'm not like them. Maybe if I was good at football rather than dancing, they wouldn't care who I liked."

"Listen to me, Eddie." His dad shifted Eddie, lifting him onto the bed and sitting down next to him. Grasping Eddie's good hand, his dad brushed a lock of hair off his face with his other before he spoke. "Dancing doesn't make you less of a man. Neither does liking boys. Hurting someone does.

Those boys who hurt Jess, who hurt you, they're scared, weak little shites. They're hooligans." Then his eyes met Eddie's, and he smiled. "As for who you like, I don't care what gender they are, as long as they treat you right. You hear me?"

"They do though." Eddie closed his eyes as more hot tears fell from them. His lip trembled, and he wanted to crawl back into his dad's arms. His dad seemed to know what he needed, lying down next to him and scooping Eddie in his arms again, and holding him close.

"I know, son," he whispered into his hair. "I want to tell you that if you ignore them, they'll leave you alone, or they'll leave you alone if you fight back." He rubbed his big hand up and down Eddie's back. The small move comforted Eddie more than he could have known. "The truth is that I don't know what will make them bugger off. But I can tell you this—you are strong. These boys... they're intimidated by how talented and incredible you are. One day you'll leave this place. You'll perform all over the world. You'll bring people happiness, and you'll be up on a stage loving every minute of it." He squeezed Eddie's hand and blushed. "And maybe you'll remember this conversation as the time when your old man was the most proud of you."

"Why?" Eddie scoffed, "I'm lying here crying because I'm scared that they'll break something next time they get their hands on me."

"No." His dad shook his head and smiled. "Because you just came out to me, and that takes guts."

Eddie opened his mouth, ready to deny it, but he'd said the words. He'd been so wrapped up in how to get away from the other boys that he hadn't censored himself. He hadn't protected that piece of him that he'd only ever revealed to Jess. "You aren't disappointed?"

"Never. You hear me? Never." His dad's gaze never left Eddie's. Never wavered. There was no hesitation in his words either. With a grin and a chuckle when Eddie groaned, his dad ruffled his hair and added, "I'll give you the safe sex talk another time. But for now, I'll tell you this—" His voice turned serious, his gaze boring into Eddie as if he was imploring him to understand. "You aren't alone. Your mum and me, your brothers and sisters—we'll always be here for you. There's a whole community of rainbow folk too. You'll find them, and you'll see that the insults those boys are throwing around are just stupid words spoken by insecure children. There's nothing wrong with being attracted to boys, or girls, or both. God made you exactly the way you were meant to be, and we love you no matter what."

Eddie let out the breath burning his lungs. The hand that his dad held shook, and he clenched his jaw to stop the sob from breaking free from his chest. Instead, he shifted closer, practically crawling onto his dad like he'd done as a wee baby and clutched him close. The tears came nevertheless, but his dad's arms around him were everything he needed. "Thank you," he whispered. "I was scared to tell you."

"Your mum and I kind of guessed a while ago."

"Why? Because I like dancing?" It was the same conclusion Duncan and Harry had reached, except they hadn't known the truth until Harry had overheard him and Jess talking.

"No." He laughed. "Because you drew love hearts on your sister's poster of that boy band. Who were they again?"

"One D," Eddie supplied, then realized that he'd just admitted to knowing exactly what poster his dad was talking about. "Adele did that," he lied.

"No, she didn't." His dad smiled and whispered conspiratorially, "Your mum saw you doodling on it but didn't say anything. She didn't want to force you to tell us before you were ready."

"Thanks, Dad," he mumbled. "I was still scared to tell you even though it's probably obvious to everyone."

"People will run their mouths without thinking and let their minds take them to some strange places. You can't stop people doing that. But you can control what you think and do. Stop living for them and live for you. Be proud of who you are." His dad tweaked Eddie's nose. "I'm proud of you, and so is your mum." He leaned down and kissed his forehead. "Now, how about we ice that shoulder so you can dance at the concert and get some ice cream into you."

* * * * *

The applause from the crowd was deafening. It wasn't the first time Eddie had danced in a theatre, but this one was bigger than anything he'd ever been in before. Tiered seating extended up with row upon row of filled seats. The two giant screens facing the audience illuminated the first few rows, letting him see the faces in the crowd. He spotted his parents and brothers and sisters cheering him on. Jess too. All of them were standing now with the other families in an ovation that rejuvenated itself like waves on a beach—cresting and washing over them again every time it started to peter out. The stage lights dimmed and screens blacked out, lengthening the shadows onstage as the long red velvet curtains on either side of them began to close smoothly.

Eddie couldn't wipe the smile from his face, even as the curtain slowed to a stop, separating the dancers and elite public school orchestra from the audience. He never wanted the performance to end. He was bouncing out of his skin, giddy with an adrenaline high. His shoulder had held up, thanks to his mum strapping it tightly, and he'd pulled every move off with a perfection he'd never dared hope for.

This was it.

His moment.

Pride welled inside him, a foreign feeling to Eddie. He'd persevered. He'd pushed through the taunts and teasing, the fear of getting beaten to a pulp again to make it this far. Now that he knew what it was like to dance on a big stage, he wanted to do again and again. He never wanted to stop.

The lessons were gruelling, rehearsals more so. Pain had become a constant. Blisters and strained muscles and torn ligaments were things he dealt with daily. But like a path being lit before him, he knew that this concert was only the beginning of his journey. Tonight's performance had crystalized what he already knew in his mind—his future was on a stage. This was him. Eddie was a dancer. He was put on this earth to perform.

And he'd done it defiantly wearing a rainbow pin.

There was no doubt in Eddie's mind that everyone had seen it. The cameras had beamed their images to the screens on either side of the stage, emblazoning him in fine detail to every seat in the theatre. He'd done it despite his dance teacher's insistence to remove it from his full-body white Lycra costume. There were important people in the audience, she'd said, and she didn't want any political statements being made. Eddie didn't care whether he was making a broader political statement. The pin for him was acutely personal. This was him owning every part of himself. His dad's support and the conversation he'd had with his mum later that same night had empowered him. She'd opened up his world, given him a name for what he was other than faggot, and called up a support line with him to prove that he wasn't alone. She showed him that his people were out there. So, this was him taking back control from his bullies. Whatever happened from then on, he'd face it head-on and be bloody fabulous doing it.

His dance teacher waited with a lady on the sidelines. Wearing a pantsuit, she looked out of place next to his dance teacher in her brightly coloured flowing kaftan layered with mismatched scarves and leggings to ward off the chill of the autumn air. The clipboard the lady held caught his attention. Bottle green with a logo emblazoned on it in gold, he couldn't see what it was, but he recognized the outline of a pointed toe in ballet slippers. His teacher waved him over. "Go get your parents, Eddie. This nice lady wants to talk to you all."

He looked at the stranger, assessing her. Why did she want to speak with them? She shifted and smiled, and Eddie's heart stopped beating. RCA—Royal College of the Arts—was printed on the folder. The school for talented artists and performers of every persuasion. The dream destination for every dancer, singer, musician, writer, artist, you name it. Eddie's eyes widened, and he looked up at her. When she nodded in encouragement, he sprinted to the edge of the stage, leaping off it, and raced out through the door into the theatre. Scanning the empty rows and crowds meandering out to the foyer of the grand old building, he shouted, "Penny, Charlie!" Heads turned, and he saw his parents. Waving at them and bouncing on his feet, he pleaded with them, excitement pitching his voice higher. "I need you. Come quick!"

People shifted, and their group bucked the tide of people, travelling towards the front of the stage once more. When they were in front of him, Eddie couldn't contain his excitement anymore. "There's someone here from RCA. They want to talk to you. About me. C'mon, let's go." He grabbed his dad's sport jacket and tugged on the sleeve, dragging him along with him.

"Calm down, son. We're coming." Eddie threw a look over his shoulder and saw his dad's excited grin. "This is it, Eddie. The next step."

And he was right.

TWO

Will

TEN YEARS AGO

Exhaustion washed over him as the lift doors slid open on the seventh floor. His blinks were getting longer, each one painful. The grit from the dry plane air scratched the sensitive surface of his eyes with each slow movement. Will needed a shower and a bloody long sleep. His three-month rotation onboard the cruise ship had been brutal. Like any FIFO worker, he needed a few days to sleep away the virtually relentless sixteen-hour days. The twenty-hour flight stuck in cattle class between two much larger, albeit shorter people, one of whom had used him as a pillow, hadn't helped. He didn't sleep a wink the entire flight.

Will slumped against the front door and fumbled the keys, dropping them onto the mottled brown carpet that hadn't been changed since the eighties. His hands weren't working properly; his brain was operating in survival mode with one message only: sleep.

He knocked, but no one answered.

Groaning as he reached for the keys, every muscle in his body protested the movement. Will clutched them and managed to slide the right one into the lock of the Seattle apartment he shared with his husband. All he wanted was to fall into Stefan's arms. He'd missed him. Missed his fiery temper, acerbic tongue, and quick wit. Missed the passion that ignited between them like an out of control wildfire when they were in the same room. He missed seeing Stefan in the morning, pulling every piece of clothing out of his wardrobe until he found the perfect combination for his mood. He had a dress sense that many would find garish, but Will was envious of it. He couldn't pull off that flamboyant a style. The mix of bright colours and pastels, tight jeans, and sexy stiletto heels were too loud for Will's more muted fashion choices.

The click of the teeth sliding into place in the lock was loud in the silent hallway. It wasn't late—barely past nine at night—but the neighbours were all safely ensconced in their warm apartments. He turned the knob and pushed the door open. The two lamps on either side of their couch were set to low, the heavy curtains drawn closed, a barrier to the winter chill that would steal through the apartment given a chance. Closing the door quietly, he shrugged off his coat and scarf and slid the gloves off his hands. Before stepping away from the tiled square at his front door, he kicked his boots off and sighed at the warmth that had already begun to defrost his bones. Winter in Seattle was brutal, especially when he'd come directly from the tropical summer of the Coral and Timor Seas. The temperature was four times the maximum daily that Seattle typically reached at that time of year.

A moan sounded from the bedroom, and Will's lips turned up. Stefan was proudly sexual, and their chemistry was off the charts. The first time they'd met—Stefan on the dancefloor of a club and Will admiring him from the sidelines—was burned into Will's brain. He'd been swept up in Stefan's magnetism and presence, and as soon as he'd gotten close, Will couldn't keep his hands off the man. It hadn't taken them long before they were hooking up every time Will was onshore, and they'd been quick to elope too. A drunken night out was to thank for that, but Will had never regretted his one act of impulsiveness, even if it did strain his relationship with his parents.

Smiling, Will stripped off his hoodie and the long-sleeved tee he wore underneath it. He unbuttoned his jeans, palming his growing erection as he listened to the sounds Stefan was making.

Will pushed open the partly closed door and froze. Like in the loungeroom, the bedside lamps were set low. But even though the light was dim, there was no mistaking the picture before him. A stranger lay on his back, the other man—his husband—straddling him. Naked, sweaty, and moving as one, Stefan rode him, the bloke's fat cock sliding in and out of Stefan with every rock of his husband's hips. Will opened his mouth, but no words came. His body flushed hot, shock boiling through his system before it instantly turned to ice when he looked to the point where they were connected. The dude buried in Stefan was bare. He'd been on PreP—they both had—but they'd stopped taking it after they were married. He didn't think it was necessary anymore; Stefan had agreed. How wrong he was.

Will slumped against the doorframe and blew out a pained breath, his chest constricting like a vice around his heart, the organ breaking into a million pieces. And in his bubble with his lover, Stefan still moved, riding the guy's dick as he arched his slim back and moaned again. "Yes, that's it," he hissed, his voice breathy. Will knew that tone. His husband was close to coming apart in another man's arms.

"So tight," the other moaned.

He couldn't watch anymore. Disgust turned his stomach, and betrayal left a sour taste in his mouth. Leaving his suitcase at the door, he staggered away, bumping into the wall as he made it to the couch, the same one they'd picked out and christened the moment the delivery blokes were out the door. They hadn't even unwrapped the plastic that first time. Defeat warred with exhaustion, and his mind short-circuited. His legs wouldn't carry him any further. He slumped in the seat and rested his elbows on his knees. Hung his head low and rubbed his eyes, wiping away the tears tracking down his cheeks. He hated himself for crying; he didn't even have the energy to, but he couldn't help it. Will tried to block the noises from the bedroom from his brain.

He failed miserably.

Moans and skin slapping together, the creak of their bed and the bang of the headboard as his husband and the stranger fucked their way to a climax. When Stefan's shout rent the air, Will lurched forward, vomiting on the rug. His guts heaved, and more came up, emptying his stomach's contents at his feet.

"What the fuck?" asked a voice he didn't recognize at the same time as his husband uttered, "Oh, shit."

Quick footsteps on the carpeted floor sounded, and Will looked up, glassy-eyed and wavering in the seat. "You're early," Stefan said matter of factly, his ire obvious. He stood before Will, naked as the day he was born, his hand on his hip and cum dripping down the inside of his leg. The man behind Stefan was a foot taller than his husband, broader in the shoulders too, a glare on his face.

"How long?" Will rasped, motioning between the two of them with a flick of his wrist.

"Doesn't matter," Stefan replied, turning his nose up at Will.

Will shook his head, his thoughts bouncing around in his brain like a bad pinball machine. "No, you're right. It doesn't matter." He stood on shaky legs and headed for the bathroom. He winced when he flicked the lights on; they were far too bright for his sensitive eyes. Will looked at himself in the mirror and groaned. Dark circles highlighted the sallow tone of his skin. He splashed water on his face, barely feeling its chill. Will looked down at his wet hands and noticed them shaking, but he couldn't feel it. Numbness had set in, giving him an almost out-of-body sensation. He blinked slowly and reached for the mouthwash, pausing for a moment when he noticed an unfamiliar toothbrush in the holder alongside his husband's. This bloke had been living in their apartment. Will wondered what Stefan had planned—would he have told him? Or would all evidence of the other man have disappeared before Will returned home?

Rinsing his mouth out, he heard angry whispers in the hallway and huffed out a humourless laugh. It was as if he was the one doing the wrong thing. Maybe it was. Maybe he shouldn't have tried to surprise Stefan by coming home a day early. It was a fluke that it'd happened at all. Will was supposed to meet his parents for the day in Sydney, but they'd cancelled at the last minute, and Will had jumped at the opportunity to change his flight and see his husband. Spitting out the mouthwash, Will wiped the back of his hand across his mouth and walked out, barely stopping to collect his luggage.

With a hand on the front door, Stefan's loud voice cut through the silence. "Where do you think you're going? You're not leaving until you've cleaned that up." Stefan pointed to the vomit still staining on the rug.

"Bite me," Will muttered. "Oh wait, you probably already bit him." He turned to glare at the man. "Did you know he was married?"

The other man shrugged. "Not my problem."

"Wow," Will uttered. He wasn't even shocked that the man, still standing naked before him with cum drying on his belly and chest, was as much of a callous bastard as his husband. "In that case, enjoy each other."

"Oh, we will," Stephan purred, bending over the couch and presenting his arse to the other man. "Come on, Chad, give me that fat cock again."

Will pulled the door closed and shuffled into his jumper and coat in the hall, preferring to do it in the chilly air without the visual or the symphony of moans as Stefan and his new lover began fucking again right there.

Thirty minutes after he'd entered, Will exited the building and hailed a taxi. Unlike their hallway, at nine in the evening, the street in front of their building was busy. The driver took him closer to the city, where there was a cluster of hotels, pulling into the first one. Assuming they had a room vacant, the historic building would be his temporary home while he untangled himself from the chaos his life had suddenly been thrown into. Hopefully, it wouldn't take long, and he could leave the US. He was unlikely to be back—his only reason had already moved on.

Will moved mechanically, paying the driver, collecting his suitcase, and checking into the hotel. When the door to his room closed behind him, enveloping him in the quiet space, Will forced himself to do one last thing before he crashed. Shower. Still operating on autopilot, Will cranked the heat up and turned on the hot water. He had the sensation of watching himself as he undressed, unfeeling of the shift of material against his skin. Naked, he shivered even as steam filled the room. His muscles protested taking another step, but he pressed forward and into the shower stall, falling against the cold tiles. Leaning against the wall, the shock of the cold had him sucking in a breath. It was only then that he noticed the heat of the water hitting him. Will's skin prickled, a thousand tiny knives stabbing him as feeling returned to his body. The numbness washed down the drain with the water, leaving a void in its wake. His legs buckled, and Will slid to the floor, heaving sobs wracking his body as his world fell apart.

* * * * *

His doctor's appointment was later that afternoon, and the lawyer assured Will he would be able to finalize the divorce without him having to return to the States. It was a good thing too; he didn't want to go back. He stood at the window of his hotel room and looked out over the sea of buildings lining the street as he sipped the coffee room service had sent up. He didn't have much of a view, but it would have been wasted on him in the last three days anyway. He'd slept, waking only to eat and use the facilities. He hadn't left his room since he'd checked in. This was the first daylight he'd spied too. But it was time to get moving now. He wanted to gather his things and get the hell out of Seattle. He'd messaged Stefan, telling him to make himself scarce while he collected his clothes, but Will knew it was wishful thinking. There was no way the man would be kind enough to leave, not when Stefan had already been so cruel. Will wondered when things had changed for his husband or if they'd ever been as Will had pictured them. Will was a romantic at heart. He'd fallen fast and hard for the beautiful man who'd watched Will, his heated gaze sending prickles of awareness through Will. Stefan's desire had been obvious, and Will had soaked it in, never having been appreciated as blatantly before. It was as if Stefan wanted to make a meal out of him.

That heat had been nowhere in Stefan's gaze the last time he'd seen him, and it sent a pang of disappointment through Will. Was it his fault? Had he done something to turn Stefan off him? Had he driven his husband away? Not satisfied him? Then he came to his senses, and Will wanted to kick himself. His only fault had been his naivety. Believing Stefan would be faithful because of a few words spoken in front of a celebrant was wishful thinking. He'd always been driven by a need for sex, and Will could barely keep up with him some days. He should have known better, thinking that Stefan would wait for him for months at a time when the man could go out and find a warm body at any club any night of the week.

Will's mum called him as the lift descended to the ground floor, and he answered it, dreading the conversation. He loved his ma, but he knew the "I told you so" was coming. He'd had to tell them what went down—he wouldn't keep that kind of information from them and risk further damaging their already rocky relationship—but now he had to face the music. His ma was no doubt seeking answers to Will's cryptic text.

"Hey, Ma," he greeted.

"Will, baby, I'm so sorry." Pity laced her voice.

"Yeah, well you told me he was no good," he mumbled, figuring he'd get the lecture over and done with sooner rather than later.

"Enough of that. We never liked him, but we never wanted him to hurt you. What a bastard," she cursed, then asked, "How are you? Are you all right?"

"I'm okay, I think. I'm getting my things from the apartment now. I'll sort them out and get everything shipped home. The lawyer doesn't need me here to get the divorce underway, so I'll come home. Can I take the couch?"

"Your old room is already made up."

He smiled for the first time since he'd opened his apartment door days earlier. "Thanks, Ma. I'll let you know my flight details."

"See you at the airport." He bade her goodbye as the taxi he'd waved down pulled up beside him. The trip to his apartment went fast, traffic flowing easily at that time of the morning, and he stood at the entrance doors what felt like only a few minutes later.

Will shook off the cold as he hurried inside, only to pause when he reached the threshold of his apartment. He swallowed, wiping his clammy hands on his jeans as he worked up the courage to knock on the door. His mind was playing tricks on him, conjuring up worst-case scenarios. Possibility after possibility flashed in his mind's eye of Stefan and his new guy tangled together and putting on a show just to spite him. But Will didn't know whether anything that Stefan did to him now could be as bad as what he'd already witnessed. That first glimpse of Stefan una-bashedly taking what he wanted from his lover had broken something inside of Will that he wasn't sure he'd ever heal from.

Finally screwing up the courage and rapping quickly on the door, he stepped back and waited.

No one answered.

Wary, his mind ratcheting up the games it was playing with his confidence and calm, he let himself in. Relief whooshed through him at the sight that met him. Stefan sat on the couch, wearing fitted leggings, socks, and a fuzzy jumper a few sizes too big for him. Will had to resist the temptation to touch him, just to feel how soft it was. With an iPod in hand and headphones tucked into his ears, he glanced at Will then quickly looked away. Will caught a flash of what he hoped was regret—not because Will wanted him back, but because he'd never thought of Stefan as mali-cious. But the man who he'd come home to a few days ear-lier was stone cold and callous.

Stefan didn't meet his gaze again, and Will tracked his eyes around the room, feeling a pang of guilt for walking out without cleaning the vomit-stained rug. Pictures of Stefan riding his lover popped unbidden into Will's mind, and the guilt disappeared. He looked over to where the rug sat and noticed it'd been replaced. Much like himself.

"Ah, hey," Will hesitated, unsure of whether he'd get as cold a reception as he'd already been subjected to. Stefan turned to him, the walls firmly in place. His glare was like ice, cutting him to the quick. Will cleared his throat, wishing he could be anywhere but there and motioned over his shoulder down the hallway. "I'm just gonna grab my things."

"Whatever," Stefan responded, dismissing him with a wave of his hand. The man he'd returned home to hadn't been the one he thought he'd married. Never would he have ever dismissed Will like a piece of garbage. It wasn't in Will's nature to fight. He would if he had to, but sadness surrounded him, sucking the life out of their once happy apartment, and Will just needed to get the hell out of there.

He steeled his spine and turned on his heel. He chanted a mantra in his head, biting his tongue. *I won't say anything. I won't lash out.* He wouldn't give Stefan the satisfaction of knowing how much he'd hurt him. Moving slowly, deliberately, he focussed on his breathing. Concentrated on pulling the two suitcases he had stored in the spare room cupboard—the one he used as his wardrobe—and tossed his clothes in it. He shook his head at the irony of Stefan having already moved him out of their bedroom a year earlier.

"But why can't they stay in the wardrobe in our bedroom?" he'd asked.

"It's a closet, not a wardrobe. And it's too crowded. My clothes are getting all creased. I have to iron them whenever I want to wear them."

Will hadn't stated the obvious—if his husband stopped buying them, they wouldn't have a problem. But shopping made him happy, and Stef sacrificed so much with Will being away as often as he was that if a little shopping made his husband happy, Will was happy too. "You're never here," he'd continued, his voice a whine. "It doesn't matter if your clothes are in the spare room. You won't even notice."

Will had sighed and begun taking his clothes out. He knew when to argue and when not to push. If he did, Stefan would have a meltdown, and there'd be shouting and banging—but not the fun kind. Raised voices and slamming of doors would proceed Stefan locking himself in the bathroom sobbing until Will gave in, followed by him handing over his credit card so Stefan could shop until he felt better. Or he'd be given the cold shoulder for days. He loved his husband—even the fiercely passionate side of him that his family thought was more diva than grown man—but Will knew if Stefan didn't get what he wanted, he'd be the one paying the debt back for months. Receiving the silent treatment for days wasn't an option. Will only had a weekend left in Seattle before his next assignment at sea began. He refused to waste it fighting over something as petty as where his clothes were kept.

With his clothes from the spare room packed, Will walked into their bedroom and paused at the end of the bed. He ran his fingertips over the cover that Stefan had chosen. He remembered the trip. It was his last day onshore, and he had yet to pack. Stefan had begged him to go out for brunch, which had turned into a day of wandering around the city, choosing trinkets in cool little stores and linen from Nordstrom for their apartment. They'd held hands and laughed together. They'd been in love. At least Will had been. How far they'd fallen.

Will opened his bedside table drawer and was confronted with another man's things. He closed his eyes, the pain of Stefan's betrayal a lance in his chest. There was nothing left for him here. Nothing left of him either. The photo that sat on the dresser of their wedding—the two of them in suits standing on the steps of the Vegas chapel, both still half-drunk from the night before—was gone. He knocked his fist on the surface gently and sighed, wondering just how long ago Stefan had moved on.

Will wheeled his suitcases out to the lounge room. There were so many questions he had zipping around in his head. The whys, the whens, and the what happeneds. But it was pointless asking. Nothing would come from knowing.

He paused at the door and turned to Stefan. He looked ridiculous sipping on a glass of bubbles dressed in what could have been workout clothes, but the hard glint in his eyes told Will he was feeling combative. Stefan raised an eyebrow at Will, lifting his chin in defiance. Will realized he didn't have much to say to this man. This virtual stranger. Although Will questioned how well he'd ever known Stefan if he was capable of this. His heart was broken, but Will had quickly stopped crying for what he'd lost. Instead, the only thing playing in a loop in his mind was that he'd been betrayed by the one person who was supposed to be on his side. Numbness and shock had set in, but the need to escape and get as far away from there as possible was winning. The part of Will that had wanted to rear up and demand that he fight for his man, that he didn't go down without trying everything to save their marriage, was silenced. The scene he'd witnessed in their bedroom had snuffed out the desire to mount that fight. Instead, looking at him, Will felt nothing. As if the man opposite him was a stranger that he had no emotional connection too. It was sad that things had ended that way, but Will couldn't help hear the whisper of sweet relief in the back of his brain. He was being gifted a freedom of sorts. It didn't come from being single—there was no way he was ready to even think about dating or being with someone else—but from stepping over the line he'd drawn because of Stefan's betrayal and not looking back. The freedom to not watch every word he said for fear of tipping his husband into a mood or opening the mail to discover his next few months' pay had already been spent. He'd walked on eggshells for much of their marriage, but it only occurred to him once he was outside of it.

He didn't want any reminders of it either. He would walk away from everything they'd built with his head held high and start over. Will wanted to focus on what was important. He would concentrate on rebuilding his relationship with his family and getting the promotion to cruise ship captain that he'd dreamed of since being a wet-behind-the-ears teenager.

The canvas of the ballet dancer hanging above the TV unit caught Will's attention. Maybe he did want something of their life together. He lifted his chin and motioned to it, deciding on the spot that he was going to take it. He'd seen the picture in a studio collection. Images of ballet dancers had lined the walls. But that photograph had spoken to him, and he had to have it. It wasn't a large print compared to many of the others they'd seen that night, but it had captured his attention and held it. The man, dressed in white leggings and ballet slippers, spun around in an industrial-style space holding a pose that no untrained dancer would manage to contort their body into. Pristine against grungy, the picture was a contrast in conflicting beauty. Untouched, unblemished skin against a gritty background. Perfect lean muscle and grace, poise and confidence; his beauty in motion had held Will captivated the first time he'd seen it. Stefan hadn't thought much of it, and Will knew it would be headed for the garbage chute if he didn't take it. "I'm keeping my picture too."

"Fine." Stefan nodded. "Chad is moving in, and we're redecorating anyway, so I don't need any of this."

Stefan's words made him pause, the armour he'd built around his heart piercing like a hot knife cutting through butter. "Why, Stef?" Will asked quietly. "I thought we were good together."

"Good together?" Stefan huffed, his tone caustic. He stood and poked his finger into Will's chest, his voice rising with every word he spat at Will. "You leave for months at a time, then pop back home when it suits and expect me to rearrange my life for you when you get back. You expect me to be celibate that whole time, then when you finally arrive home, you sleep for days!" He turned his nose up at Will and walked away, moving into the kitchen to refill his glass.

Will nodded. "How many have there been?"

"Enough to know what I want from a man, and it's no longer you."

"You were never going to move home with me, were you?" That had been their plan. Will would be working out of Sydney for years to come. Stefan had promised him that they would move to Australia. Will had wanted to live near his family, to rebuild the close bond he'd had with them. Stefan didn't get along with his own family, so Will thought it was a perfect solution.

"Not a chance." Stefan drained another glass of bubbles and glared daggers at Will.

Will nodded, took the picture off the wall, and clutched the two suitcases. "My lawyer will be in touch. Sign the paperwork when you get it."

He let the door slam behind him and walked the hallway, not regretting for a moment that he hadn't said goodbye. He knew without a shadow of a doubt that it was the last time he'd ever see the inside of the building. It was just as likely the last time he'd be in Seattle. He'd loved the city, but he'd grown homesick. Leaving granted him a sense of relief when his marriage becoming unsalvageable had been cold comfort.

THREE

Eddie

Six Years Ago

The curtain had closed on his final performance as a student of the Royal College of the Arts. It was bittersweet. Eddie's shine had sparkled at the school. He'd been able to be himself. Unashamedly so. No one blinked an eyelid when he'd worn make-up the first time to his classes. Instead, they'd complimented him on how his high cheekbones and pouty lips were highlighted. If he walked with a swish of his hips and a cut-off tee with his training tights or giggled a little more effeminately than even his sisters, no one criticized him. He wasn't at risk of being hurt by someone for it. In fact, there would be a dozen other boys and girls doing exactly the same thing. It wasn't all roses, though, and that's what he'd loved about it. The teachers demanded perfection. He, himself, had demanded a standard above that. Competition in the school was fierce. Performances were important—the gateway to being seen by agents and talent scouts in an industry even more vicious than the most spiteful of competitors in the school—but they'd never been Eddie's problem. He blitzed every audition, crediting his drive and focus to prove every one of his childhood bullies wrong. There had been no room for stupid errors, lapses in concentration, or weakness of any kind, and that suited Eddie to a T. He'd thrived in the cutthroat competition, consistently winning leading roles in performances.

But now he was leaving his safe haven.

He was heading home for a few weeks. He loved his family, and he didn't see enough of them, but fear niggled at his throat, clawing at it like that scary clown in the drain as the seats next to and across from him on the train he was on filled up. He closed his eyes and concentrated on slowing his heartbeat, clearing his mind of all the interference like he did before a performance.

It didn't help.

The clutch on Eddie's throat gripped harder, closing his windpipe. He sucked in an urgent breath. That's when he smelt them. Peanuts. He gasped again, panic gripping his chest and seizing his breath. His heart thundered, pumping blood through his veins. The allergic reaction took hold as his body went into shock from the lethal concoction in the air. Eddie fumbled through the pockets of his bag, searching for his EpiPen. "You right, mate?" a man asked from next to him. Halos tinged Eddie's vision, and the sight of the man before him blurred.

Eddie tried to answer, but he was too far gone. His throat had closed completely, the blotchy patches that had broken out on his skin standing stark against his pale arms. Lightheaded from the lack of oxygen, Eddie shoved his hand deeper into the pocket and sifted through its contents, hoping he wouldn't pass out before he found it. Old pens and chocolate wrappers, plasters, and even compression bandages filled the space. Where is it?

His hand shaking, Eddie pushed through the litter in his rucksack and his fingers closed around the one thing that would save him. Wrenching it out of the pocket, he knew the needle would punch through the denim of the jeans he was wearing if he had the strength to push it hard enough. Darkness tinged his vision, and he pressed down on the trigger. His fingers slipped, the EpiPen nearly clattering to the floor. Saved only by it falling onto his lap, he willed his mind to clear of the cottonwool, and he reached for it, his fingers closing around air. He fumbled for it again and had it pressed to his leg, but the rush of adrenaline didn't come. His vision didn't clear. His breathing didn't come easier.

Mustering all his fading strength, he tried a third time to depress the button. As he slumped in his seat, feeling unconsciousness tugging him into oblivion, there was a commotion before him. A woman's voice. Calm and authoritative. Clear. Pressure on his leg, the rush of the medicine flowing through his veins. "You're okay." Eddie heard through the white noise in his ears. "My name's

Beatrice. I've injected you with your EpiPen. You're going to be okay." Eddie tried to reach out for her, and a warm hand closed around his. "I need to know what you're allergic to."

"Nuts," Eddie rasped as loud as he could manage, but his voice was barely a whisper. He sounded like his dad had when they'd spoken last—raw from shouting at the football match his family had gone to see. Eddie had missed all the games. He'd missed their banter, his sister's overprotectiveness, and his brothers' boisterousness. Only moments earlier he'd feared going home. Now he feared not being alive long enough that he could get there.

Another commotion. Voices that didn't register as they should have in Eddie's fuzzy brain. He concentrated on breathing, but the smell was still there. Roasted peanuts, salty and still warm. They were moreish and delicious but deadly to him. A poison that would kill him nearly as fast as falling under the train he was on would.

"What's your name, love?" she asked. He blinked open his eyes, his vision clearing enough to make out her features. She was older—around the same age as his mum. Her hair was a sweeping mass of grey-blonde curls surrounding her rounded face, her lips a soft pink that gave her a gentleness. She was a carer, and he innately knew that he was safe with her.

"Eddie." He tried to move, to sit up on the seat, but her hand kept him steady.

"It's okay, Eddie. Stay lying down. You won't get dizzy that way." She patted his hand and motioned to the seat he now had his legs on. "The man who sat next to you with the peanuts has moved, but the air is still likely contaminated with particles of them. We need to get you off this train at the next station and to a hospital. That was a severe attack." She waited until he nodded his understanding and continued, "Can I call someone for you? Your parents, a friend?" He reached inside his bag, his trembling fingers closing around his phone. It took two goes for Eddie to unlock it, hitting his mum's number before Beatrice took the phone from him and spoke to her. She held his hand, her calm seeping into his psyche. She was exactly what he needed in that moment—someone to take control and steer him away from the danger when he couldn't help himself. He didn't register much of the conversation, drifting in and out of awareness as she spoke.

The train slowed, and Beatrice returned Eddie's phone, placing it into his hand and closing his fingers around it. "Your parents are on their way. They'll meet you at the hospital, love." Another person reached over and helped him up, wrapping his arm around Eddie's waist. With the stranger lifting him bodily out of the seat, and Beatrice on his other side holding his bag for him, Eddie stumbled forward and sagged into the man's strong hold.

He didn't know how long he'd been out of it for, but the waiting gurney and paramedics surprised him. Eternally grateful, he looked for Beatrice, and she was right there, placing his giant bag between his feet as he was helped onto the trolley. She was explaining his reaction and treatment to the paramedics, talking in medical terms that didn't really make sense to Eddie in his hazy state. But seeing the professionals standing side by side, he noticed she was dressed in scrubs—pink pants and a top with cartoon characters printed on it. As one of the paramedics listened, with her stethoscope to his chest, the other strapped a blood pressure cuff around his arm. They nodded their thanks, and Beatrice squeezed his free hand. "I'll check in on you when I get a moment during my shift, but Ford and Anna here will look after you. You get well, Eddie."

"Thank you," he choked out, tears forming in his eyes and running down his cheeks. He'd been worried. Scared that even after he'd made himself look as masculine as he could in his wardrobe of pastels and soft knits and fabrics, he'd become a target. Instead, the kindness of strangers had shone through.

* * * * *

His mum told him that the telephone call from his agent had come when he'd been sleeping. The man who'd taken Eddie under his wing halfway through high school had been sending minor gigs Eddie's way for years, as well as getting him auditions for small parts in West End plays. He hadn't landed any of the bigger parts he'd auditioned for, but that was mostly because of the rehearsal and performance demands clashing with his schooling. His parents had insisted that he finish his final year, much to Eddie's frustration, but now that he was done, he'd been sure to tell anyone who'd listen that he was free. He didn't know what his agent wanted to tell him, but whatever it was, it would have to wait. His mum looked like she'd aged a decade and his dad's normally chilled vibe was nowhere to be seen. "Dad," he croaked, his voice still scratchy from the constriction of his throat. He reached out and snagged a hold of his shirt to tug him closer. "I'm okay now." He smiled, and his dad blew out a breath and leaned down to wrap Eddie in a hug.

"I've never been more afraid than when we got that call." His voice shook, and Eddie squeezed him harder, letting his dad know that even though he'd had a close call, he was still there. Still fighting.

"I'm yet to become a darling of West End, Dad. I'm not going anywhere." Eddie winked at him and reached for his mum, taking her hand in his. "I was scared too. I thought it was nerves about coming home, but then I couldn't breathe."

"Why are you nervous?" His mum sat on the bed next to him and brushed Eddie's hair back off his face. "It's no different to any other time."

Eddie looked down, embarrassed to admit his insecurities. He'd been out and proud at school, but going home, he knew he needed to tone it down. Not because of his parents—they'd joined him in London to march in every Pride Parade since he'd been accepted to RCA. More because of the risk of bumping into old foes. They didn't run in the same circles anymore. Jess, his childhood friend, had introduced him to her group of girlfriends, and they'd all clicked. Eddie was a ring in, but he talked make-up and boys with them too. He'd been welcomed to every party and eventually the sleepovers too when their parents realized he was no risk to their daughters' innocence. But now they were legal, and Jess wanted to celebrate by going to a club. One that his brothers had warned him was popular with his old school friends. Eddie stood out. He always had. Even if he toned down his personality and even his clothes, there was no doubt that he was as gay as they came. And in the working-class area of Leeds where they were from, that was not exactly the most acceptable thing to be. But how did he tell his parents that without sounding... like an upper-class snot looking down on them, rather than an insecure teenager who was scared of being beaten again. Either way, his dad would be disappointed that he was even thinking about changing who he was to fit in.

"Jess wants to go out." He shrugged, trying to play down the fear knotting his stomach up. "Jack told me that the club she's planning to go to is where all the lads from our old school go. I haven't exactly been to a club where all the masc straights go, if you know what I mean."

His mum and dad both frowned. "Honey, are you worried about Duncan and his friends?" When he nodded, his dad sighed, and his mum rubbed her eyes beneath her specs.

His dad spoke, his voice both sad and tired. "Duncan and two of his mates are in jail. Sentenced a few weeks ago. They went to a party and got in a fight. Beat up one of the girls there pretty badly, and when her friend stepped in, they put him in the hospital. They've been bad news for a long time, Eddie."

The news stunned Eddie. Horrified him too. While he'd been in London, living life to the fullest, thriving under the stage lights and eating up the pressure to achieve perfection like it was his morning Weetabix, people he'd once gone to school with—albeit those same boys who'd terrorised him—were landing themselves in jail. Relief that they were off the streets shook him to his core. He may have been acting a little selfish, but knowing he wouldn't be running into them anytime soon shook the weight off Eddie's shoulders and let his smile come more genuinely.

"So, now that we've sorted that out, you planning on calling your agent back anytime soon? He's called again." His dad pointed to the light flashing on Eddie's phone charging on the moveable table.

Eddie picked up his phone and dialled his agent's number. "Grant, hi," he greeted when the older man answered. "It's Eddie Taylor."

"Eddie! Glad you called me back." He spoke fast; he was always on the go. Life for him was one series of fast-paced meetings after another, and everyone around him was expected to keep up with his boundless energy. Excitement coloured his tone, and a second shot of adrenaline passed through Eddie that day. "I have an audition for you. This one is big. One of the main dancers in a musical on West End. The director was impressed with the video I sent him of your senior performance."

Eddie was silent for a moment as the words sunk in. A smile spread across his mum's face, and she squeezed his free hand so hard that it snapped him out of his shock. "Eddie," Grant called. "You still there?"

Eddie blew out a breath and looked from his mum to his dad. "Yes, I'm here. I'm just…. Are you serious?"

Grant chuckled. "Yes, son. I'm serious."

"When do they want me? I'm in hospital. I don't know when they're releasing me."

"What happened?" the older man asked, now alarmed.

"I had an allergic reaction to nuts. There was a fella eating them on the train, and I didn't realize until I'd already gone into anaphylactic shock. I'll be fine within a few hours, I'm sure, but they may keep me overnight."

"Oh, thank goodness you're okay. The audition is the week after next." Grant gave Eddie details of dates and location and instructed him to have an original piece to perform. Two weeks wasn't long to choreograph a perfect audition piece for a major role, but he'd make it work.

* * * * *

An arm reached out from the shadowed alcove to the side of the stage, snagging his wrist. Eddie smiled and heat bloomed through his body. Henri Dubois—star of the show—wanted him, and what Henri wanted, Henri got. Especially when it concerned Eddie.

He let himself be pulled in and tugged back against Henri's chest. Twisting so he could look up into Henri's heat-filled gaze, Eddie licked his lips, his dick already standing at attention. He was in a perpetual state of arousal when around Henri, and performing left Henri suffering the same fate. It made for fireworks between them when the star demanded that Eddie satiate him. It was no hardship either. The man was sex on a stick. Older, with greying temples and a magnetism that made Eddie melt into a puddle at his feet, Eddie was more than happy to submit to Henri's demands.

Henri dominated on and off the stage, sucking all the air out of Eddie's lungs and leaving him in awe of the man. His ability to sweep into a room and instantly become the centre of attention didn't just end with his performances. Eddie was flattered that Henri had chosen him to give his body to.

Every time he looked at Henri, Eddie's cock reacted, need pulsing through him. Wearing tights had never been so embarrassing, but right at that moment, he was grateful for the easy access.

Running a hand down Eddie's front, Henri leaned in close, whispering to him in French, his heated breath raising gooseflesh on Eddie's skin. He could have been uttering nonsense; Eddie had no idea what he was saying, but his body understood the message like it was written in neon. Henri licked the column of his throat in a move as dirty as the hand he slipped down the front of Eddie's tights. He rocked his hips and Henri pinned him close, grinding his erection into the cleft of Eddie's arse.

It had hurt at first. With only a pre-lubed condom and little prep, Henri hadn't taken it easy on him—especially considering Eddie had never bottomed before—but he learnt how to enjoy it. They had to be quick. Eddie understood that, so he never complained, especially when Henri would keep an eye out to make sure they weren't caught while Eddie finished himself off.

He moaned quietly, the laughter from the stagehands breaking into Eddie's bubble of sensuality. It was risky, Eddie knew that, but Henri made him brave. Probably a little reckless too. He'd been performing on West End for only a few weeks and he really shouldn't already be shagging the star of the show, but Eddie couldn't resist. He found himself dropping to his knees to swallow Henri down, lathering his sheathed cock in extra spit.

"Let me spend the night with you," Eddie gasped when Henri dragged him up, spun him around and tugged Eddie's tights down to expose his arse.

"No." Henri shook his head and rubbed his cock over Eddie's hole before pressing forward until he was buried balls deep in him. Barely allowing Eddie a reprieve to get used to the girth impaling him, Henri moved, slowly dragging his cock back out until Eddie's hole was stretched as wide as it ever had been. Eddie's objection died on his lips when Henri punched his hips forward drilling Eddie's prostate hard. He wanted nothing more than to take the man to bed and explore what it was like to have sex with Henri while horizontal. But Henri refused. He always refused. Eddie didn't think his request was a big deal. He wanted to stay with his lover and wake up with him.

For now, he had to be satisfied with what he had. The sex was exhilarating and life-affirming. Performing, even more so. He was born for it, thriving with every moment under the spotlight.

He didn't understand why Henri insisted they not go home together. He kept their relationship a secret too. Henri had done him a favour, Eddie supposed. He didn't particularly want to be the focus of the tabloids for being Henri's boyfriend. He'd rather it be for his own talent. The star had said he didn't want to constrain their relationship with unnecessary labels either—why conform to others' expectations? But was Henri doing exactly that when he refused to tell anyone about them? Henri's secrecy wasn't because he was in the closet—he was an out and proud bisexual man. But he was a firm subscriber to the adage that an attainable lead was a successful one. Women loved him, and men either wanted to be him, or be with him. If Henri announced they were together, that notion would be shattered, and he was unprepared to risk his popularity.

Regardless of whether anyone knew about their relationship, there was no question they were in one—however it was defined. In Eddie's mind, they'd passed the point of dating and were firmly into the B-word territory. He smiled at that. Eighteen, with a steady boyfriend and doing what he loved. Eddie's life was full.

Right at that moment, as Henri sank into his willing body right there in the alcove, the definition didn't matter so much to him.

FOUR

Will

FIVE YEARS AGO

Will reported to the captain—the man who'd become his mentor—at precisely oh-nine hundred, dressed in his officer's whites. The exhaustion from his latest fourteen-hour night shift had been shocked out of him with the sharp knock on his door half an hour into his break. He was already in bed, his quick shower just enough to wash away the sweat of a long night's work.

He shook out his hands and wiped sweaty palms on his pressed pants, then looked down to make sure he hadn't put smudges on them. The last thing he needed was to be late when a formal summons had been made. Captain Bugeja rarely exercised the privilege. He preferred a much more casual approach, simply calling someone and having them meet him if he had to pass on important messages face-to-face. But this time was different. The captain of the MV Dreamchaser, the largest ship in the fleet of cruise liners that had employed Will for the last six years, had sent two of the ship's guards to his quarters, ordering him up and dressed in formal whites and at the Captain's office within a sharp fifteen-minute deadline. Will was nervous—not because he'd done anything wrong—but because he'd heard whispers of the first mate on the ship retiring. Was his dream of becoming second in charge within his reach? Captain Bugeja had taken him under his wing once Will had demonstrated time and time again his unwavering focus and dedication to his profession. He'd set his sights on captaining a ship, but he knew it would be a decades-long pursuit to get there. It didn't matter, though. Will had all the time in the world and an endless fountain of dedication. Captain Bugeja had helped him achieve promotion from third mate to marine captain since he'd joined the MV Dreamchaser. Was this another potential step up?

The guards knocked and opened the door when a muffled "Proceed" sounded from the other side. One of them, Mario, gave an encouraging nod to Will as he passed. He wondered whether the nerves were showing. His reflection in the mirror of his stateroom was one of exhaustion—dark circles under his eyes, and pale skin stared back at him. He barely recognized himself anymore, but it was in a good way. He'd grown a beard in his first two months of being single after his disastrous marriage had ended. He hadn't shaved since. It was trimmed short, perfectly manicured to keep with the high standards set by Captain Bugeja, but it was starting to grey.

He'd beefed up too, taking up a rigorous routine of workouts to keep himself fit and focussed. Bulking up had been easier than he'd expected too. Will liked to eat healthily, but his weakness was protein. Give him steak, and he was happy. He'd never aimed for perfect definition in his muscles—getting and keeping the cut look that bodybuilders had was too laborious for his career with its long hours and shift work, but the size he'd gained had done wonders for his confidence levels and his mental health. He understood now that his relationship with Stefan had been toxic right from the start. It wasn't a partnership of equals. Rather, one of them—Stefan—had held all the cards, demanding something, and Will giving in to him. He'd thought of himself as spineless for years, getting angry at how weak he'd been. But he was young and naïve too. The couple of friends he'd kept in contact with had filled him in on enough gossip over the years to learn that his laid-back, people-pleasing personality had made him a target for Stefan. The man was manipulative to the point of abuse and had no compunction throwing away his toys when he'd gotten sick of them. His relationship with Chad, the political lobbyist, had only lasted a few months, except this time, it was Chad doing the tossing away. When Stefan could no longer afford their old apartment on his meagre wages, and his credit cards were maxed out, Chad had walked, and Stefan had bummed a couch off whatever friends he still had left.

But his history was so far in the past that Will hadn't thought of his ex-husband in years.

The door to the captain's office closed behind him, and Will jolted back into the present and looked around. The captain wasn't the only person gathered inside the spaciously appointed meeting area. The first, second, and third mates were in the room, together with the managers of each of the various divisions on the ship—entertainment, food and beverage, hospitality, and engineering. All were in their dress uniforms. All were standing at attention. Will's heart beat harder, his nerves ratcheting up. Stopping before Captain Bugeja, Will saluted him and stood at attention, waiting for the older man to speak.

"Marine Captain," the captain started. "At ease." Will relaxed his pose, clasping his hands behind his back, and waited with bated breath. Captain Bugeja grinned at him, and Will smiled back. It took everything in him not to plead with Captain Bugeja to explain what was going on. His pulse thundered in his veins, and sweat broke out on his brow as the silence stretched out. Captain Bugeja paced, walking away from him only to turn back again with something the size of an envelope in his hands. "Do you know what today is, William?" he asked but didn't pause long enough for Will to answer. "Today is the day Head Office made the announcement on staffing for the newest ship in the Dream Liner fleet. We're having some staff changes as a result of the MV Dreamcatcher's launch."

"Yes, sir," Will croaked, his mouth dry and throat scratchy from nerves.

"Congratulations, William," he said warmly. "This came for you." He handed Will a folded piece of paper printed on thick card stock in a rich cream. When he opened the first fold, Will saw the Dream Liner logo, the silhouette of a large capital D in navy blue with two flowing silvery lines representing the swell of the ocean and a sail. On the top right, a star. Will sucked in a breath and, with shaking hands, unfolded the rest of the letter. It was short, barely half a page, but its impact had Will staggering and reaching for the closest chair. It was new orders. A request to report to Finland in two months to begin the final preparations for the maiden voyage of the MV Dreamcatcher. As her captain.

"Sir..." Will began and lost the words in his throat. He hadn't applied for the position. He didn't think he was ready. Four years as a marine captain wasn't enough to make the jump to captain. How had his name been put forward?

"You're ready for this, Will. I have absolute faith in you. All of us do." Captain Bugeja held his hands out, motioning to the rest of the people in the room who were standing at ease, wearing smiles to match the captain's own. "Officers, may I introduce Captain William Preston of the MV Dreamcatcher."

They clapped, and Captain Bugeja squeezed his shoulder. All Will could do was look around the room in shocked silence. Will reread the letter, hoping he'd understood it correctly, and then looked back at Captain Bugeja. "This isn't a joke, is it?" Captain Bugeja's booming laugh and the shake of his head reassured Will that he wasn't being pranked, but it was a lot to take in. When the champagne cork popped and a glass was passed to him, Will gulped the drink down, the bubbles fizzing his nose and burning a trail down his throat. Stifling a cough, he held his glass out for a refill and looked back at the letter. "Captain, how did this happen? I didn't put my name forward."

"I did. William, you've given this company your all for, what, six or seven years? You do every educational course you can enrol in, and you have jumped at every opportunity to get more experience. You're one of the most highly qualified marine captains I've ever had the pleasure of working with. Executive management asked me why you hadn't applied. They've had their eye on you for some time."

He slid into the chair he'd been gripping, Will's legs finally giving out at hearing his words. "I didn't think I was ready." He looked up at his mentor, still trying to make sense of all that had happened.

"The rest of us did. Congratulations, William, but I'm going to miss having you on my ship." He held out his hand, and Will stood on wobbly legs to shake it. The man had been a source of inspiration for Will for as long as he'd known him, and Captain Bugeja had just managed what Will thought impossible for at least another five years.

Charcuterie boards and platters of hors d'oeuvres were laid down by wait staff, and Will managed to mingle, making his way around the room. Pure shock kept him upright and still functioning long after he would have been fast asleep, but even as the party wound to a close an hour later, Will couldn't stop his mind from racing or his head spinning. He made his way back to his stateroom and undressed, collapsing face first into bed in just his underwear. Grinning, he dialled his mum. She'd want to know the moment he knew. He'd rebuilt his relationship with his parents brick by brick over the last decade. They'd been there for him, helping pick up the pieces of his life when his marriage had fallen apart, and he'd moved halfway across the world to come home. Even through their own amicable divorce, they'd been his number one supporters.

"Will, baby, how are you?" she answered on the second ring. "Where are you?"

"Hi, Ma. We're out at sea, still partway between Brisbane and Bali. We're about even with Broome," he explained. "So, I have a suggestion for you. Would you and Brett like to come on the maiden voyage of the MV Dreamcatcher with me? As the captain's guests?"

"Oh, baby, we'd love to," she breathed. "And as captain's guests? That's incredible. You must know them well to have been given that privilege on the maiden voyage. I didn't even realize you knew who it was yet."

"I found out today." He paused and waited, counted it out in his head until his mum put the pieces together. One, two, three, four—

"Will? Are you there?"

"Yeah, Ma. I'm here. It's tradition for the captain to give the staterooms on the first voyage to people who mean the most to them. I was going to ask Dad and Pam too. That is, if you feel comfortable—"

"You know your dad and I are still the best of friends—"

"Ma," Will interrupted, dragging her name into two syllables, his frustration and excitement pouring out of him. "If you feel comfortable with me captaining the ship."

"What?" she screeched. "Oh my God, holy shit. Will, are you serious? You got your own ship?"

"Yeah," he said with a laugh. "I did it, Ma. We did it. I couldn't have gotten there without you and Brett, and Dad and Pam."

"Oh, baby. I'm so thrilled for you. You've worked so hard for this." A shuffling sounded, and a muffled yell of "Brett" nearly split Will's eardrum. He conveyed his news to his mum's boyfriend and hung up, repeating the same with his dad and Pam, his dad's partner. Smiling broadly when he hung up, he knew the messages from his sister and brothers would begin soon enough, but until then, he needed sleep.

* * * * *

"Oh, hey," Will said as he answered the door to his mum's house to a petite lady and two men holding a large rectangular box. They were preparing for that night's get-together—welcoming Will home and celebrating his promotion—but his mum hadn't told him anything about a delivery. She'd insisted on catering for the event, and he'd compromised, agreeing to keep it simple with a few store-bought salads and a barbie so she wouldn't go overboard. He hoped she hadn't gone to too much trouble.

"Hi, I'm Katy," she said as if he should know her. She held out her hand, and Will shook it, desperately trying to remember if he'd met her before. His answer came when she asked, "I'm guessing you're Will?"

"I am." He nodded, smiling.

"Great! We're here to drop off the cake for your cele- bration. These are my partners, Connor and Levi." She mo- tioned between them.

"G'day," the taller man, Connor said, giving him a nod while Levi greeted him with a "Hi."

"Where are my manners? Come on in." Will held the door open and motioned for them to enter.

"Keep it steady," she directed. "One step up over the threshold."

Connor was walking backwards. He bit down on his lip and shot a quick glance over his shoulder as he walked back- wards.

"S'all good, Connor, keep going," the other man, Levi, said. "I'll let you know when you have to turn." Will lived in a duplex, with his mum on one side and his smaller unit on the other. Her house had a long hallway at its entrance, with the living areas at the back next to the patio. His was de- signed the same, except for the two fewer bedrooms. The backyards were joined, a large undercover patio area with an outdoor kitchen, firepit, and gardens with a small lawn area leading down to the waterfront finishing the area off. It made for the perfect spot for drinks.

"Katy," his mum exclaimed in a flurry of loose linen and hugs for the woman he'd only just met. "We're setting up outside. Come, come," his mum directed before pausing and asking, "The cake doesn't need to be refrigerated, does it?"

"No, don't put it in the fridge. It's fine as is until you cut it, then just an airtight container will do. You can freeze as much of it as you like." She explained the steps his mum would no doubt follow and watched as Connor and Levi manoeuvred the board into place, gently removing their hands without jostling it any more than necessary.

Katy let out a breath, and her shoulders relaxed. When Levi ran a hand through her dark hair, smoothing it down, Will saw a flash of adoration pass between them, and Will was, for the first time since his marriage had ended, jealous of another couple.

Connor had stepped away, looking out at the wide waterway behind the house. "This is a beautiful spot. Beautiful house too, Mrs Preston."

Will snorted out a laugh as his mum gave Connor the lecture that Mrs Preston was her ex-mother-in-law, and she'd never liked the old biddy. The only time she'd seen her happy was when his parents had separated. Now his nan had Pam to contend with, but the joke was on all of them. His nan had received the shock of her life when she'd met Pam—tattooed and pierced, she was half his father's age and a hell of a lot of fun. She made his mum look like an angel, but wouldn't you know it, his nan and Pam had become fast friends, getting along like a house on fire.

"Should we have a look?" Katy asked. "It wasn't the easiest thing to get to balance being so top-heavy. I'm really hoping you like what I came up with, Cheryl." She carefully lifted the lid on the box and stepped back. Will's eyes widened, and he let out a low whistle.

"My God, that's incredible," he murmured as he walked around the cake. On a board about the size of an A3 piece of paper, the cake was shaped into a cruise ship, long smooth lines of the bow and stern with tiny windows painted on, decks filled with miniature deck chairs and swimming pools, water slides, a movie screen, and the Dream Liner logo on its stacks. Aqua-coloured water that looked deceptively translucent surrounded the ship, smooth except for a low rolling swell and the ripples from the wake.

"She's pretty amazing, isn't she," Levi commented, sending one of those adoring smiles to Katy while casually leaning into Connor as he rested his forearm on Levi's shoulder. Will's gaze bounced between them, and he realized that when Katy meant partners, she didn't mean business partners. The two men looked at him as if checking his reaction before they looked down to his tee. The black shirt had a simple message emblazoned down its left side. "Love" was written in rainbow colours. Levi nodded to it. "Your shirt's cool."

Will smiled back. "I like it. It's a nice way of saying 'fuck you, I still exist' to all the haters."

Connor coughed out a laugh and ran his hand down Levi's back, settling it on his waist. That small move was full of intimacy. Will smiled and ducked his head away until Connor asked him, "So, what's the significance of the ship?"

"Did I not tell you?" Katy exclaimed excitedly.

"I work on cruise ships. Just got a promotion." He grinned, still giddy when he thought about the letter proudly framed on his dad's wall of models of classic sailing ships. While his mum passed around a few beers to them, he smiled gratefully at her and murmured his thanks.

"To what?" Connor asked.

"Captain." He grinned, and Levi choked on his mouthful. "That's never gonna get old saying that."

"Congratulations, man. That's brilliant." Levi coughed into his elbow and held out his other hand to shake. "You're really young to be captain, aren't you?"

"Yeah, a little, but I've been working towards it since I was a teenager. Went to a specialist high school and then two degrees at uni, and I've been on cruise ships working my way up the ladder ever since."

Will motioned for them to sit, and they kicked back on the loungers by the water's edge.

"We should do that," Connor murmured. "Go on a cruise together. Maybe a big group of us."

"You should."

FIVE

Will

PRESENT DAY

Still half asleep, Will squinted in the unforgiving light of the bathroom attached to his stateroom. He was not a morning person at the best of times. But having woken up after a few sleepless nights and thirty-two hours of shifts in two days, Will was not his chipper self. His body clock had also been knocked for six. It was the middle of the night, yet he was waking up ready for another long shift.

The last night of a cruise was always wild. Everyone was out partying until dawn, but this time a guest had overdone it. Will had been about to knock off when the call came through from Ezio Dimitriades, the on-board doctor. *Unconscious male, early twenties, suspected drug overdose.* As much as they screened passengers coming on board, they could never guarantee they were completely drug-free. So, fearing for what the young man had taken, Will made the call and pulled the ship out of its chartered course. He detoured along a shipping channel, travelling due west until they were close enough to rendezvous with the Coast Guard chopper and medivac the patient off Will's ship.

Will smiled. *My ship.* Even after five years of captaining the MV Dreamcatcher, he still got a kick calling her his.

After they'd docked in Sydney Harbour, they smoothly disembarked a thousand passengers, refuelled, restocked everything a cruise ship needed for a seven-day trip, looked after waste disposal and urgent maintenance works, had a staff changeover for those finishing their three, five, or seven months at sea and boarded another thousand guests. Will was responsible for ensuring everything ran flawlessly, but he didn't do it alone.

His team was second to none, and Will trusted their judgement implicitly. He'd built up a solid working relationship with all the managers, and Will knew that when they said the ship was good to go, he could rely on them and the crew. This time they'd also had a visit from the police, who were working with border control to piece together how the drugs got on board and who knew about it. Thankfully, that was the easiest part of the day; their electronic records and passenger manifests more than enough to facilitate the police investigation.

Aside from the hectic first day of each cruise, Will loved his job, and he wouldn't change it for the world. How could he not love the majesty of sailing through deep oceans to paradise? They were only a small cruise ship—the smallest in the Dream Liner fleet—but he'd worked hard to ensure the ship was the best of the best. Their guests were young, fun, and energetic, and their staff showed them how to have a great time. The ship had the best reviews around, and the revamp of food and entertainment services would up the ante even more.

But at that moment, the only thing on Will's mind was getting the hot shower he desperately needed to wake the hell up. He flicked the tap on, but it shuddered and spluttered before water gushed out the wall. The showerhead above remained stubbornly dry. He sighed. Whatever was wrong with it was not going to fix itself.

He turned the tap off and, still naked, made his way through the luxurious suite to the phone on the desk. Dialling maintenance, Will waited for them to pick up. He had half an hour before he needed to be on deck, and in that time, he had to shower, shave, and eat breakfast—one that came with a strong cup of coffee. Early morning start times were horrendous but necessary. Although they were beginning a day at sea, day three of the cruise would see them port in Noumea at oh-six hundred, so if Will wanted a break between shifts, he needed to start this one now.

Two rings, and Eli, the maintenance manager, picked up. "Good morning, Captain Preston. How may I help you?"

"Hello, Eli. My shower is leaking at the wall. Nothing's coming out of the head."

"I will have someone come over immediately, sir." There was a groan and a hiss from the attached bathroom. Eyebrows furrowed together, he stepped closer to the noise, craning his neck to try and see inside the smaller room.

"You'd better make it qu—" Will's words were cut off by the crash and sound of water gushing.

"Sir, are you all right?" Eli called through the telephone, concern in his voice. Will dashed through his suite to the bathroom only to see water was rushing from the point where the tap was formerly mounted. Instead of being joined to the wall, the piece of chromed metal was lying on the floor. A crack pierced the wall of the shower, leaving a hole gouged into it. Water gushed into the crack and over-flowed out of the stall onto the tiled floor and carpet of the bedroom he was standing in.

"Shit," he muttered, snagging the towel set on the van-ity and balancing the cordless phone between his shoulder and ear as he wrapped it around him. "Eli, I need someone over here now. It's overflowing everywhere. And can you please find me somewhere I can shower?" Will hung up, his lack of caffeine and the rude awakening making him a hell of a lot grumpier than he normally was, even in the morn-ing. All he wanted was to get ready and have a coffee, but apparently, it wasn't the day for things to happen the easy way.

He slipped on a pair of cargo shorts and a fitted white polo with the ship's emblem on it before donning his thongs. Tossing all his toiletries and the towel into a bag, he hung them with his dry-cleaned uniform and hat on the hook, ready to head out.

His telephone rang just as he was zipping his bag. It was housekeeping. "Hello, sir, Eli called me to arrange an alternative place for you to shower and change." Will's staff were top-notch and knew the key to wonderful service was to be prompt and, although polite, to the point. He certainly wasn't a bastard, not even crabby most of the time—especially when they were on their way to paradise—but they knew he was on schedule. She didn't bother waiting for Will to respond before continuing. "All the executive suites are occupied, as are the remaining rooms in the staff and crew quarters. All the guest suites are also occupied. Unfortunately, the only place I can send you with a little privacy at this time of night are the entertainers' change rooms on the theatre level."

"Thank you, I'll head there now."

* * * * *

He walked through the dimmed staff-only halls to the opposite end of the ship near the back entrance of the theatre. The show had finished hours ago, so both the staff and guests had long ago left. Most of the entertainers had either moved to the nightclubs or bars to continue their shifts or had finished up for the night.

The artwork hanging at the intersection of the two hallways made the corridor look like it terminated with a dead end. It was striking and held his attention as he neared it. While the guest corridors had modern interpretations of the masters, the staff-only walkways were filled with photographs of performers from dancers and singers to fire breathers and acrobats. Each image was different—black and white, splashes of bright colour, dark and brooding or filled with laughter. It was pure coincidence, but the framed picture of the ballet dancer that Will had carried with him halfway around the world and now hung in his stateroom was the perfect match to those mounted along the hallways he was currently walking down.

Will swiped his card to gain access to the room at the end of the corridor. The door slid silently open and closed behind him with a whoosh, but any sound would have been drowned out by the deep bass from the sound system reverberating through the studio. Will closed his eyes and let the temptation in Bruno Mars's voice wind seductively around him. The song "Gorilla" made Will want to get hot and heavy, experience desire again. Raw and hypnotic, the song was pure sex.

Curiosity piqued, Will stepped silently through the neatly organized props and into the warm-up room.

His breath caught.

The room as a whole was dim, shadows still dancing in the corners from the stark spotlights pointed at the pole affixed in its centre. A man, if that entirely inadequate description of his perfection could possibly suffice, spun on it. He held his body weight perpendicular to the pole, his arms outstretched and his legs in a split. His toes were pointed, touching the pole on either side of his strong grip. Letting one arm drop, he rolled like he was going to hit the floor, and Will couldn't help reaching out for him. The speed he moved with was death-defying, but his muscles strained, and it was obvious he was in complete control.

Catching himself at the last moment with a hand to the floor, the man twisted his hips, moving from a side split to a forward one. Toes still pointed, he paused, holding himself there.

Will was spellbound, his feet fixed to the floor, frozen in a trance.

The subject of his fascination dropped down and rolled up to standing, his back bending at an angle Will had no idea was even possible. With one hand still on the pole, he froze, looking at the shadows where Will was still watching. He reached into the back of his training tights, and the music cut off. "Who's there?" he asked cautiously, his British accent lilting.

"I-I am," Will stuttered, transfixed by the greenest of green eyes he'd ever seen, rimmed with black eyeliner. Lust shot through Will, and his dick thickened, hardening from the sight of the beautiful creature in front of him.

The desire to drop to his knees, strip the man out of those sexy as sin tights, and lick every inch of his lean frame assailed Will. He wanted to worship the stranger, to touch and tempt him, to taste him. Need shot through Will like a lightning bolt, waking up parts that he restrained when working, like a dog on a tight leash. Will didn't date when he was on the ocean. He didn't fuck around, made sure he didn't even take a second look at another staff member, and certainly not a passenger, but this man made him want to throw caution to the wind.

Just the sight of the beautiful dancer had Will's palms sweating and his heart thundering. He itched to touch him, want and need warring for domination.

All before Will even knew his name.

The man ran his fingers through his hair, wiping away the sheen of sweat on his brow, and stepped forward. "You wanna step into the light so I can see you, rather than standing in the dark like a creeper?"

Will smiled, the guy's spunky attitude making him even sexier. Even though it was expected and necessary to ensure the ship ran smoothly, the problem with being the captain was that the staff and crew did exactly what he asked, usually without question. So, having this man, this hottie, speak to Will like he would any other person was refreshing.

The man, Will's wet dream come true, took a step forward, and Will was drawn to him like a moth to a flame. He mirrored the other man's actions until Will stood in the light. Their eyes locked, and they moved closer together.

The man's smooth chest rose and fell, a rivulet of sweat dripping from his clavicle between his pecs and down a perfectly flat stomach. He was shorter than Will, slimmer too—almost to the point of being petite—but Will had seen with his own eyes the strength those wiry muscles held. Dragging his gaze up before he could get past the low waist of those training tights, which he knew would leave nothing to his imagination, Will focussed his attention on the dancer's lips. They were plump. Totally kissable and shiny like he was wearing gloss. Will wanted to bite down on the bottom one and devour him whole. Did he taste of berries? Or was it some other flavour?

Everything about the man before him was such a damn turn on that Will unconsciously found himself eliminating the gap between them. *Who are you?* Chest to chest, Will breathed him in as the man sized him up, his gaze lazily trailing a path down Will's body. Every inch he took in was like a physical caress, lighting Will up.

Breathing deep, Will shivered as the man's musky scent hit his senses and he barely contained a moan. The man's eyes snapped up to meet Will's. Instinctively, Will licked his lips, and those emerald greens darkened in response, a low growl coming from the back of the other man's throat. *Oh God.* Will's breath hitched.

"What's your name?" Will rasped.

"Eddie." His voice was quiet, and Will leaned closer to him, wanting to hear more.

SIX

Eddie

Movement in the shadows had Eddie pausing. He didn't think anyone would go down to the warm-up room so long after the show finished. His shift had just ended—he'd danced in the main theatre performance, then on the pedestal in the nightclub, and needed to wind down. This was his time; Eddie's chance to dance the way he loved best rather than the choreographed moves all the dancers pulled in the shows. The performances were at least as good as the West End plays he'd danced in, but over the years, pole dancing had become one of Eddie's passions.

Eddie paused the music and called out, "Who's there?" He cursed himself for letting the tinge of anxiety that plagued him show. He'd come a long way from that scared teenager, but knowing he was being watched and having no clue who it was had Eddie's heart thudding a staccato rhythm in his chest.

"I-I am," the person answered. It was a man, his Australian accent a deep rumble, and Eddie's dick twitched. *Damn.*

That accent. It got him every time, and the hesitancy in the man's voice, as if he might possibly be in the wrong place even though the man clearly worked on board, was even sexier.

Eddie was hot and sweaty, and he craved a drink of the water stashed in his bag. But his visitor had piqued Eddie's curiosity. He stepped forward, trying to coax the shy boy out. "You wanna step into the light so I can see you, rather than standing in the dark like a creeper?" Eddie taunted him, teased him in an attempt to draw him out, but the man's voice drew Eddie forward.

The silver fox who came into the light was not at all what Eddie expected—he was so much... more. Wearing a deer-in-the-headlights expression and clothes that looked like they'd been tailored to fit him despite being deceptively casual, he was the picture of style. Broad-shouldered with thick biceps and forearms, rounded pecs, and a flat stomach that tapered down to slim hips, he was an Adonis. Mussed up grey-blond hair and rich chocolate brown eyes, with a short beard and a perfect nose, completed the package. He was beautiful enough to model for any fitness magazine, lust spiked through Eddie. *Fuck me, he is gorgeous.* He was tall, so tall Eddie had to look up into eyes that were piercing yet warm at the same time. He was in trouble. Big, big trouble. Eddie hated acknowledging he had a type, because differences were what made the world an amazing place, but Eddie had a type. And the man in front of him ticked every. Single. Box.

Eddie was checking him out and not being subtle about it. Who the hell could when this sexy, stacked piece of gorgeousness was standing in front of them? When the man shivered, Eddie's eyes instinctively snapped to his. Did the guy do it because of Eddie's inspection? Was the man feeling the same insane lusty connection he was? The silver fox licked his lips, and Eddie nearly pounced. He used all his restraint to stop himself from climbing the guy like a jungle gym, but Eddie couldn't help the growl that escaped.

"What's your name?" the man rasped, his voice all dark and sexy.

"Eddie." He spoke a lot quieter than normal, but it had the desired effect; the silver fox leaned in closer, and Eddie smirked. Clearing his throat softly, Eddie added, "My, my, my, aren't you a handsome one? And what might your name be?"

"Will," he responded immediately, and Eddie smiled at the name. It suited him. Clean-cut like a William, but he was loose enough not to introduce himself with his full name. Eddie had only been on the ship a total of twenty-four hours, and he was generally hopeless with names, but Will was the sort of person Eddie wouldn't forget in a hurry, and now that he was there….

"And what are you doing down here, Will? You lost, or are you looking for little ol' me?" Eddie smiled and fluttered his lashes, touching his fingertips to his chest in an exaggerated caress. Will sucked in a breath, and Eddie took the opportunity to check him out again, this time dropping his gaze straight to Will's crotch. He had a nice bulge, the length of his shaft clearly outlined in the shorts he wore. Either he was going commando, or he had loose boxer shorts on, because there was no way that snake was being contained by anything.

Eddie licked his lips, imagining what it'd be like to drop to his knees right there and taste him.

"I, ah..." Will shifted his weight, and Eddie noticed for the first time he was carrying something. Clothes in a dry-cleaning bag, a duffel, and a hat balancing on his fingertips. But it wasn't just any hat. It was the same hat that the executive staff wore.

Will.

Executive staff.

No, it can't be.

Eddie's eyes shot to Will's, and Eddie knew exactly who was standing before him. It served him right for missing the captain's briefing for the incoming staff, listening to it being broadcast instead. He had a good excuse—an appointment with the on-board doctor to discuss Eddie's severe nut allergy kept him indisposed.

"Captain Preston, my apologies. I didn't.... How can I help you?" Eddie stuttered. Fuuuck. His first assignment on a cruise ship—Eddie's dream after experiencing the best and worst of West End—and on the first day on board he was hitting on the bloody captain. *God, could I be any more inappropriate?*

"Eddie," he murmured, looking oddly disappointed. He seemed to turn in on himself, to not stand as tall. Whatever spell had weaved itself between them, Eddie had broken it.

"It's okay. I'm just here to shower. I apologize for interrupting you. Please, continue." He gave Eddie a small smile and took a step to the side to pass Eddie.

But Eddie couldn't keep quiet. He couldn't let the man pass him by without reaching for him. Brushing his fingertips over Will's muscular forearm, Eddie swooned and asked the first thing that popped into his mind, "Why? I mean, why here? Why not your stateroom?"

"Shower's broken. It's only for tonight, though, I'm sure. I'll be in and out before you know it. Please don't let me stop you from continuing." Will was so apologetic, and yet Eddie was convinced it should have been him begging for the captain's forgiveness for his behaviour. Eddie may have been out of line, but there was no denying he'd acted on instinct to try to capture a moment of the gorgeous man's time.

"No, sure. I understand." Eddie smiled brightly and added, "I'm actually finishing up anyway. I'll show you." He pointed to the men's room and moved forward, holding the door open for the captain.

"I don't need formalities, Eddie. Not when it's just us." Will spoke quietly. When Eddie met his gaze again, his eyebrows furrowed, and Will shook his head and sighed, closing his eyes.

Eddie didn't understand what he was saying. He was the captain of the ship; a position in which formalities were expected. But Will changed the subject before Eddie could ask.

"Are you finished for the night?"

Eddie nodded, deciding that any conversation with his superior officer was better than none. "Finished up an hour ago. I just came down here to unwind. What about you? Just starting?" *Stupid question, Eddie. Of course he's just starting.*

"Yes, twelve-hour shift, then a short break before I do another shorter shift to get us into port." Will hung his things up and pulled a towel out of his bag, together with a couple of bottles—shampoo and body wash by the look of it.

"I'll, ah…" Eddie left the rest unsaid, knowing how inappropriate it would be to ask the captain if he could wash his hair for him. His back. Hell, everywhere. Eddie fished around in his bag for the bottle of water stashed in there and gulped it down, suddenly parched. But it had nothing to do with the pole workout. No, it was entirely the captain making Eddie desperate to quench his thirst.

Will paused, watching everything Eddie did, and heat flared in Eddie's gut. But the difference in Will was so pronounced that it gave Eddie pause. In the studio, he'd been standing there all tousled and sexy, with a shy smile and desire staining his cheeks an adorable pink. But since Eddie had recognized him, he'd become a walled-off ball of tension.

Eddie wanted to see that sexy smile again. The heat in his eyes.

He knew he shouldn't think about the captain that way, but it didn't matter. His body overrode any rational thought floating in his mind.

Without thinking, Eddie blurted, "I'll be dreaming of you tonight, handsome." Eddie disguised his horror at himself at the likelihood he'd blown any chance at a permanent position on the ship by sauntering out, adding a swish to his hips, and throwing a wink over his shoulder. Eddie hoped Will would think it was a joke, but he'd never been more serious. However the captain took it though, it was worth it when Will smiled.

It was breathtaking.

Eddie stumbled, tripping over his own feet.

"Sweet dreams, Eddie." Will blushed, and Eddie had the insane urge to kiss those sweet lips. Instead, he just smiled and stepped away from the door, letting it swing closed and break their connection. His stomach flip-flopped, his grin ridiculous as he thought about the cute captain and how endearing he was.

SEVEN

Will

Will hadn't been able to wipe the smile off his face for his entire shift, even when maintenance called to give him the bad news about the shower in his stateroom. The crack in the wall wasn't just cosmetic—the whole shower lining needed to be replaced, but they didn't have the materials on board to match the décor in his stateroom. So, they were putting up a temporary fix until they could get the parts when the ship next docked in Sydney. But the temporary fix was still at least two days away from being completed because of the need to drain the water and thoroughly dry the steel frame before the crack could be sealed.

Until then, Will would be shower-hopping. He should have been a lot more upset about it, but the sliver of excitement at the possibility of seeing Eddie again washed it away. He was like a breath of fresh air, clearing the cobwebs from a rickety old house. It was obvious that the young man lived every moment being authentically himself, and while Will wasn't in the closet, no one really knew which way he swung. He'd never given in to any of the offers that had been tossed his way or bothered answering any of the whispered questions about his sexuality, mainly because it was irrelevant. He'd vowed never to date anyone on the ship. The temptation that Eddie presented was far too alluring for Will's own good.

He smiled, remembering how the make-up had highlighted Eddie's best features—his eyes and those pouty lips—and the almost slight figure that hid the sheer strength in his body. The whole unapologetically flirty and utterly sexy package Eddie presented was alluring, and Will was crushing hard.

It was laughable, though, that crush. Will had sworn he wouldn't be one of those people. Executives that bed-hopped with the staff or crew complicated things, and Will wanted to run a smooth ship. Relationships between staff and guests were absolutely prohibited—one of the few offences that would result in a person's immediate sacking—but it was a different story if the two people worked on board.

"El Capitan," Will's first mate, Felice, teased as she grinned broadly. She was second in charge on the ship, and they always got along well. "Someone had a good shift." She nudged him playfully, and Will tried unsuccessfully to stifle his laughter. "You feel like giving me the rundown before you head out partying for the night?"

Will couldn't help but roll his eyes. "I have a wild night of working out, dinner, and an in-room movie planned, and if I'm feeling adventurous, I might even read a book."

"You should watch the performance tonight, Capitan. It's the new one that's been choreographed by whoever does Bruno Mars's concerts." At the mention of the singer, she had Will's attention, but it wasn't the show on stage that night he was thinking about. No, it was strictly a private viewing—one of Eddie stripped naked and dancing just for him on that pole. God, if the show was anything like what he'd seen of Eddie the night before, it'd be a hit.

Will had seen all the performances before, but it wasn't something he often indulged in. This time though, the possibility of seeing Eddie in action was too tempting for his own good. He was taunting his "no dating on board" rule, poking it with a stick. He should avoid the performance; he should keep to his original plan and have a quiet night in. But... yeah, nah. There was no way he was missing out.

Was Will hyping himself up, though? Talking up the man?

He was sure that if he saw Eddie again, it would prove his crush was just that—a crush that wouldn't go anywhere. It wouldn't mean anything.

It was easy to convince himself he'd over exaggerated how sexy Eddie was. No one was that perfect. Surely he'd just built the other man up so much that Will was fixating on him.

Think things through rationally. Will couldn't just break his rules—rules he'd put in place so his professionalism could never be questioned, and he was never the subject of a conflict of interest. Will had to get Eddie out of his head.

He was going to the show. If for no other reason than to prove that he was being ridiculous.

Will nodded and smiled. "I might just do that."

* * * * *

Two hours later, Will had run five kilometres of laps around the track on the top deck and was in the staff lift heading down into the bowels of the ship. His destination was the performers' change rooms for a shower.

When Will swiped his card against the lock, the door opened to a hive of activity. Racks of costumes were lined up with each performer's name on them. Not one person in the room looked up from what they were doing, checking and rechecking the clothes that would be moved into the backstage changing area.

He was just about to ask whether the bathrooms would be occupied when Eddie pushed through the door, and their eyes met. Will was kidding himself thinking he'd been over exaggerating the man's beauty. Lust sparked like an inferno inside him.

The dancer was even sexier than Will had let himself remember.

Eddie pulled off the preppy uniform for the entertainment staff like no other person Will had ever seen, especially when he paired it with his dark-lined eyes and glossy, kissable lips. Salmon shorts, a pale blue button-down shirt, and boat shoes had never looked so good. And damn, Will had to hold himself back from peeling Eddie out of his uniform right there.

"Hey, ah…" Will hesitated, blushing furiously. "Busy in there?" He motioned to the bathrooms Eddie had just come from. When he shook his head, Will's grin stretched across his face. "Great."

Eddie's smile matched his own, and it set the butterflies in Will's stomach fluttering. "Everyone will start to arrive in the next twenty or so to get make-up started for the show, so unless you want to be sharing the change room with them, you'd better be quick."

"Thanks for the tip." Will hitched his gym bag onto his shoulder, suddenly nervous. He didn't want their conversation to end, but if he had any hope of continuing his self-imposed on-board abstinence, he had to walk away.

Going to the show was a bad idea. Seeing Eddie again in his element would have Will's libido working overdrive, but instead of "goodbye" or "see you 'round," he blurted, "I'll be watching the show tonight. Looking forward to seeing you on stage."

Eddie's chest puffed out a little at Will's comment, and Will could see how pleased he was from his sensuous strut. Sauntering towards Will, Eddie ran his fingertip down his chest all the way from collarbone to navel, and Will sucked in a breath, his skin quivering from the other man's touch. "I'll make sure to shake my arse just that little bit harder for you then, handsome."

Eddie smirked and stepped away, swaying his hips to music only he heard as he stepped out of the studio. When

Will looked around, he was alone with the costumes. The studio had been an old storage room, but the sets for the shows were now too elaborate, too large to fit in there. By the looks of it, though, it was still used daily, and not just by sexy pole dancers who Will desperately wanted to feel against him.

* * * * *

Will had always understood why the reviews the ship got were high. The on-board entertainment was nothing short of spectacular, but the show unfolding before him was on a whole other level. Sitting in the second row, Will watched enraptured as the lead singer belted out a P!nk song, and the dancers turned aerialists swung from sheaths of material hanging from the scaffolding mounted to the roof. Eddie was right at the top of one of those swaths, and he had it wrapped around and around his body. Will knew what was coming, but he held his breath nevertheless.

Eddie let go and spun down, reaching so close to the floor that Will let out a squeak of panic before Eddie effort-lessly halted. It was only when Eddie's feet were firmly planted on the floor that Will relaxed the white-knuckled grip on the armrest. Will's breaths were heavy as he watched Eddie dash off the stage and appear a moment later, confidently sashaying down the aisle.

"Step right up, step right up," the singer announced from the stage, and Eddie's hand closed around his.

Confused, Will looked up at Eddie as the lithe dancer tugged him up.

"Come on, handsome. I need a volunteer."

"Oh, hell no." Will tried to pull away, shaking his head. That was the last thing he wanted to do.

"I'll make it worth your while." Eddie gave him a smile that held so much promise. But it wasn't his cockiness that had Will nodding. It wasn't the bravado or the charisma that Eddie exuded, but rather the genuine hope in his gaze. Will knew without a shadow of a doubt that Eddie genuinely wanted him to do this.

Will let Eddie lead him up to the stage, and he stood with the three other volunteers—two men and one woman—who'd been persuaded to go up there. Four chairs sat in a line facing the audience, spotlights on them. "What's your name, honey?" Katya, the lead singer, asked the woman.

"Aimee," she replied with a confident smile. Katya repeated the questions until she reached Will and her eyes widened before he gave a slight shake of his head. She recognized him—they'd known each other for years—but he didn't want her announcing to the entire theatre that it was him up on the stage. There were some things guests didn't need to know, even if he was up there during his downtime.

"And what's your name?" She paused, holding the microphone out.

"William," he offered up, smiling politely at her.

"Okay, folks. Let's give a round of applause for our volunteers Aimee, Sharman, Tom, and William." The audience clapped, and Will took his cue from the others, who gave a small wave to them.

Eddie was back by his side, now dressed in shiny black skin-hugging tights with sparkly stripes down the outside. Chunky, loosely laced black boots and a bowtie were the only other things he had on. The other male dancer was wearing exactly the same thing, and the two women looked like Playboy bunnies. Even though they were dressed similarly, Will took no notice of them. He couldn't take his eyes off Eddie.

He was riveted.

Every single muscle in Eddie's limber body was defined, and his damp skin looked downright lickable. His stage make-up gave him a come-hither vibe that made Will want to not only break his self-imposed rule but shatter it into a million pieces.

Eddie grasped Will's hand, directing him to the chair at the end of the row. The other dancers did the same for their volunteers, and the lead singer started singing Christina's "Dirty."

Just like with the last song he and Eddie had been chest to chest to, the lyrics washed over Will and wrapped him in a haze of longing.

Eddie pushed him down into the chair with a flourish, and in time with the beat, spread Will's legs wide, stepping between them. With a finger under his chin, Eddie lifted Will's face to his and leaned in close while he shook his ass. It took Will every ounce of strength in his body not to reach out and touch Eddie, to pull him close and kiss the ever-loving fuck out of him. But from the gleam in Eddie's eyes, Will knew he wasn't allowed to touch.

Yet.

"Hope you're ready for a wild ride, handsome," Eddie whispered seductively in his ear. When the rumbly groan bubbled up from deep within Will, Eddie hummed. "Oh, I like that. I wanna hear that again." He snapped his hips from side to side and trailed his fingertips across Will's collarbone, stepping around his knee.

"And again."

Straddling Will's leg, they locked eyes, and Will bit down on his lip, lest he pulled Eddie on top of him to feast on the man. If Will thought Eddie was gorgeous dancing up on the pole or standing a foot away from him in the studio, that close he was stunning. The dark kohl around his emerald eyes made them pop. His pupils flared, and a puff of his breath tickled Will's face. Eddie leaned in and rubbed himself along Will, and he instinctively shifted, need propelling Will to eliminate the distance between them. Hands on Will's head, Eddie pulled him close, holding him just out of reach of Eddie's skin. Eddie arched back and stood, rolling his hips seductively. This close to him, Will was powerless to resist the allure. He forced himself closer and pressed his lips against Eddie's belly, breathing in his musky scent. Before Will lost any more of his self-control, Eddie shifted, spinning away from Will.

He strutted behind the chair. Eddie hooked his leg over Will's right shoulder, and Will instinctively reached for Eddie's calf, squeezing as Eddie's other foot slipped over his left side. Will wanted to see him, wanted to do more than touch his legs, but he would take what he could get. Eddie straightened then and moved away, the chair jerking as he slid underneath it and through Will's legs. Writhing on the floor in front of Will, a sexy as fuck grind and slide, Eddie looked over his shoulder and winked at him before pushing up on his arms and rolling his hips. Will didn't need to use his imagination to know what Eddie would be like in bed. Seductive, teasing, and sexy as hell.

Will hoped that his boner was hidden from the audience. He was so grateful that they had no idea who he was, because he was harder than he'd ever been before when Eddie snapped his hips forward. He bit down on his cheek to stifle the moans that wanted to break free and held tight to the chair so he didn't palm his dick.

Will could do nothing except hope the song would end before he came in his pants. He was already on edge, pre-cum leaking from his dick like it was a tap. But at the same time, he never wanted it to stop; he could watch Eddie's moves forever.

Jumping up, Eddie stalked forward, coming at Will like he wanted to devour him. His green eyes blazed, and Will wanted to chase Eddie's pink tongue, tasting and teasing him, when he swiped it along his bottom lip. Pushing Will's knees together, Eddie straddled him, pressing against him. From the corner of Will's eye, he could see the other dancers. He saw just how much farther away from their volunteers they were. Will was up on stage with Eddie in a theatre full of people, but this was no act for the two of them. This was them both giving in to the desire playing out between them. And Will's self-imposed rule of not dating the staff or crew?

Gone.

Obliterated beyond recognition.

Will ran his hands up Eddie's legs and cupped his arse, feeling the play of firm muscle against his hands as Eddie moved. He was so freaking beautiful that Will's breath caught. God, he wanted to take his time with him, to love on him until they were both mindless with lust and completely satiated. But Will's connection to Eddie was broken far too quickly. The dancer next to them started rapping, and Eddie pulled away, he and the two other performers moving in sync and breakdancing.

Will's chest heaved, his fingers itched to reach out for Eddie again, but instead, he waited. Impatiently.

Eddie finished the choreographed moves on the floor of the stage and crawled towards Will on his knees. Pulling Will's knees apart, Eddie slipped between Will's legs and pulled his bowtie off, wrapping it around the back of Will's neck, using it to pull him close and rub his face against Will's. "I really wanna kiss you right now," he murmured before hopping up, pushing Will's legs together and sitting on his lap, crossing one leg over the other and resting his chin on his fist. The smirk he flashed Will was adorable. Naughty and far too tempting for his own good.

As the music came to a close and the audience clapped, Eddie stood and grasped Will's hand, quickly leading him backstage after they bowed. He saw the stairs that led down to the seating area, but Eddie held onto him, waiting for the other guests and dancers to move away. He stepped close, his chest still heaving. Eddie ran his fingertips down Will's cheek and kissed him. It was just a press of his lips against Will's, but it was enough to make Will swoon.

"Go," Will murmured, pushing Eddie away but keeping a hold of the bowtie. "This is mine now. You'll have to get another one." Eddie smirked and turned, taking a step before spinning back to Will, gripping the back of his neck and kissing him again, another hard press of his lips. Will laughed as he pulled away, the lightness in his chest matching the butterflies fluttering in his belly.

Will licked his lips and moaned when Eddie's flavour hit him—something irresistibly sweet mixed with strawberry lip gloss. It was Will's favourite. Eddie's nostrils flared, and he visibly clenched his jaw before spinning around and dashing backstage into the change room. Will watched the rest of the performance from that very spot, not wanting any more distance between them than was absolutely necessary.

He'd never had such an innate draw to someone before, not even his ex. But that's what cruise ships did to people— it was literally an island, and being in close quarters with people 24/7 stirred the melting pot. Will had held out for so long, but suddenly he didn't want to anymore. He wanted this, wanted Eddie with every fibre of his being.

EIGHT

Eddie

"**W**hat the hell were you thinking, Eddie?" Katya hissed at him as the curtain drew to a close, gesticulating wildly and her eyes flashing. "The captain? Your first assignment on a ship, and not only do you not pick a woman, so we've got even numbers on stage like the show calls for, but you pick Captain Preston to give a lap dance to? Are you insane?"

"I'm sorry," he mumbled. He knew he was playing with fire. In his head, he knew that reaching out for Will when he'd seen him sitting in the second row was a bad idea, but he couldn't help it. And it wasn't like Will resisted. Hell, Andrea had asked three men before one of them agreed to come up on stage, and that was only because his friends pushed him out of the seat. Eddie had just asked, and after a moment's hesitation, Will had followed him up. Had he done it because he didn't want to cause a scene?

"Look, I know I was supposed to pick a woman, but when I saw Will, I thought it'd be fun to have him up there. Next time I'll do what I'm supposed to. I can take orders.

Really, I can. But I've seen him before, spoken to him as well. I didn't think he'd mind."

"I didn't mind." Will spoke those words in that warm voice of his from behind Eddie. The tension in Eddie's muscles relaxed, knowing Will wasn't upset. Coming to stand beside him, Will was close enough that their shoulders touched. His warmth seeped through Eddie's skin, and he found himself leaning into the bigger man, trying to get closer. "Eddie and I have spoken before, and there's nothing for you to be upset about, Katya. Eddie's gay, I assume. I'm gay, and there are passengers on board who identify as LGBTI. I think it's good he was his authentic self. He made the dance his own while still doing everything he was required. Don't you agree?" He inclined his head, waiting for an answer from her. In that moment, he was a consummate professional, and Eddie could see why so many people looked up to him. He was, quite literally, the ship's fearless leader. He carried himself with quiet confidence. There was no empty bravado about him, no aggressive authoritarianism either, just mutual respect for every person in the room.

"Yes, Captain, I apologize. I didn't want you to feel uncomfortable." She didn't meet his eyes as she expressed her regret.

"It's fine, but truly, I enjoyed myself." Will brushed his fingers against Eddie's hand, sending tingles through his body. The two kisses they'd shared were innocent and quick. They weren't enough, but even though it'd be easy for them to fall into bed together and shag each other's brains out, Eddie was intrigued. He really wanted to get to know Will a little better. Then the other man added, "I do appreciate your level of professionalism, though, Katya." She looked up at him and smiled, genuinely relieved. Eddie, on the other hand, swooned. Just a little.

Will motioned to Eddie, and with a hand on the small of his back, guided him to a quieter part of the backstage area. He looked down and away, blushing slightly, that adorable, shy boy Eddie had first met making an appearance again. "What time do you finish up?"

Giddy excitement pulsed through Eddie, and he couldn't help but smile. "You wanna see me again, handsome?" He paused, waiting for Will's response. When he looked at Eddie through lowered lashes with a small smile playing on his lips, Eddie sighed. "'Cause I'd really like it if you did."

"I thought maybe we could get a drink together, get to know each other a little." Then he frowned and looked at Eddie, adding, "Unless you didn't want that. I mean, if you just want to… well, I'd like to, but I'm not really into that kind of thing." He winced. "It's really hard having a private conversation when there's a million people around all the time."

Eddie put a hand on his forearm, squeezing it and enjoying the firm, warm muscle tanned to a golden glow, a smattering of light hairs dotting his arm. His skin tone contrasted beautifully with the rolled-up sleeves of his light blue button-down shirt. "Just for the record, I'd love to have a drink with you. But my shift runs for another few hours yet, and I know you mentioned having an early shift tomorrow. What about tomorrow night?"

His smile was disappointed, but he nodded. "I'll look forward to it."

"Goodnight, Will." Eddie wanted to kiss him again, but this time he wanted a proper kiss. Lingering and sexy. He wanted to press himself up against the wall of muscle that Captain Preston was and rub all over him like a cat.

"Night, Eddie." He squeezed the hand Eddie was still caressing along Will's muscular forearm, and Will's eyes darkened as Eddie licked his lips, imagining setting fire to the sheets with this man. Those muscles were just delicious, and he wanted more of them. But he also wanted to see just how far the shy blush that stained Will's cheeks spread over his body and what would make the colour flare the hardest.

Will disappeared down the stairs, exiting the stage, and Eddie smiled. He knew he looked love-struck and all gushy, but his sexy silver-fox Captain did that.

"I bet he'd be a good fuck." Eddie whirled around at the comment and stared down the only person still standing on the stage. Holding the mic stand in one hand, Gerard flicked his eyes back to Eddie. "Then again, you might be too with how flexible you are. With your ankles up around your ears..."

Eddie gritted his teeth and stalked towards the other man until he was standing chest to chest with him. The bastard knew he was good-looking and used it to his advantage. But Eddie had been surrounded by arseholish, self-centred types his whole career. Hell, Gerard was enough like his ex-lover—the one who was allergic to any type of commitment, especially monogamy—that he knew to keep well away from him.

"Shut your mouth. Now. Before you say something you regret." Eddie stood straighter, hardening his gaze and mentally preparing himself to duck a punch. But one never came. Instead, Gerard cupped him, squeezing Eddie's cock and balls a little too tight, before leaning in and licking the sweat drying on Eddie's throat. Eddie pushed him away, masking a shudder with his anger as he lunged for Gerard, aiming to plant his knee in his groin. Gerard dodged him, and the look he aimed at Eddie had him pulling up short. He was a predator, sizing Eddie up as if he was going to eat him. Cold and calculating. Eddie was instantly transported back to his teenage years when he was that vulnerable kid getting beaten up by Duncan and his cronies.

"Pine after the captain all you want, but you'll be my pretty little cocksucker soon enough. I can wait." Gerard aimed a smile that was more of a bearing of teeth than anything remotely friendly and strode away. Eddie's knees just about gave way, fear and anger a potent combination with the adrenaline coursing through his veins. Memories collided with the present, the scabbed wounds caused by his childhood bullies reopening. The adult part of his psyche told him to get help. To report him and let the HR Director sort him out. The child in him cowered under the bed. The last time he'd been in a wildly different, yet similar situation, he'd confided in his parents.

Look where it got him.

He could still feel the pain from each blow and kick where they landed. The fear and the looking over his shoulder. No, this time he'd do it differently. His dad had once told him that sometimes if you ignored a bully, they'd leave you alone. That's what he was going to do. It's what he needed to do.

Eddie was the newcomer on the ship. Gerard was a veteran who had the respect of all the entertainers. He probably knew all the right people too. No one would believe him. But worse still, they might believe him. Then what? He'd be back in school again, terrorized by the bully. What if he was putting his job at risk too? No, he just needed to suck it up. Put on a brave face and not give Gerard anything else to target him for.

He took a deep breath, centring himself, and went straight to the changing rooms. The sooner he was in his costume for his performance at the bar, the sooner he'd be away from Gerard.

* * * * *

"Did you still want to get that drink together?" Will looked around at the entertainers slowly filing into the warm-up room and frowned when he noticed more than one set of eyes on them. His consternation was ridiculously adorable, but he was right. The only place a person ever had any privacy was in their stateroom, and sometimes not even then. Eddie was one of the lucky few. As an enter-tainer, he had his own room. The crew—waiters, cleaners, machinists, and the myriad other people who made the cruise possible—all shared rooms, some bunking with three other people.

Eddie rested his hand on Will's side, smiling as he leant in close, resisting the urge to nuzzle into Will. Eddie was drawn to him. He wanted to cuddle Will close and make the best of any opportunity to touch all that warm skin and solid muscle. But that wasn't all Eddie wanted to do. He wanted to get to know him better. Captain Preston was intriguing. An alluring mix of shy and sweet, yet strong and capable, Eddie was captivated by the juxtapositions in his personal-ity. There was no way he'd turn Will down for any offer of a date, but he couldn't deny that he would have preferred somewhere quiet and out of view of anyone who could start rumours.

"I'd love to. If you can give me ten minutes to shower and change, we can head to the bar."

Will's smile was a mix of relief and embarrassment, and Eddie couldn't help sliding that hand around Will's waist and hugging him close just to touch him.

"Actually, I thought somewhere a little quieter than the bar."

Eddie lit up like a Christmas tree at Will's suggestion. He hadn't had a chance to fully explore the ship yet. The crew areas he'd visited were always full, no matter what time he was there. So, finding a gem where he could switch off and avoid people for half a minute seemed like a dream. "I'd love to."

This time Will's smile was genuine. "Go then." He motioned to the changing rooms, and Eddie grinned, adding a swish of his hips as he dashed through the doors.

And walked straight into someone else.

Eddie stammered out an apology, straightening himself up as he cottoned on to who he'd walked into. Gerard.

The man's hand landing on his arse and kneading it made Eddie squirm, and not in a good way. He tried to pull free of Gerard's grasp, but it was no use. The other man was stronger and used his bulk to push Eddie away from the changing room doors. They were alone, and a pang of fear pulsed through him.

Eddie's skin crawled with disgust when Gerard leered at him. "So keen to get in my pants that you're throwing yourself at me, little cocksucker?"

"Fuck off, Gerard."

He laughed, a cold, calculated cackle, and let Eddie go, adding loudly in a singsong voice, "Someone's getting lucky tonight."

Eddie stepped away from him, hesitating before dashing into the changing rooms, dodging the performers in various stages of undress to get to the showers. The last thing he wanted was to get stuck alone with the vile sleaze again, but if Eddie was quick, he'd be in and out while the others were still there.

Within a few minutes, Eddie was slipping on his shoes and straightening his silky black pants and pale pink satin shirt with cap sleeves, a cute tie at the throat, and a plunging neckline. The material was glorious against his skin, soft and smooth where it clung to him, highlighting his trim waist.

He pushed back into the corridor where Will was waiting, chatting with Seamus, one of the other singers. He was a good guy. Friendly and with years of experience, Seamus had offered to answer any of Eddie's questions and given him the rundown of who's who on the ship. Shame he hadn't warned Eddie about Gerard.

Will's gaze snagged on him and the warmth in his eyes enveloped Eddie in an embrace like drinking a hot chocolate, wrapped in a fuzzy blanket by the fire on a cold winter's evening. He bade Seamus a goodbye and turned his attention to Eddie. "You look lovely." His smile lit Eddie up, and he swooned a little. "Shall we?" He motioned in the direction of the lifts and placed his big hand on the small of Eddie's back as they walked. Warmth curled low in Eddie's belly, making it flip flop, the butterflies flittering around in an exciting kaleidoscope of colour. Eddie loved a gentleman, especially one who lived and breathed chivalry, and so far, Will had been charming.

Will didn't remove his hand even when he pushed the button on the wall of the lift, nor when the carriage started ascending through the belly of the ship. Eddie was sure his smile was giddy, childish excitement pulsing through him at the chance to discover something new onboard and sharing it with the captain. The air between them sparked with anticipation, and Eddie wondered if Will could feel it too.

The numbers flashed above the doors until they reached the top floor, and Eddie smiled, meeting Will's gaze when he reached for Eddie's hand. Will tugged him along the corridor through unfamiliar territory. He hadn't been in that part of the ship before, and he took it all in, wide-eyed with excitement. They couldn't see much from where they stood—only the walls painted in the same colours with doors on either side of them. Photographs were hung at regular intervals, and royal blue carpet lined the floors. There was more of a lurch in the ship that high up, the rolling of the swell of the Pacific so much more noticeable so far above the waterline.

Will led him to a white metal door marked Authorized Personnel Only, and Eddie stopped short.

"Will, I don't want you bending any rules for me," he hesitated.

"Staff can enter. Crew aren't authorized, except to clean the area. I wouldn't ask you to risk your job for me, Eddie. Not when you've got so much talent. You've obviously worked hard to get here. I wouldn't jeopardize that for you."

Eddie didn't expect Will's understanding or recognition. But he was quickly learning that despite unintentionally setting the bar extraordinarily high, he had completely underestimated Will. And with every little part Will showed him, Eddie liked him more.

"Where are we going?" Eddie asked, much more curious now.

"The officer's deck. It's the only semi-private part of the ship, apart from our staterooms, but it's visible from the bridge, so not completely secluded." When he held his ID card against the door lock, and it flashed green, Will pushed through, holding the door open for Eddie. His heart swelled, joy filling him. His captain was a sweetheart.

The deck was sparsely furnished. A couple of loungers were pushed to the side, overlooking the water that stretched in front of them for miles. Sheltered from the buffeting winds was a small round table with a long white tablecloth flapping in the lighter breeze decorated with a vase and a single red rose. Two chairs were pushed in, and standing aside one of them was a bucket with a bottle and two glasses perched in it. Strands of fairy lights were hung along the pergola-type structure overhead. It was as if a million stars lit the sky.

When Eddie looked beyond the deck, he gasped. There literally were a million stars overhead. Without the light pollution from a city, every star was visible against the ink-black sky. It was magical.

"It's not much," Will murmured, but he was entirely wrong. He'd taken Eddie somewhere truly special.

Eddie smiled softly, reaching up to kiss Will on the cheek. The blush that stained the captain's cheeks in response made Eddie grin more. "It's perfect. Or it will be once we put some music on." Eddie retrieved his ship cell from his pocket and hit Play on a classical music playlist, adjusting the volume to low and placing it on the table.

Will set about rolling up the sleeves of his shirt and showed Eddie the bottle of bubbles. "Is this okay? We can get something else if you'd prefer."

Eddie could only nod, focussing instead on the sight of those muscular forearms bulging from under his shirt sleeves. When Will peeled the foil off the bottle, Eddie wanted to reach out for him. To touch him. Realizing he could, Eddie placed his hand on Will's hip and stepped closer, leaning into him.

Will didn't hesitate, dumping the bottle and glass back into the bucket and turning his undivided attention to Eddie. His hands on Will's broad chest, Eddie smoothed them down to his waist and pulled the man close. Will's arms went around him, and Eddie reached up, cupping his face in his hands. "I'm glad you chose me, Will." This time when Eddie kissed him, it was slow and sweet. He licked his bottom lip, relishing the taste of lime and soda, minus the kick from the vodka and something uniquely Will. When he opened for Eddie, their tongues touched gently. The tartness mixed with his flavour was intoxicating, and Eddie moaned, wanting to get closer. He wanted to climb the older man and wrap himself around him like the cute koalas Eddie had seen at the zoo in Sydney.

Eddie didn't want to pull back. He hated the idea of putting any distance between them, but if he didn't, he knew it'd get hot and heavy real quick. There was no way he wanted Will to think Eddie was using him for a casual lay. He'd only just met him, spent all of twenty minutes in Will's presence, but even in that time, he could see how special Will was.

And Eddie wanted his date night.

He opened his eyes and smiled at Will, brushing his fingers along the line of his beard. "You're so handsome."

Will ducked his head and laughed self-consciously, and this time Eddie let him go so he could retrieve the bottle. He handed Eddie a flute once he'd poured it and half a glass for him. Hand in hand, they wandered over to the railing and looked out across the darkened ocean. The moon shimmered on the surface of the water, barely a ripple breaking as the ship sailed through the inky ocean waters. Will stood behind him, pressing his warm body against Eddie's from shoulder to hip, and wrapped an arm around Eddie's waist. The soft swish of wash against the hull of the ship and the music playing on the deck enveloped them in their own little bubble. For the first time since he'd arrived onboard, Eddie was truly at peace. He was exactly where he was supposed to be in that moment, and the rightness washed over him like a gentle lapping wave. Will giving them a moment alone without the prying eyes of the other crew and without any rumours that would be stirred up by them being seen together was perfection.

Eddie sank into Will's embrace, loving the strength of his arms surrounding him. They stood quietly, watching the gentle rise and fall of the ocean swell. "This is my favourite part of the ship," Will murmured in his ear, raising goosebumps over Eddie's skin.

"Thank you for sharing it." Eddie sighed happily, turning so he could wrap his own arms around Will, and snuggled into him, rubbing his cheek against the thatch of hair poking out from Will's collar. Eddie wanted to run his fingers through it, to explore every inch of him and show him just how infatuated he was.

"Dance with me?" Will asked after they'd watched a few clouds washed in silver moonlight roll across the sky.

Will led him in a slow waltz. His moves weren't fancy, but Eddie appreciated that more than if it were a perfectly polished choreography. Although shy, Will was daring too. He didn't hesitate to put himself out there, to do something Eddie loved, even though Eddie might have been an arse and criticized him.

They stayed like that, swaying softly in the moonlight for hours, whispered conversation between them and soft laughs as Will charmed Eddie with stories of his early career and Eddie spoke about RCA and his experiences in West End.

Eddie yawned and nuzzled into Will's chest, holding him tighter so he could feel the rumble of Will's words against his skin. "Come on, let's get you into bed."

"Hmm, yes, please," he mumbled into Will's chest. "Will you stay?"

Eddie blinked and raised his head, suddenly wide awake. He hadn't meant his question like it sounded. As much as Eddie wanted to strip Will down and worship every beautiful part of him, he didn't want to jump straight into it with him. Will was regarding him, but Eddie couldn't get a read on the man, his poker face completely devoid of emotion. His expression was inscrutable. "I meant to sleep, that's all," Eddie blurted. "I don't want to rush this, whatever it is between us, but I don't want tonight to end either. Never mind, it's stupid. I shouldn't have asked." Eddie was rambling, his words tumbling out without any pause between them. He never rambled, but it seemed Will had him tongue-tied, babbling, and wanting to flirt all at the same time. He was suddenly a ball of nerves and uncertainty all rolled into one.

"Eddie," Will murmured, tugging his hands away from his heated cheeks. "I'd love to go to sleep with you."

As suddenly as it had descended, the worry lifted, and he smiled at his captain.

They walked hand in hand to the lifts. "I'm guessing you only have a single bed in your suite?" he asked. "But a working shower."

"Yes, and you've got a big comfy bed and no shower." Will laughed and nodded, blushing again. "How about we sleep in yours, then you can use my bathroom in the morning?" When Will agreed, Eddie grinned happily, hooking his fingers through the belt loops in Will's dress pants. He leaned in for a slow kiss as the lift descended to their quarters.

They wandered down the corridor to Will's stateroom, and when they entered, Eddie couldn't help but take it all in. The bathroom was off to the left, and he could see the fan blowing into the cavity in the wall, drying it out. In the suite itself, a queen bed took up most of the space, and on the other side underneath the windows was a couch. A TV and a desk and chair were positioned on the opposite side. But it was the picture hanging on the wall at the head of his bed that spoke volumes about Captain Preston's type.

"Can I get you anything?" Will asked.

"So, you're into dancers?" The confident façade Eddie presented to the world—the one of the successful dancer and unrufflable character—crumbled, and he sounded defensive even to his own ears. He winced, hating the uncertainty that crept into his mind.

Will reached for Eddie's hand, and he hesitantly let him grasp it. His grip was warm and firm, the same as it had been before. "I found that picture a decade ago when I was married. I loved the contrast in it—the grungy background against the beauty of the artist. It spoke to me, and it was literally the only thing I took when I left my ex. I wasn't desperate to have it, but I knew he'd throw it out simply because I'd chosen it. Stefan was spiteful like that." Will pointed to the lines of the dancer's body, the curvature in his pose. "I love how fluid his body looks, how beautifully he holds himself. But that's all. He's no fantasy that I jerk off to if that's what you're asking."

"So...." Eddie trailed off. Will had stumped him with his earnestness. "Wait, you were married?"

"Yeah. It was pretty toxic to begin with, but when he cheated, I walked."

"Know that feeling. Henri, my first lover—" He rolled his eyes. "—he wouldn't let me call him my boyfriend— couldn't keep it in his pants. If they had a heartbeat, he'd do them. He always said that he needed to appear attainable. I didn't realize that appearing attainable meant shagging anyone. We never made a commitment to be exclusive, but I thought that once you were with someone, you stopped being with other people. I was straight out of high school and far too naïve for my own good."

"I was a little like that too. Older, but no less naïve. Stefan was using me right from the word go."

"Does the picture bring back bad memories? I mean, you got it when you were together."

Will shook his head. "Nah, not anymore. Especially not when you're here."

Eddie swooned. Just a little. All the happy fluttery butterflies alighted, the weightlessness in his belly giving him the sensation that he could float right into Will's arms. But above all that, he was grateful Will had been able to move past his break-up and see it for what it was. He batted his lashes. "So, tell me more about me."

Will laughed and wrapped Eddie up in an embrace that had him giggling. Becoming serious, Will tilted Eddie's face to his and joined their lips together, kissing him until he was drunk and starved for air. Will didn't just kiss. He was like an ocean that you could fall into and get lost in exploring its wonders. "You captivated me when I saw you dancing for the first time, and since then, I've been spellbound. You're an artist, perfection in motion."

In the space of a few minutes, Will had rendered Eddie speechless twice. But this time, Eddie was able to let go of the insecure part of him—the gift from Duncan and his cronies, the wound torn open again by Gerard. But Will's words filled him with new confidence. To take back part of himself. He stood straighter and preened. Will reminded Eddie that he was fabulous. He was fierce. And he certainly wasn't a basket case freaking out over a picture. Internally shaking his head at himself, Eddie winked at Will and tried to lighten the conversation. "Good answer. So, I could do with a spare toothbrush?"

Will's answering grin had him smiling too, and when he kissed Eddie's fingertips still laced with his, Eddie pressed a hand to his chest and sighed dreamily. He watched Will move into the bathroom, and after rummaging around, he held up a toothbrush in a box with a flourish and added a bow after a giggle escaped Eddie's lips.

"Bravo," Eddie called out, laughing and clapping at the same time.

NINE

Will

Will sat on the bed, waiting for Eddie to finish in his bathroom. He couldn't decide whether he was suffering from nerves or excitement. Probably a little of both. He'd never had a date like this before, and he hated the idea of it ending. But when Eddie had asked him to stay, Will's walls had slammed back into place. He had rules in place for a reason—no fraternizing with the staff or crew—and Eddie had crashed through those walls so quickly that Will was still standing there dumbstruck and assessing the rubble when Eddie had thrown him for a loop again. Will didn't want them to just be about sex; he didn't want to start making the same mistakes that his mentor had warned him about.

But everything in Will's body screamed for him to dive headfirst into Eddie. Lord knew he wanted him. But he was scared too. After his relationship with Stefan had fallen apart, Will realized that they'd had no substance beyond good sex. He desperately wanted things to be different with Eddie. The thought of walking away from Eddie with only a painting tore Will up more than it ever had when it had happened with Stefan.

Hook-ups were one thing, but this was the first time Will had found himself wanting more. And that terrified him.

The toilet flushed, and he heard the tap running. Eddie walked out a moment later fresh-faced and clear of the dark eyeliner around his eyes. He stopped dead in his tracks and did a slow perusal of Will's body. The hunger in his gaze was incendiary, lighting Will up from inside. He'd taken off his shirt and tossed it on the chair but left his dress pants on. In bare feet, Will padded over to him and ran his fingertips down Eddie's cheek before tipping his chin up and giving in to the need to kiss him.

"I'm really glad you chose me," Will murmured, closing his eyes and hoping against hope that the man before him would understand Will's reticence to drop trou and jump into mutual blow jobs, or whatever else they could come up with.

Will savoured the moment when Eddie's breath caught.

"Go do something with all this perfection." Eddie waved his hands at all of Will, making him smile. He could tell Eddie was trying to be playful, trying to respect the boundaries he'd set, but the gravel in his voice told him just how much Eddie was struggling. Will sympathized. The desire was overwhelming. That spark between them heating to supernova status.

But was Eddie in it just for sex? Just for the kudos of sleeping with the captain? He hadn't seemed like the type, but Will had been wrong about a person's character before.

The last person he'd trusted so easily was Stefan, and the man had abused that trust for years. What if Will was wrong again? He stepped away from Eddie and gave him a small smile before heading into the bathroom, needing the privacy and space to collect his thoughts that the small room afforded.

After brushing his teeth, he closed his eyes and took a cleansing breath. Decision made, he hoped Eddie would respect it. Opening the door, the first thing Will noticed was that Eddie had dimmed the lamps to a more intimate level. Lying half under the covers, he could see Eddie was still wearing briefs, if that's what they could be called. They were tiny. A scrap of bright yellow material that followed the curve of an arse Will wanted to bite. He almost wanted to slap himself silly when he realized how happy he was that Eddie wasn't stroking himself in the middle of the bed. Because that visual... damn. Will could get on board with that, even if it would have made waiting an impossibility.

He stripped down to his boxer briefs and looked to Eddie to gauge his reaction.

"Get in here," Eddie spoke, his tone warm. Will slid in next to him, and they rolled onto their sides, facing each other. "This side of the bed okay for me to lie on?" Will nodded his answer and mirrored Eddie's position, slipping a hand under his pillow and smiling at him. Eddie reached out for Will's other hand, lacing their fingers together, and complained playfully, "I'm not tired anymore."

Will bit down on his lip and willed himself not to blush, but he knew it was futile when his cheeks were awash with heat. He had no idea why the hell he was so shy around Eddie, except that he was crushing hard. The crazy butterflies he got every time he thought of Eddie were exciting, especially when the man before him was beautiful and sexy and lovely all at the same time. Will wanted to swoon and laugh and learn everything about Eddie. There were so many questions he wanted to know the answers to while wrapped up in his arms.

"So where did you grow up?" Will asked with a smile.

"Leeds," he explained. "My parents are both in warehousing. They fell in love, got married, and had five kids. I'm in the middle. You?"

"The Gold Coast. Ma and Dad were big on fishing and boating. I grew up on the water, spent all my spare time at Currumbin in the estuary and on the beach. My younger brother and I are both in the maritime industry." Will pointed to the photo of his extended family on the desk facing them, everyone in swimwear and lounging around on the deck of a boat, blue water, white sand, and cerulean skies in the background. "That's everyone. Ma and Dad are divorced, and they both have new partners now, but they're still friends." Will stroked his thumb along Eddie's hand, enjoying the smooth skin that met his own. Eddie's eyes softened when he turned back to Will and smiled.

"So different from where I grew up." Eddie paused and pursed his lips in thought. "When did you know you were gay?"

"Pretty late, actually. I did all the stereotypical things masc boys do, but as a teenager, I never felt comfortable in my own skin. Then I was channel surfing one night and ended up watching the Sydney Mardi Gras. Right then I knew. All the pieces that I couldn't make fit and didn't understand about myself suddenly slotted into place. Ma took a bit to get used to the idea, but Dad just smiled at me and told me it'd taken me long enough to figure it out. I was twenty."

Will placed his free hand on Eddie's hairless chest and stroked him there, loving the smooth skin that met his touch. He couldn't get enough of exploring him, but it wasn't sexual. Not entirely anyway. Will wanted to get close to him. To press himself against every inch of Eddie's body and take his time to explore.

"Is your mum okay with you now?" Eddie's concern— the furrowed brow and the way he bit down on his bottom lip—was touching.

"Yeah. She tried to say I was mistaking my attraction for men because there were so many half-dressed women there. It wasn't that, though. When I let myself look, really just let go and watch, it occurred to me that the women didn't hold my attention. It was the men. I couldn't keep my eyes off them. It was as if I'd adjusted the focus, and I could finally see clearly. I was anything but confused." Will huffed out a laugh and grinned at Eddie. "I told Ma if I was just distracted by the half-naked women, I wouldn't be imagining sucking cock."

Eddie barked out a laugh and scandalized, whisper-shouted, "You did not. No way." The glint in his eyes and his bright smile took Will's breath away.

"I did." Will's voice was rougher than normal, but he cleared his throat and continued. "My parents are pretty open about sex. They always told us to ask any question we wanted to know and then, later on, insisted that when we were dating someone, we bring them home instead of going somewhere unsafe. I'd been with a few women, but it wasn't exactly mind-blowing. Never anything like my friends raved about. I thought there was something wrong with me. Back then, we didn't really have terms for being asexual or demi. But it wasn't so much that. I'd just been looking at the wrong people. When I let myself think about who I found attractive, I finally admitted it wasn't women. It was men." Will shook his head at himself, remembering how confused he'd been as a teenager. "I was so completely clueless."

A shudder of need passed through Will when Eddie rubbed his foot along the length of his calf.

"I was a bit the same, but far younger—I was like twelve. My bestie and I were talking about which boys we wanted to kiss, and the brother of our mutual crush overheard us. Didn't go down well, but we were both okay in the end. Few bumps and bruises." His words were flippant, but a haunted look flashed in his eyes. Will drew him closer, wishing he could protect Eddie from the arseholes he'd clearly encountered. Will had never been picked on—he'd always been a jock. He hadn't played traditional sports himself, but he'd been active in the sailing club, surfing, and surf boat rowing. If it was on the water, he was doing it. It made him popular with both guys and girls.

"We didn't really see what the problem was—Jess is bi so she liked girls and we both liked boys—but everyone else did. I was picked on at first for being a dancer, then for being a faggot. I didn't even know what that was, but everyone was pretty quick to throw it around. It was like the go-to insult. But Mum and Dad were great. Dad told me how much he loved me, and Mum talked terminology. She gave me the words to describe myself, and we called a helpline, so I knew I wasn't alone. Then they marched in every pride parade with me. This will be the first year I won't be there, but they're sending photos."

"We're lucky we've both had supportive families. What about dancing? How'd you get into it?"

"A bit like you with water. I was dancing before I could walk. Music has always spoken to a part of my soul. When I was a toddler, I'd put on concerts for my family and make everyone watch me while I twirled around. I even had the tutu. When I was four, Dad asked me if I wanted to play football like my older brother, but I told him ballet. Then, later on, I added hip-hop and dance gymnastics. I haven't looked back." He paused and smiled fondly. "I've been dancing for twenty years now."

"So you're twenty-four?" Shit. Will had known there was a big age gap between them, but he had no idea it was that big. Will looked at where his hand brushed over Eddie's chest and swallowed. He loved seeing it there, but he was far too old for him. It wasn't like he felt his age, but still....

"Okay, now you look panicked. What's the problem? I'm legal everywhere." He smirked. But it didn't make Will feel any better.

"I'm forty-three. I'm probably the same age as your father." Will grimaced, pulling away from him.

"Two years older, actually." At Will's horror, Eddie cackled and reached for his hand, squeezing it. "God, you should see the look on your face right now. Dad turns fifty-five this year. Like I said, older siblings. But even if you were older than him, it doesn't matter. We've got enough in common that our ages haven't been a problem so far. It's just a number. I like a silver fox anyway." He raised his fingertips to Will's face and gently scratched his beard, then touched his temples. Will's heart beat a staccato rhythm with his soft touch. "Do you have any grey besides here? Because seriously, I'd love on you so hard if you were a full silver fox." Will blushed and looked away. "Oh my God, you do, don't you? Your beard? Chest hair?" Will looked down self-consciously and nodded. He'd noticed a few grey hairs coming through a couple of months earlier, and he'd been tossing up whether to wax it ever since.

Eddie pushed him to his back, straddled him, and leaned over to the lamp, bringing up the light in the room. Will's hands went to his hips, and he sucked in a breath when Eddie leaned down and dropped a few light kisses on his chest and licked his nipple, lining up their cocks at the same time. Eddie's moan had Will squirming under him, and as his fingers tightened around Eddie's hips, he ground his teeth. Forcing himself not to rock against Eddie, Will's mind whited out when the other man whispered in his ear, "I want to make love to you, Will. I want to make you shout my name when you come. I want to explore everything that you like and love, and I can't wait to do it, but as much as I can't wait, I'm forcing myself to. I want more with you than a one-night stand."

Any uncertainty Will had in being with him dissolved—his position, their age gap, everything—and he wrapped his hand around Eddie's nape and brought their mouths together. Their kiss was ravenous, desperate as they let the chemistry between them ignite into an inferno. The way his tongue stroked Will's, the way Eddie's lips melded to his were heady. Intoxicating. Will was already addicted. Want and need slammed into him, and he ached to get closer. Will didn't care whether Eddie was over him or under him as long as they moved together until they couldn't figure out where each of them ended, and the other began.

His body, tight and small against Will's more muscular frame, was so utterly sexy. Lean and strong, compact and so fluid in his movements, the simple thrust of his hips against Will's as Eddie ground down, dragging their dicks together had Will arching into his touch. Will's cock was hard, throbbing under Eddie's weight.

Never mind waiting. Will wanted it all, and he wanted it now. But the whispered promise of more was a temptation he couldn't ignore. He hadn't been looking, but now that he'd stumbled across someone who called to him on a level beyond just sex, it was difficult to walk away from the possibility. Except that the need to touch him and let him touch

Will amplified, multiplying exponentially until it was all he could focus on.

Eddie pulled away and rested his forehead against Will's. Out of breath, he groaned when Eddie rocked his hips again, and their hard shafts slid alongside each other through the thin fabric of their underwear. "Push me off you, or I won't be able to stop."

Eddie's words made him stall in the best possible way. The echo of more in Will's head grew louder. Eddie had heard him. He'd listened and understood exactly what Will needed. And he respected him, not trying to push boundaries.

It took every speck of willpower Will had, but he rolled them to the side, and with their legs still tangled and arms wrapped around each other, Will breathed deeply. He palmed his dick, adjusting himself, and moaned, "Fuuuck."

"Tell me about your ex," Eddie rasped, killing Will's boner in an instant. His eyes popped open, and he looked at Eddie incredulously.

"Way to kill the mood," Will muttered.

"I had to do something. You moaning like that and touching yourself? Fuck, I nearly came in my pants." He ran his fingers through Will's chest hair, making him arch into Eddie's whisper-soft stroking. He felt so damn good; it was as if Eddie was electrifying Will's skin with every brush of his fingertips.

"You really want to talk about him?" When he nodded, Will sighed. "I met him on one of my days off when I was working out of the US. We both lived in Seattle. I'd dock there all the time, and we'd see each other for a few hours every week or so. Because of where I was sailing—along the West Coast—we could speak all the time. We did a lot of video chatting too. He was a diva, but I liked fussing over him, so it didn't bother me. I should have stayed the hell away from him." Will shook his head and scrubbed a hand over his face. "I worked for three months, then had a few weeks off. I only went home once a year, so during my downtime, I'd stay at my apartment. We lived around the corner from each other—we met at the coffee shop near my place. We'd been seeing each other for a while when I tried to clarify that we were exclusive. He'd said something that night that made me think he'd been seeing someone else, but he swore he hadn't. Then in the same breath, he told me it wasn't necessary to promise exclusivity to each other. When I pushed, he caved and finally agreed. That should have been my second warning. During my next break a few months later, we were drunk and in Vegas for the weekend with friends. I don't even remember who suggested we get married, but that was it. We did the whole Elvis chapel thing and were married that night. Ma and Dad were furious. There I was, on the other side of the world dating a man they'd never met—never really even liked if I'm being honest—and suddenly we were married.

"My contract with the cruise company ended a few months later, and I got a job with Dream Liner. I was working out of Sydney and flying to the US on my breaks. Mum and Dad were meeting me in Sydney one day, but they had to cancel, and I managed to get a last-minute change to my ticket. I went home early and found him in bed with another man. I packed my stuff, filed for divorce, and got the hell out of there. I haven't spoken to him since."

"What a bastard," Eddie fumed. His loyalty was noble but no longer necessary. It had taken Will a long time to get over Stefan's betrayal. But a lot of good had come out of their divorce too. His relationship with his parents and siblings was repaired, and he was happy. He hadn't realized how unhappy he'd been until he'd found himself alone and could rediscover himself.

"Don't waste the energy hating him. I'm better off without him. What about you? Tell me about Henri."

He laughed, but it held no humour. "I was starstruck. And young and dumb. He was the lead, and I was a newbie dancer on set. He refused to tell anyone we were together because he said it damaged the fantasy of him being attainable. He wouldn't even let me stay the night. I caught a woman leaving his townhouse one night, and I could smell her perfume on him. I confronted him, and he admitted sleeping with her. In fairness to him, we'd never agreed to be exclusive. I just assumed it." Eddie slowly stroked his fingertips down Will's chest, looking lost in his thoughts. Will doubted he was even aware of what he was doing, the move one of comfort more than arousal. "After we split, there were more men than I care to count. One after another who were just like Henri. The same thing happened over and over. We'd hook up, I'd want more, and they'd walk away. Henri hurt me the most." Eddie sighed and looked down, no longer meeting Will's eyes. "I thought I was in love with him." Eddie shook his head and smiled sadly. "Bastard took advantage of me being so idealistic." Then his smile became more genuine. "Jess saw a pattern forming and complained that she needed a personal trainer because of all the ice cream we were eating after my breakups. I was spiralling, constantly miserable and she begged me to get out. I'd seen it too, and I never wanted to be one of those lads who moved onto a new boyfriend with every show, but that's what was happening. I had to get out of West End. I'm too much of a bloody romantic to keep that up for long. I loved it—the performances, the lights, the stage, the crowds—but it was a toxic environment for me."

Will ran his fingers through Eddie's hair, pulling him close for another lingering kiss. He wanted to rid Eddie's eyes of their haunted look. Wanted to replace the disappointment with contentment. Will grinned when Eddie laughed and fanned himself.

"Do I get you hot under the collar?" Will teased, running fingertips down the curve of his spine until he had a nice handful of Eddie's arse in his palm and squeezed.

"Yes, Captain. You do." He narrowed his eyes and smiled before running his nose down Will's and kissing him again. They quietened then, holding each other close. Eddie curled into him, resting his head on Will's arm and burying his nose into Will's chest. As he lay a trail of opened-mouthed kisses up Will's pec to his throat, then across his cheek, Will turned and captured Eddie's mouth.

Will lost track of time as they lay there making out. Neither took it any further, even though both were tenting their underwear. Content with just being close, Will nuzzled into Eddie, who returned to his spot against Will's chest.

"Sweet dreams, handsome."

"Night, Eddie."

* * * * *

"So, I heard a rumour last night." Felice's attempt at feigning casual was terrible. "And I might have seen a bit of evidence to back up the claim."

"That's nice," Will muttered, triple checking the charts to make sure they were still on course. Noumea was the only country on his route that they docked at. All the others, they simply moored in the channel and had smaller boats called tenders transport the passengers to shore. Walking back to the windows surrounding the bridge, Will checked the ship's progress into the deep seaport. The shanty huts of the nickel mine workers passed them on one side, and on the other was the capital city of the most developed of the Pacific Island nations, New Caledonia. "Slow to two knots," he ordered, spying the dock up ahead. They were pulling into an industrial shipping port, but they were welcomed in true traditional islander style with singers and dancers greeting the ship with song.

Most of the passengers would disembark for a few hours, heading over to the tourist sites and swimming in the quiet bays. Will was two hours into his shift and had another ten to go, but it would be a day filled with maintenance, meetings, and communications with head office rather than sailing.

His mind returned to the beautiful man he'd left in his bed that morning. Eddie was in a deep sleep when his alarm had gone off, and Will had quickly silenced it. He'd picked up his uniform and slipped out, heading straight over to the dance studio to shower and dress for the day. Eddie hadn't even moved when Will had stopped back in to drop off his things before his shift started. He liked knowing Eddie was there, that he'd been able to stretch out on Will's sheets and...

"Thrusters off. Prepare for reverse thrust as we dock."

"Yes, Captain."

It wasn't long before they had the ship moored against the dock, and Will waved hello to the performers as the guests stood on their balconies and around the public decks to get a glimpse of the island welcome. He had no time to waste, and he busied himself with the long list of tasks that needed completing before they departed again.

TEN

Eddie

The talk at lunch seemed to be about one thing—the lap dance Eddie had given the captain two nights earlier. He was doing his best to block out the whispers and ignore the pointed stares, but it was difficult. He didn't mind it for himself. Being the subject of constant critique, reviews, and social media commentary had made him develop tough skin. But the captain hadn't ever had that thrown at him, and Eddie was determined to shield him from anything that could tarnish his reputation or expose him to negativity.

He snapped out of his thoughts when Gerard dropped into the chair next to him, scooting it close. He leant into Eddie's personal space. "So, did you fuck him?"

Eddie repressed the shudder that shook through him and clamped down on the unease of being around Gerard. He was in public. He was okay. "Do me a favour and don't ask me questions like that. I'm not gonna tell you anything about my private life. If you see something I do, make of it what you will, but I'm not telling you shit." Eddie's tone was short, his words clipped and louder than normal. He sounded a lot braver than the terrorised teenager he was inside.

Not one person who'd stopped to talk to him had any interest in him. All they were asking, most in a more tactful way than Gerard was, was whether he and the captain were together. He'd heard some debating who was the pitcher and who was the catcher, and others were asking in a not-so-subtle way whether he could pull some strings now that he was Will's apparent plaything. He'd expected gossip but he'd hoped for a little more tact and maturity.

Eddie needed to get out of there. To get away from Gerard. He stood abruptly, his chair tipping and crashing to the floor. Snatching his tray of food off the table, he stepped over the fallen chair and away from Gerard, who'd moved even closer.

Every eye in the room was trained on Eddie, watching him like a hawk. Waiting for him to react. Frustration and impotence stole through him. He was sick of the gossip mill firing and the ruminations over everything about Will being muttered in hushed words. He ground his teeth together, glaring at every person in the room, daring them to start another one. He spoke loud enough that the dozen or so tables surrounding him heard, "All of you need to butt the fuck out too."

"Eddie," Katya called, motioning him over. He reluctantly went. He didn't want to tell his superior to do the same as the others, but he was at the end of his tether. "You're welcome to sit down here. I won't ask any questions other than whether you're excited about to-night's show."

"Oh my God, yes." He beamed, sitting down. The first night's show was an interpretation of an island holiday, and he couldn't help being reminded of the *Gilligan's Island* re-runs he'd seen his old man watching years back. The second night—the one that had sparked all the tongues wagging in the room—was a tribute to all the queens—Beyoncé, Chris-tina, Brittney, Whitney, Madonna, Diana, and so many oth-ers. There had been two more spectaculars and that night's performance was 1980s hair bands. It was wild fun, crazy costumes, dance moves like no others, a whole lot of strobe lights and wigs that were so full of hair spray they were fire hazards. It was the sort of show Eddie had dreamed of being a part of as a young dancer.

They talked mostly about work—the activities they were running that day and what the other shows had in store for them. Katya was good people, not once asking him about Will, and Eddie appreciated that more than she could know. Eddie wanted to shout to the world how wonderful the captain was, but he could only imagine how twisted a rumour it would become within only a matter of whispers. There was no way he would risk Will's reputation because Eddie couldn't keep his giddy mouth shut.

* * * * *

Will

THE NEXT DAY

Whispers stopped as Will walked down the corridor after his shift. He smiled and nodded where staff and crew looked at him, and he bade those that turned away quickly a good evening. He'd never been the subject of rumours like this before, but there was a first time for everything. The whispers had been following him around like a bad smell, the staff, and crew all wanting to get a look at him, then scurrying off as soon as they did. Will had no idea why, but it was laughable.

It was still going, and Will was getting frustrated. How had nothing else interesting happened? Why was he still the subject of all the gossip? He wondered whether Eddie was faring any better; they'd had little chance to catch up. Their shifts crossed, and downtime was scarce for both of them. All he wanted to do was fall into Eddie's arms, but it seemed that the schedule demanded by the cruise was conspiring against them. Even when they'd both had a ten-minute break and had arranged to meet for a coffee in the staff room, Will had received an urgent report from the doctor regarding a patient who was admitted with suspected food poisoning. It was enough that Will was a few minutes late and, as a result, they'd been like ships passing in the night. The stolen kiss they'd shared made Will ache for him even more.

But he was on his way to see Eddie again. Another shared ten-minute break would have to do, but it was better than nothing, and he had a proposal that would have them spending a little more time together that evening.

The figure walking up the hallway was familiar, and when Will realized who it was, he barely kept the groan at bay. "Will. Good morning." Gerard's words were jovial, but they put Will on the defensive.

"Gerard, while I'm in uniform, you'll address me by my title, please." Will wasn't usually a stickler for protocols. He was happy to have a more relaxed approach when he was in civvies, but there were certain expected behaviours, and he needed to comply with them as much as everyone else did. Calling him Captain, and every one of the other executive staff by their titles was a requirement when in uniform. The hierarchy existed, and it needed to be complied with. No level of disrespect could be tolerated onboard. There was a good reason—it wasn't because Will got off on a power trip but because in an emergency, he needed the complete cooperation of everyone on board. He needed to know everyone would follow the lines of command and do exactly what was required without hesitation. The alternative meant that people could die, and Will would never be okay with that.

"My apologies, Captain." Gerard gave Will an exaggerated bow right there in the corridor. He didn't wait for Will's response, instead just stalking away. Sarcasm laced his tone when he muttered just loud enough that Will could hear, "I try to be nice, but it's not good enough for the captain."

Will grasped the door handle to the exit, his grip tight, and groaned. Gerard couldn't make it easy. He couldn't just apologize and let it go. Why was he pushing a whole new level of inappropriate now? Gerard wasn't someone he'd call a friend. They didn't interact all that much, but even if they were friends, there was a time and place for sarcasm. This wasn't it.

And now he'd forced Will's hand. Reacting angrily or getting frustrated would only give Gerard ammunition; Will knew his type. But he couldn't afford for it to escalate into insubordination. "Gerard," he called out to his retreating form. "Report to HR."

"What for?" The snark in his voice was enough to have Will squaring his shoulders and staring him down.

"Keep speaking to me like that, and it will be insubordination. Right now, it's a caution to keep your attitude in check. Understood?"

"Yes, Captain." He sounded suitably chastised, but the eye-roll let Will know it was a façade. Will sighed and shot a text to Eddie, apologizing for having to miss their coffee date again. His plans had changed—he now had to stop in and see the HR director.

Eddie's response was quick.

Eddie: *sad face*

Will was going to ask him face-to-face, but doing it by text would have to do. At least if Eddie could make it, they'd be spending more than a short coffee break together. Excitement pooled in Will's gut, and heat crept over his cheeks. There was something about Eddie that made him shy and fluttery, and Will kind of loved it.

Will: Wanted to ask you f2f, but I have an event in The Loft at five. It's black-tie. If you can make it…

Eddie: I don't have a suit *another sad face*

Deflated, Will trudged back up the stairs to the executive level and knocked on the HR director's door.

"Come in."

"Hello, Director. You got a minute?" He shot her a small smile from the doorway.

"Of course, Captain. Always." Her answering smile was genuine. Emira was a people person through and through. She was incredible at reading everyone and knowing just how to respond. Hopefully she could share some insights with him. "What can I do for you?"

"I wanted to report a situation to you. There's no need for formal action, but if it escalates, there will be."

"Okay."

"Gerard—the entertainer, I'm not sure what his family name is—anyway, he's… I don't know. Pushing his luck would probably be a good way of describing it. I, ah… had a date a few days ago, and Gerard pulled me aside and warned me about my date." When Emira opened her mouth to speak, Will held up his hand and shook his head gently, halting her comment. "The warning wasn't the problem. I appreciated him telling me. It's what happened afterwards that has been. Gerard adopted a familiarity with me that crosses professional lines and is bordering on insubordinate." He retold their most recent run-in, and she arched her eyebrow at Will, tapping her pen on her chin in contemplation.

"Captain, may I speak freely?"

"Yes, Director, it would be appreciated."

"Thank you." She adjusted the knot of her tie at her throat and smoothed it down. "I heard the rumours floating around the ship. First of all, congratulations. I won't make any notes about your date in the record, but I appreciate knowing so I can navigate any conflicts of interest that may arise." Will nodded, relief washing over him that she didn't need specifics, like Eddie's name, just yet.

It wasn't that he wanted to keep them hidden. He'd never do that to Eddie, especially when he'd suffered that fate time and time again. She probably already knew, but Will wasn't quite ready to tell the director the full details of their budding relationship. Eventually, it would happen. He'd tell her when things got a little more… formal. He wanted to get there with Eddie, but he didn't want to jump the gun. Both of them needed to be certain about where they were headed before he subjected Eddie to whatever formalities would, no doubt, be attached to dating the captain. It was a little premature for that after one date; any sane person would probably run for the hills if HR had to get involved in their private lives.

Would Eddie put up with the intrusion? The flicker of hope flared in his chest. The man made him want to giggle like a kindergartener in time with his belly flip-flopping every time Will thought of him. It was the first time in a long time any man had affected Will like that.

"Secondly, I'm glad you came to me. I'll have a chat with Gerard. The level of disrespect he's displaying certainly isn't appropriate. I'll sort that out for you. In the meantime, I'll see you at the function this afternoon."

"You will. Thank you."

ELEVEN

Eddie

Eddie palmed the phone and sighed. He was disappointed. That morning he'd already helped with disembarkation and was now headed to run on-board activities for those who elected to stay on the ship. Later that afternoon, he would be helping people back on board, scanning identification cards and checking bags for banned items until they accounted for each and every passenger. Then a pole dancing exhibition and finally a break for a few hours, right when his captain had a function at The Loft. He could have spent some time with Will, except that he didn't have the right clothes. He couldn't very well show up in anything less than the required dress code, which meant that going was an impossibility. He understood exactly how Cinderella felt about the ball now. Deflated and defeated, he knew he wasn't going to be his bright, chirpy self in the class, but he'd plaster on a smile and fake it.

In the five-minute break he got to move between locations, he'd sprinted up an extra two levels and checked out the onboard clothing stores. Predictably, they only stocked souvenir T-shirts and ball caps. It was no use.

He ran, racing through the staff-only corridor to the open lobby where he was due to preside over a mass game of Twister.

"Hey, Katya," he called as he sprinted the last of the way catching up with her.

"Why are you running? Class go over time?"

"No, needed to dash up to the clothing store."

"The guest shops?" she asked, puzzled. "What for?"

"Oh, I was looking for something." Her eyebrows drew down at the dismissive wave of his hand, and she paused at the door. Eddie took the opportunity to smooth down his dishevelled uniform. "Hey," he mused, not sounding at all casual like he was trying to be, "What's on at The Loft this evening? And where do I get a suit?"

She looked at him, and a small smile tilted one side of her mouth upward. "I don't know, but we've got suits in the costumes room. It's part of your uniform. We rarely use them, so no one keeps them in their staterooms."

She could have knocked him over with a feather. Shock, excitement—no elation—filled him, and a joyful grin split his lips. "You're kidding, right?"

"No, not joking. We only wear them if we're chaperoning the formal nights' dances or attending the Captain's Dinner." Her eyes lit up, and she clicked her fingers. "It's the Captain's Dinner tonight. It's always held at the midpoint of the cruise."

"Oh, okay. Wow," he mumbled.

"You'd have to leave early, but you could easily be ready for the seven-thirty show if you got downstairs at, say, ten to seven," she offered. "I could have make-up do you last."

"You'd do that?" he asked, giddy at the thought, before it came crashing down. Suspicion muted his happiness. "It's not because of who my date would be, is it?"

She squeezed Eddie's arm. "No, I'm just happy for you both. Consider it an apology for snapping at you for the lap dance." There was a genuineness in her tone that had Eddie believing she really meant those words. Even if she didn't, he would take it. "Enjoy yourself, okay." Katya pushed through the door, and they were on.

* * * * *

The day flew by. Helping guests back onto the ship was fun. Eddie was surprised how many people recognized him from up on stage.

After a few hours following the embarkation protocols, Eddie headed over to the main theatre for his pole dancing exhibition. It was the first time he was working with Andrea on the poles, but he'd learnt all the moves, practicing endlessly every spare moment he had.

There were two poles erected side by side in the middle of the stage and a high bar table with a couple of bottles of water and Seamus's microphone sitting ready, so he could emcee the session. With the curtain still closed, Eddie checked the stability of the setup. He was impressed, but he had been from the first moment on board. Nothing was half-hearted, every effort made to ensure a spectacle for the audience, while making safety a priority.

He had also seen the list of music tracks, playing as a background accompaniment to their demonstration. This exhibition wasn't a performance like those showcased every evening, but rather a display of the strength and athleticism needed to pull off some of the moves.

When Seamus introduced Eddie and Andrea to the small crowd of people, the performer in him came alive. Feisty, flamboyant, and full of fabulousness, he had a blast.

But it was the close of the curtain he'd been waiting on. It had barely come to a halt when Eddie dashed off stage, heading straight for the showers. Water poured over him, the cool stream refreshing after the heat of working under the spotlights. Time was running short, though. He hadn't had a chance to look for his suit in the dressing room, and he now had thirty minutes to get cleaned up, find it, and hopefully wear it to dinner. Nerves assailed him. He didn't want to be late. He also didn't want to make a fool of himself in front of the passengers or the other executive staff.

Eddie ran through the dressing rooms in a blind panic and rifled through the costume racks until he finally found the hangers that Katya had mentioned. Wrapped in plastic, with his name neatly printed on the label, the black pants and white jacket with matching white shirt and the black bow tie was elegant. He would look smart in it. Shoe boxes lined the bottom of the rack, one marked with Eddie's name.

Slipping into his outfit, Eddie was instantly pleased—the tailoring was comfortable and near perfectly fitted to him. He gave himself the once over, checking how the slim fit pants followed the curve of his arse and hugged his thighs and calves closely. The black buttons and bow tie were a stark contrast against the white shirt and jacket.

He was kicking himself. His dream had once been to perform on West End. It wasn't all it was cracked up to be, and Eddie had quickly learnt he wasn't meant for a life like that. But this—cruising through paradise on tropical oceans and mixing it up between performing and taking activities to keep the passengers entertained—was a blast. Even without dating the captain, Eddie was the happiest he'd ever been. He couldn't wait to experience everything this career offered.

He made his way up to The Loft restaurant on the top level of the ship. It was uber elegant, and even in a suit and bowtie, he felt underdressed. Uncomfortable in his own skin, he wished he'd put on some make-up or was wearing those heels that made his calves look hot as fuck. Instead, winding his way through men in top hats and tails and ladies in evening gowns, he swallowed hard and hoped he didn't embarrass the captain when he finally found him.

The lady who stopped in front of him raised her eyebrow. "Can I help you, ma'am?" he asked.

"I think a round of champagne would be nice, would it not?" She was wearing jewellery which had to have cost the equivalent of six month's rental, and Eddie blinked, taking in her words. Oh. His heart sank, and he looked down at himself. Swallowed hard and faked a smile.

"I'll see what I can do."

"You made it." Will eased himself between two groups of people, and when Eddie got a look at him... holy. Fucking. Hell.

Will reached out to Eddie with a gloved hand, and never mind Cinderella, he was Julia Roberts. Eddie was literally having his very own Pretty Woman moment. He took Eddie's hand, lifting it to his lips and brushing a kiss over his knuckles. "I'm so glad you came."

When Will's other hand landed against the small of his back, all Eddie managed was a whispered, "Hi."

Will grinned happily and tugged Eddie closer, and Eddie swooned. Lost for words, he grinned happily up at Captain Preston, sinking into his presence. The smooth rumble of his voice and that damn Australian accent had his insides doing cartwheels again.

Turning to the woman eying them from down her nose, Will added with a smile, "I see you've met Barbara."

"Not formally, no."

Will's smile was charming. And fake as hell. "Well, allow me. Barbara, this is my date, Eddie. He's one of our performers. Eddie, Barbara is on her fifth cruise with Dream Liner Cruises. First time on the Dreamcatcher, so a very special guest."

"Pleased to meet you." He nodded with a polite smile. Before conversation became too painful, Eddie looked around, spotting a waiter. He flagged them over. "Would you please have some champagne served to Barbara and her group, please?"

"Certainly, sir." The waiter nodded and hurried away, and they excused themselves. Will guided Eddie forward with a hand on his lower back and leaned in close, bringing their heads together.

"She thought you were a waiter, didn't she?" he asked Eddie in a whisper.

"Mmhm."

Will snorted out a laugh, and Eddie grinned, leaning into the captain when Will wrapped an arm around him. Pulling back, he eyed his date from head to toe and licked his lips. Damn, the man was fine.

Dressed in a white uniform, the fitted jacket buttoned up to his throat, and his epaulettes proudly showed off his rank as captain. He looked stunningly handsome. His black and white hat, rimmed with a band of gold to match the stripes on his shoulders, sat casually under his arm.

He smelt amazing too. His touch was warm and affectionate, and the shy smile he looked down at Eddie with had him fanning himself. Eddie was sure he was blushing, but who wouldn't? In casual clothes, Will was attractive as hell. Even in his everyday uniform, he was good-looking. But put him in a dress uniform that looked like every stitch had been hand-sewn to fit his spectacular body, and the end result was perfection. He was breathtaking. And that was only the top line in a long list of what made Will such a catch. Kind and caring, loyal and down to earth, yet incredibly intelligent, Eddie's captain was a beautiful man inside and out.

Eddie was the luckiest person on the ship.

They joined a couple and introduced themselves. No older than their late forties, they held an air of intelligence and quiet confidence that drew Eddie to them, much like he was to Will. As long as Will kept an arm around him or hand on him, Eddie was content to listen to the guests' opinions on just about anything from their walk around the island to where they lived and what they did for work.

It took nearly an hour before Eddie got a moment alone with Will. The Captain steered them to a dimly lit corner of the restaurant and hooked his finger under Eddie's chin before pressing their lips together in a chaste kiss. "You have no idea how much I needed that kiss." Eddie sighed dreamily. "You light up this room, handsome. I'm so damn lucky to be here with you."

"You look dashing too. I'm so glad you could make it." Will smiled, and Eddie's heart somersaulted in his chest, soaring high at his words.

Eddie cupped his face, running his thumb over Will's bottom lip, marvelling at how the beautiful man before him welcomed his touch. Knowing he was the first person Will had let close to him in such a long time—and at work no less—made Eddie especially grateful. He'd had barely anything more than a hook-up in the last few years, and yet, there Eddie was with him. Date number two and in his arms being introduced to people who, albeit they'd never see again, were important. Their opinions mattered, not because either Eddie or Will cared much about what they had to say, but because they could rock the boat, so to speak. Will's professionalism could be called into question. He was taking a risk asking Eddie to be there with him at the dinner, and Eddie was determined to not let him down.

In fact, Eddie wanted to show him just how much of a privilege it had been to be on his arm that evening. Reaching up to kiss him again, he let his lips linger, keeping it chaste but hoping Will understood what it meant to Eddie that he'd gone out on a limb to extend his trust.

Reality intruded when the alarm on his cell sounded. Silencing it, he explained, "I have to leave early to get ready for the show tonight. Will you be able to be there?"

He sighed softly and leaned into Eddie. "My shift doesn't finish for another couple of hours." Will squeezed his hips gently and nuzzled his beard against Eddie's smooth face. He fought to stop his eyes rolling back in his head as Eddie tilted his jaw to give Will better access and flat out purred when Will kissed along his jaw.

"Want to join me in the staff bar later?" Eddie asked hopefully. "I'm killer at air hockey." He knew that if he met Will somewhere private, he'd take things too far too fast— he was stretched thin, gathering every shred of self-control just to hold back a moan from the warmth of Will's breath against his cheek.

Will hesitated, then smiled warmly at him, and once again, Eddie found himself falling a little harder for his gentle captain. He couldn't pull away from Will if he tried—he was like the sun, and Eddie was Mercury, orbiting so close that he'd go up in flames if Will reached out to touch him.

"I don't usually spend too much time in the common areas, but I'd love to if you'll be there." Will's shy smile and Eddie's corresponding grin left nothing to the imagination. Anyone looking at him would think he was as giddy as a teenager at a K-pop concert. Will kissed him again, just a press of their lips together, and stepped away from Eddie. "Go, or you'll be late."

Eddie laughed and walked out of the room on a high, his feet barely touching the floor. He was five minutes earlier than the deadline Katya had given him, but he didn't want to push the boundaries too far, especially when he was being watched like a hawk.

TWELVE

Will

Will waited for Eddie at the bar. He'd dressed down, hoping that wearing casual clothes would help him blend into the crowd more easily. No one seemed to be looking, but Will was crawling out of his own skin. He didn't fit in there. He was at least a decade older than everyone else in the bar—or it felt like he was anyway—and he was obviously out of the loop on whatever mating rituals his staff and crew had. He could imagine himself narrating the scene like a David Attenborough special, except that he didn't understand a lot of what was happening around him.

He sipped his lime and soda and kept an inconspicuous eye on the door. The laughter met his ears before he saw them. All the entertainers flooded in together, some with arms around each other and every one of them high off what he knew was a favourite performance.

The smile that lit up Eddie's face when their eyes met was like the sun emerging from behind a cloud. It warmed Will from his belly through every tingling nerve ending to his fingertips and toes. It was exciting and fun, and Will grinned right back at him, enjoying the view of tight jeans and an aqua-coloured shirt with just the right amount of frill to look enticingly feminine against his lithe muscles.

Will found himself in the fray within moments, caught up in Eddie's magnetism. Soon shot glasses littered the high-top tables that the group stood around, and the conversation between the performers became more animated.

Eddie nudged him away from the group and took his hand, leading Will over to the pool tables in a dim corner of the bar with a hand low on the small of his back. When he slipped his thumb under Will's polo, touching the sensitive skin along his spine, Will sucked in a breath. That was all it took for Eddie to shift and grasp Will's hips, hauling them against the wall. With a hand pressed against the smooth timber panelling, Will leaned down and nuzzled the man who had intrigued him from the moment he'd laid eyes on him, pinning him against the wall. Will breathed him in and nibbled along Eddie's jaw, the other man tilting his head to give Will better access. When Eddie's grip on his hips tightened, and he let out a breathy moan, Will ground against him, his entire being desperate to get closer to the man before him. He wanted—needed—to be skin on skin with him. To learn every peak and valley of Eddie's toned body. How far could he go before they would be indecent? Grateful for the bulk he had over Eddie, he knew it would be further than either one of them should entertain.

Opening his eyes again, Will's gaze snagged on Eddie's, and the heat between them flared. Eddie moistened his glossy lips with a swipe of his pink tongue, and Will's self-control snapped. He slammed their mouths together, thrusting his tongue into Eddie's mouth and taking what he needed, while trying to convey to Eddie just how much he'd missed being close to him.

Will had no idea how long they stayed there tucked away in the corner and making out like teenagers, but the noise in the bar grew louder in ebbs and flows. The volume of the music increased too. He was hard and aching, tempted to throw Eddie over his shoulder and steal away somewhere private so he could strip the man naked and worship his body. Instead, he pulled back, breathing hard, and groaned as Eddie clutched at him and dragged his hips along Will's leg, using him for friction.

"Need you naked," he said with a gasp as Eddie sucked a mark onto his collarbone.

"God, yes."

That was all Will needed to hear. He clutched Eddie's hand and marched him out of the bar, grateful for the dimmed lights and packed room. Walking with a hard-on wasn't easy—his eyes were almost crossing with the concentration it took not to adjust himself—but when they spilled out of the darkened bar into the brightly lit corridor, Will hesitated. Which way was the closest to their suites?

Eddie didn't pause. Taking the lead, he tugged on Will's hand as he walked in the opposite direction to the one Will expected. He pressed the button on the bank of lifts, but when doors didn't immediately ding open, he turned for the stairs, leading them up a level and towards the aft of the ship. The theatre.

Swiping his staff card, Eddie led them into the darkened warm-up area and through the doors to the change rooms. Flipping the light switch, then the lock, he cocooned them in silence, the only noises their ragged breathing. Will didn't hesitate, scooping Eddie up in his arms and carrying him over to the lockers. The metal banged as he pressed Eddie into them and took his lips in a needy kiss. Rocking their bodies together, Will moaned as Eddie's hardening length rubbed against his own.

Skin.

He needed naked skin against his own.

Will tugged on Eddie's shirt, and Eddie slid his legs down, his feet hitting the floor just as Will reached for his buttons. Seeing him there, panting, lips swollen and glossy, with his eyes glazed over, had something snapping in Will. He wanted his hands on the man until he came apart in his arms. He wanted Eddie entirely debauched. Ruined for anyone else but him.

Will reached for his shirt and gripped it with both hands. Eddie's eyes slipped closed, and he arched into Will's touch, encouraging him with a moan. The material tore, coming apart as buttons pinged around the room. Eddie's bare chest tempted Will, the heaving breaths he was sucking in alluring. Will wanted—no needed—to touch. Falling to his knees, Will licked a path up Eddie's abs, using his shirttails to pull Eddie into a crouch and his chest to Will's greedy mouth. Swiping his tongue over Eddie's nipple, Will moaned, the taste of Eddie's skin bursting onto his tongue.

Will dragged his hand down over Eddie's flat stomach and pressed the heel of his palm against the bulge in his tight jeans. Eddie gasped as he massaged his cock. Will lapped his skin, moving lower and lower until he ran his tongue along Eddie's low waistband.

Flicking the button open and dragging the zip down, the twines loud in the quiet room, Will breathed him in, his mouth watering with the smell of sex in the air. Nuzzling the hard bulge, he rubbed his beard against Eddie's prick and shuddered. Will opened his eyes and looked his fill, moaning when he spied the blue lace framing his cock. A pearl of pre-cum wet the delicate material and Will nearly went wild. His mouth watering, Will pulled Eddie's jeans down, his movements jerky and barely controlled. He freed Eddie's arse and ran his hands over the crisscross of elastic straps framing Eddie's cheeks in perky perfection. Will massaged the smooth, warm skin and stared as Eddie's shaft visibly throbbed through the lace. The wet patch grew, and Will shuddered, a sliver of need passing through him. "Please," Eddie begged, and Will couldn't resist anymore.

Tugging the exquisite material down, Will freed Eddie's cock and nuzzled him again, licking his length. Salty pre-cum burst onto his tongue as Will licked his slit and closed his lips over the head of Eddie's cock, sucking him into the cavern of his mouth. Eddie moaned, pressing his hands against the metal lockers as he fought not to thrust his hips. Will wasn't having any of that, doubling down and sucking harder. Eddie cried out and rolled his hips, and Will hummed, his hand instinctively going to his own hard-as-nails cock.

"Yes, touch yourself," Eddie moaned. "I want to see you jerk off."

Will sucked him deeper and roughly yanked open his jeans, freeing his shaft and jacking himself urgently as he swallowed down Eddie's cock. He traced the veins in Eddie's dick with his tongue, and he buried his nose in Eddie's pubes, taking his length deep into his throat. Will's cock pulsed in his hand as he jerked himself, and he brought them both to the brink. Eddie's moans pushed him over, the tingle beginning at the base of Will's spine, radiating outwards in waves as Eddie stiffened in his arms.

"Will," he gasped, but Will didn't give him a chance to pull away, grasping a handful of the man's arse and running his fingers along Eddie's crack as Will shuddered and his balls drew up tight. Then he was coming, swallowing down Eddie's essence as he emptied himself onto the linoleum floor.

Dizzy with the endorphins pulsing through his system, he let Eddie's dick slip from his mouth and caught himself before he face-planted. Eddie slid down the locker, landing on his knees, and drew Will into his arms. Nuzzling their cheeks together, Will kissed him softly, sated, and yet still unable to get enough of Eddie.

THIRTEEN

Eddie

The second-last night of Eddie's first cruise arrived quickly. The show went off without a hitch, but Eddie was excited for another reason.

The staff party.

He raced through his shower and dressed in the same tight jeans that Will hadn't gotten enough of a few nights earlier. He folded them up to show his ankles and paired them with a capped-sleeved T-shirt and a waistcoat. After applying pink lipstick, and black kohl around his eyes, Eddie was nearly ready to go.

There would be a lot of hooking up tonight, and Eddie's fellow entertainers were itching to get their freak on. This time, he'd be tasting Will if he had any say in it.

He warmed some wax in his hands and swept his hair back into a coif, checked his arse out in the full-length mirror, slipped on the hot-pink heels, and hurried out the door.

Will was waiting for him at the entrance to the staff bar, having only just come off his shift. Still wearing his dress whites, he stood there smiling and shaking hands with all the staff and crew, greeting them as they came in. "I like casual on you just as much as I like the captain look, handsome," Eddie teased, sidling up next to him. Eddie's blood warmed and a shiver passed through him from the heated inspection Will gave him from head to toe. The man was all intense desire and sexy sophistication, and Eddie couldn't get enough of it.

"I was going to tell you that I'll go change and come back, but maybe I should stay like this." He quirked an eyebrow, and Eddie smiled sheepishly. Turning to him, Eddie tugged Will's hat out from under his arm and popped it on before unbuttoning his jacket and slipping it off his shoulders. "Ah, no," he cautioned as Eddie went to step away. "You don't want to be seen wearing that around." Will plucked the hat off Eddie's head and took his jacket back before moving over to the bar. The crew standing in line for a drink parted, and Will thanked them, embarrassed, before handing both items to one of the bar staff. "Can you please find somewhere safe to store these?"

"Absolutely, Captain. I'll hang them in the office out back." When Will turned back to Eddie, there was only one thing he wanted to see him do at that moment—dance. Snagging Will's hand, Eddie dragged him onto the makeshift dancefloor where a remix with an insane beat was hammering through the speakers. Dressed in a white tee, white pants, and shoes, he glowed blue under the iridescent lights, the lighter strands of his blond hair shining.

Will laughed happily when Eddie shook his arse, lifting his hands above his head and beckoning to Will closer. He took the hint and wrapped an arm around Eddie's waist before hooking his finger in the one Eddie still had curled. Tugging his hand up, so it was around Will's nape, Will ran his big palm down Eddie's arm and slowly along his side. Will stared into his eyes and Eddie sucked in a breath at the intensity there. Eddie rolled his hips, moving to the music, his legs straddling one of Will's, and got lost in the rhythm. Eddie tugged on his neck, bringing Will closer, and kissed him slowly, aligning their bodies.

It wasn't just his leg between Eddie's and his thick thigh rubbing on his nuts that was making Eddie harden; it was Will. The whole package—the need simmering in his warm brown eyes, his parted lips, and the dart of his pink tongue as he held himself back from devouring Eddie, from tasting the lipstick now smeared onto his lips, the flex of his hand at the small of Eddie's back.

Will's self-control was impressive, but Eddie didn't have the same restraint. Practically climbing him, Eddie kissed him again, this time not holding back. Their teeth clashed, tongues tasted, and as Eddie's fingers found the warm, firm skin under his T-shirt, he moaned.

The music kicked up, a heavier beat reverberating through them. It matched the *thud, thud, thud* of Eddie's heart as he stared up at Will and smirked. "You look pretty pleased with yourself there, beautiful," he murmured, the sound shooting straight through Eddie like a bolt of lightning.

"Mmhmm." Eddie nipped Will's earlobe and chuckled at his shiver. "I have the sweetest, sexiest, smartest man on the ship in my arms. How did I pull that off?"

"You haven't yet, but I'd kill to feel your hands on me." Will moaned, punching his hips forward. He was hard, that cock Eddie wanted to get his hands and mouth on tenting his perfectly tailored pants. Eddie's breath caught at the thought of touching Will. Worshipping his golden skin.

"You're kidding me," a cold voice slurred. "He hasn't put out? Cap, you're missin' out." The husky laugh was full of derision.

Eddie froze and Will's grip on him tightened as he stiffened in Eddie's arms. Will straightened, his shoulders pulling back as he ground his teeth together. "Out of line, mate."

"The little cocksucker swallowed me good."

Anger, fierce and fiery, pulsed through Eddie's veins. He spun in Will's arms and poked the drunken man before them in the chest. "Fuck you, Gerard."

Will moved him to the side, gently pushing Eddie behind him as he stood looking deceptively calm face-to-face with Gerard. "Enough, Gerard. You've already been given a warning. Now I'm telling you to back up."

From Eddie's place pressed up against Will's back, he caught the cold glint in Gerard's eye as he leaned in closer to Will's ear. "When I sank my dick into him, he screamed my name. He'll be thinking of my dick when you fuck him later."

Eddie scrambled, trying to get to Gerard from behind Will, but even one-handed, as Will pinned Eddie to his back, Will was far stronger than him. It would have been hot had Eddie not been so damn angry.

"Eddie." Will squeezed him tighter, his tone filled with warning in that single word. "We're leaving."

"Aw, doesn't the poor captain like getting reminded that his boy's a slut?"

Eddie didn't have time to react. One moment Will was holding him to his back, and the next, he'd let Eddie go and stepped away from him. Eddie stumbled before righting himself after a moment, but in that split second that he'd looked away, his world tilted on its head. Will shouldered Gerard, pushing the man away, and Gerard's eyes hardened further when Will spoke into his ear. Eddie didn't hear the words. He didn't need to. The hatred radiating off Will was palpable.

But it was Gerard's reaction that he feared. Nostrils flared and teeth bared, he looked like a wild animal as he reared back, fist clenched.

Eddie reacted purely on instinct, the need to protect Will rearing its head. His heart hammering in his chest, fear clawed its way up his throat. But it wasn't fear for himself. It was for Will.

Launching himself at his man, he pushed in front of Will, trying to fend off the attack from Gerard.

But Gerard stumbled.

He crashed into Eddie, and in slow motion, Eddie's arms cartwheeled. He fell backwards, his four-inch heels slipping on the tiled floor.

He watched, powerless, as Gerard landed a messy punch to Will's face as Eddie landed against the wall of solid muscle of his date. His momentum propelled them backwards. Will's arms went around him, and he stumbled back, hauling Eddie to him. On one foot, Gerard pivoted, losing his footing like a spinning top slowing its rotation. Falling into the crowd of people surrounding them, Gerard roared and floundered to get up.

But as quickly as the scuffle started, it was over.

The man next to them dropped a knee onto Gerard's back, and barely a moment later, security converged on them. Will held Eddie close, guiding them backwards, away from the commotion. Then with a hand low on his back, he pointed Eddie towards the exit.

Eddie paused, instead diverting to the bar. He pushed to the front of the queue, Will in tow behind him. Annoyed glances were tossed his way, and a few people muttered, "Dick," under their breaths, but Eddie ignored them.

"Captain's hat and jacket, please," he asked the closest bartender. The man looked up from the drink he was making with a raised eyebrow until he spotted Will pressed behind Eddie. Putting the drink aside, he turned and went to retrieve it. Eddie took them when they were handed over, and Will passed his staff card over his shoulder.

"Let me get the drinks you've just poured."

Eddie looked over at the sweet man, only for concern to grip him. Will was pale, his lip swollen and blood oozing from it. He was shaking too. Eddie needed to get him out of there.

After Will got his card back and had a serviette pressed to his lip, Eddie led him out and into the quieter corridor. Pressing Will up against the wall, Eddie grasped his face between his hands, brushing his thumbs over Will's cheekbones. "Close your eyes, handsome. Breathe for me. Just for a moment."

"What did I do?" Will murmured, a deep furrow marring his brow. "I lost my shit. I nearly hit him. Laid him out on the floor."

"He hit you!" Will opened his eyes, a haunted look passing over him, and Eddie pressed on. "You warned him. You told him to back off, and he didn't. He kept pushing. Whatever you were tempted to do, he's the one that struck you. You're not in the wrong here."

Will drew him close, wrapping an arm around Eddie's waist and resting his forehead on Eddie's shoulder. His touch was comforting, but Eddie knew Will needed the contact perhaps more than he did. "I need to speak with the HR Director again. This isn't going to go away."

"We'll fix it."

Will pulled back and sighed before rubbing his forehead and pressing his thumb and middle finger into his temples. He reached into his jacket pocket and withdrew his phone, dialling a number. It rang a few times before Eddie heard a quiet murmur, and Will apologized, requesting an urgent meeting. Eddie was expecting to go to the executive level offices, but Will took them to his suite instead.

Will's hand shook as he tried unsuccessfully to swipe his card a second time against the lock. Eddie wrapped his hand around Will's and gently extracted the card from his grip. "Let me help."

He opened the door, guiding Will over to the large bed in the centre of the room. Will sank down on the end, resting his elbows on his knees and his forehead in his hands. Eddie fetched him a glass of water and pressed a wet facecloth to his lip to stem the bleeding. Will took it at the same time a knock on the door sounded.

Eddie opened it, and dressed in a pair of tattered jeans and a slouchy jumper, her hair in a messy bun on top of her head, was the woman he'd met on his first day onboard— the HR Director. "Hello, come in." He held the door open for her, and she passed him with a small smile and nod in thanks.

"Captain, are you okay?" The concern in her voice was a relief to Eddie, but a stab of unwarranted jealousy pierced him when he turned and saw her down on one knee with her hand on Will's arm.

"No, Director, I'm not. I messed up." Will's voice was quiet, broken, and Eddie didn't hesitate then, sitting on the bed next to him and wrapping an arm around his bulky shoulders.

"Will," he started, then thought better of it while he was still in uniform with the HR Director kneeling in front of him. "Captain, this isn't your fault."

"How isn't it my fault?" When Will turned to him, Eddie's heart broke with the unshed tears in Will's eyes. "Gerard got drunk and couldn't keep his mouth shut, and I lost it—"

"He hit you. You told him to stop. You put yourself between him and me so that I wouldn't be his target. You asked him to back off twice and when he wouldn't—"

"I shoved him."

"He punched you."

"In retaliation. I should have known better. I shouldn't have reacted."

"Captain, I need you both to tell me what happened step by step. Should I get the chief security officer involved?"

"Yes," Eddie requested. "Please, and the doctor too. I want Will's lip looked at." He reached for Will's chin, turning his face, and took the wet cloth still pressed against his lip. Blood still oozed from the cut, but it had slowed significantly. Pressing it against Will's lip again, Eddie cupped his face.

The director was already on the phone, talking quietly in the background as Eddie smoothed his thumb over Will's cheek. "You didn't do anything wrong."

"Feels like it." Will closed his eyes and leaned into Eddie's touch. He kept stroking the soft beard under his fingertips and giving him as much comfort as he could in front of the director.

"Can I get you anything?" Eddie asked.

"Just a hug." Eddie smiled and leaned in, kissing Will's forehead. Will responded by tugging him onto his lap and burying his face in Eddie's neck. He ran his fingers through Will's hair and massaged his scalp one-handed while Will groaned.

"Headache?"

"Mmhmm."

"The doc will be here soon."

The chief security officer arrived first, and they recounted the story of their night to him. His brow furrowed, and he asked Will, "The director mentioned that you feel a degree of fault here. I'm failing to see where, sir. What, exactly, do you feel like you've done wrong?"

"I didn't walk away."

"I have to watch the security camera footage and speak to a few other people who witnessed what happened, but by the sounds of it, you exercised the necessary restraint. At the very least, based on what you've told me, Gerard was provoking you. He seemed to be spoiling for a fight." He shook his head and sighed. "I'm aware of your prior report of him. Has anything else happened?"

Eddie spoke up then. "Yes, he's been trying to get a rise out of me too." He detailed the run-ins he'd had with Gerard, and by the time he'd finished, Will was vibrating, anger radiating from him as he clenched and unclenched his fists.

"Why didn't you tell me?"

"You can't fight my battles for me." Eddie smiled softly at Will. "It's okay. I've dealt with people like him before."

"No, it's not okay," the chief security officer assured him. "The cruise company and every executive on this ship has taken a hard-line stance against bullying, sexual assault, and harassment, and what you've reported to me clearly fits within all of them. I'll be investigating this further and adding it to the other complaints from tonight. I'm positive that Head Office will confirm termination of his contract."

Eddie shook his head. "No one ever took any notice of what he was doing. I doubt that they even saw what happened."

"Leave it up to me to gather the necessary evidence, Eddie. That's my job. In the meantime, Captain, if you need anything, just call. I will update you as soon as I have news."

Another knock on the door sounded, and the chief answered it on his way out. In bustled another man, this one dressed in a white lab coat with a stethoscope hanging around his neck. It was clear from the warm squeeze of Will's shoulder that they knew each other well. "Evening, Captain. What can I help with?"

Eddie answered, motioning to his own face, "His lip. It's still bleeding. I haven't put ice on it, but he's had a cold compress on it for—" Eddie checked the time on the clock perched on the desk. "—over an hour, and it's slowed, but still oozing."

"Nice to see you again. Ed, right?" When he nodded, the doctor smiled. "I remember faces and allergies, but names usually aren't my strong suit."

Will groaned and whispered, "Ez, I need something for a headache too, please."

"Sure." He nodded, pulling up the desk chair in front of Will. "So, how'd you get the split lip?"

"Fist to the face. Could have been a ring or something, maybe. I don't exactly know."

"What the?" The doctor's face shot up, concern lighting his features. With a furrowed brow and wide-eyed shock, his gaze pinged to Eddie's, who nodded unhappily. "Okay, let's get you fixed up then."

The doctor donned gloves and prepared saline solution and a gauze patch while Eddie took the cold compress Will gave to him. A surge of protectiveness shot through Eddie when he saw the bruise that was already forming. Will's lower lip was swollen and still bleeding slowly.

"It's quite a deep cut." He tilted his head, looking at Will's chin from another angle, and gently pressed the skin below his lip together. Eddie couldn't look. He couldn't bear to see the wince of pain crinkling Will's eyes closed and yet be unable to do anything for him. Eddie pressed a kiss to Will's shoulder, holding his hand and rubbing his back with the other. The doctor was speaking about steri-strips and scarring, and Eddie took it all in, repeating what the doctor had said so he'd remember to tell Will when he wasn't so overwhelmed.

Once he was finished patching up Will's lip, he paused and asked, "How bad is the headache?"

"Eight out of ten. I've got the aura and I'm nauseous."

"Anything to drink tonight?"

"Nothing," Eddie answered with a shake of his head and worry riding low in his belly. "Is he going to be okay?"

"He will." The doctor smiled reassuringly and directed his attention back to Will, asking him more questions about when his shift started the next day and how often he'd been getting migraines. "I don't carry it with me, but I do have treatment in the clinic that will help. Give me ten minutes. I'll run down and get the syringe loaded, then bring it up for you. In the meantime, Eddie, if you could get another cold compress for William's forehead, some ice for his lip, and dim the lights right down, that will help."

"Will do, Doc."

FOURTEEN

Eddie

The doctor had been and gone, injecting Will with medicine to stop the headache, and Eddie stood between Will's spread legs, rubbing his shoulders while Will rested his forehead on Eddie's belly.

As the door clicked closed behind the doctor, Eddie asked, "Will, can I stay tonight?"

"I'd love you to." Will took Eddie's hand in his and pressed a lingering kiss to his knuckles. Eddie sighed and swooned a little. Even in pain and struggling, Will was a sweetheart. Then he leaned forward, nuzzling into Eddie's flat stomach as Eddie gently massaged his temples. "I'm sorry. I'm not sure I'm up to anything tonight."

"I don't expect anything to happen between us tonight, handsome. That's not why I'm here—I'm not ready to leave you alone, and I'd really like to wake up with you."

"I really want to touch you again. I wanted to take things a step further." When they'd walked to his room, the halls had been quiet of people, but there were moans and shouts behind closed doors. Before everything went pear-shaped,

Eddie had pictured in his mind's eye what he would have liked to do to his captain when they took the party back to a more private setting. But the unexpected detour had derailed his plans, and while Eddie was upset that Will was hurt, he wasn't upset that nothing further would happen between them that night. As ridiculous as it sounded, Eddie wanted his first time with Will to be special. He wanted to take his time and worship him. He didn't want to make Will feel cheap or think he had to put out because it's what happened after these parties, and it was even more important to Eddie that Will understood his intentions.

Eddie tilted Will's face up to his with a finger hooked under his chin and pressed his lips to the uninjured corner of Will's mouth softly and sweetly. "It will happen when the time is right. Let's not rush." At Eddie's words, Will nuzzled his face, drawing Eddie closer and humming. As much as Eddie hated that Will's bastard of an ex had hurt him, breaking his trust and making him more cautious than a man with as beautiful a soul as Will's should be, he was also grateful. If he hadn't, Eddie would never have been given the chance to care for him. Cupping Will's face in his hands, Eddie bent and kissed him gently, pressing his lips chastely to his cheek, temples, and forehead.

Running his fingers through Will's blond locks, cut short at the back and a bit longer on top, Eddie kissed along his jaw and pressed another lingering kiss to the corner of his mouth. Goosebumps broke out on Will's skin as Eddie moved to his ear and ran his nose along the shell before kissing the soft skin just below. Eddie kneaded his shoulders and pulled back, concern filling his heart when Will groaned in pain.

"Headache getting worse?" he asked, worried he was hurting him.

"I always carry tension in my shoulders, but with a migraine, it gets worse."

That wouldn't do. "Get naked and roll over on your belly. You'll never want another man's hands on you once I've given you a massage." Eddie was trying to lighten the mood by being playful, but he was also deadly serious. Will needed this, and Eddie wanted to do whatever he could to relieve Will's pain.

Eddie went in search of something he could use as massage oil and, when he discovered the coconut oil sunscreen, returned to see Will sitting awkwardly, dressed in a pair of white, hot-as-fuck Calvin Klein's. He hesitated and blushed, and Eddie grinned. His shy boy was back, and Eddie loved him dearly.

Eddie stumbled, the thought sideswiping him. It was far too early to be talking like that, but he couldn't deny that even in a few short days, Will had completely overtaken Eddie's world. The captain was all he thought about, and the fluttery, flip-floppy thing Eddie's chest did when he thought about Will, and the smile he couldn't wipe from his face, told him that he was crushing hard.

"Ah... how do you want me?" Will asked quietly.

Eddie held up his finger. "One minute." He dashed back into the bathroom and pulled a white towel from the rail. Coming back out, he turned down the crumpled covers from the once neatly made bed and motioned for Will to lie down. "Leave them on. Just lie on your belly." Once he'd done that, Eddie laid the towel across his hips and reached up underneath, tugging the waistband of his tiny briefs down. He couldn't help his hum of satisfaction when the towel slipped, revealing the curve of a gorgeous arse and a faded tan line. Eddie kissed the spot and, when Will's breath caught, did it again. "You make behaving really hard," Eddie grumbled teasingly.

"You named your cock 'behaving'?" Will tossed a grin over his shoulder, and Eddie couldn't help the bark of laughter he let loose until Will hissed when his lip stretched.

"Shh," Eddie encouraged, laying the cold compress on Will's neck and giving him an ice block to press against his lip.

Eddie poured a generous amount of the oil on his hands, and as the aroma of coconut filled the air, he straddled Will once again and went to work, doing his best to give Will some relief. His strong muscles were firm under Eddie's fingers. Tight too. He kneaded every inch of Will's back and shoulders, concentrating on the parts along his spine which sent him rearing up whenever Eddie touched them. When he focussed on Will's neck and head, Will choked out a groan, and Eddie ran his fingers through his hair, giving him a reprieve from the pain. When Will whimpered, Eddie's heart broke. He hated seeing him like that. "Do you get many massages?" he murmured softly in Will's ear.

"No," he mumbled. "Don't usually enjoy them."

"Want me to stop?" Will gave a miniscule shake of his head, and that was all the confirmation Eddie needed. He moved to Will's arm, rubbing down the muscles there. He could map every single bulge, ridge, and valley that Will had worked tirelessly on. His body was a piece of art. Sculpted perfection.

Shifting to Will's hands, Eddie kneaded them, pressing down on each of the pads of his fingers before moving to the other side and repeating the motion, then returning to his back and rubbing him down again. Will was relaxed, his face turned to the side. His eyes were closed, long blond lashes fanning his cheeks. He was beautiful. "You want me to keep going, handsome?" Eddie whispered. When he didn't answer, Eddie smiled. Will was asleep. That was him. Eddie had done that. He'd comforted Will enough to get him to sleep. Eddie didn't ever want to stop.

He squeezed more oil onto his hands and warmed it before shifting down and working Will's hamstrings and calf muscles. He didn't know if Will's feet were ticklish, but Eddie supposed he'd find out. Pressing firmly on the arch of his foot, he alternated between his thumbs, rubbing the spots where his own feet hurt the most. The satisfied moan Will let loose curled low in Eddie's belly, hardening his cock even more than it had been before the night took its turn. Eddie didn't think he had any more blood left in his brain at that stage, but he'd survive, if only to keep touching Will.

He finished up with Will's other foot and lifted the towel, using it to wipe down his skin. He tried not to stare, but it was impossible. Will's arse was simply perfection, even more so than the rest of his body. High and tight, he had the butt of a man who did a hell of a lot of squats. The dimples above each cheek had Eddie wanting to lick them, and truth be told, that wasn't the only part of Will he wanted to devour. He wasn't just beautiful. He was magnificent. Eddie wished he was an artist. A poet, so he could write about him, a painter, a photographer, or a sculptor so he could preserve the flawlessness of his skin, the curve of firm muscle and soft warmth of his soul in art that would last forever. Sitting there, admiring him, Eddie knew. He'd known this man for barely any time at all—a single drop in all the oceans of the earth if time was measured in water—but his heart recognized its counterpart. Will's body was flawless, but it was his inner beauty that called to Eddie, that had him falling hard and fast for Will.

"Stay," Will whispered when Eddie moved away from him. He kissed Will's cheek and shimmied out of his own clothes before washing off his make-up and turning out the lights. Eddie slipped in behind Will before pulling the covers over them. Eddie needed the closeness, unable to bear the separation, so he wrapped his arm around Will's waist and nuzzled his arm, planting a kiss against his skin.

FIFTEEN

Will

ddie's warm body pressed against his did all sorts of crazy wonderful things to Will's insides. Eddie was hard, wanting, but he'd made no move to wake Will from his relaxed drunk state. The care Eddie took in giving him a massage and making him feel good despite the migraine banging around in his skull made Will's insides dance around happily.

He was disappointed. Will had ached to get closer to Eddie again. The fight, the stress, and the worry about just how badly the executive members of his team would perceive his screw up all had Will's head pounding. It was as if piledrivers were battling it out to see which could rattle his brain more. The headache, combined with the aura floating around his vision and the queasiness, was overwhelming, wiping out his ability to function.

But then Eddie was understanding and had wanted to look after him, staying to make sure he was okay. Will wanted so much more with him than just sex—as amazing as it had been so far. He'd settled for his ex. They'd had a great physical connection. At the time, he'd been the one to handle Will in exactly the way he liked, but they'd never stopped to get to know what was below the surface. When Will eventually saw the person Stefan really was, he didn't like what he saw—from either of them. Will had become someone he didn't recognize, and he'd tried to turn Stefan into someone he wasn't. Then they were over, and Will had re-evaluated everything. He'd reinvented himself, working on both his mind and body until he was happy with what he saw staring back at him in the mirror every morning. Now when Will saw himself, he knew who he was and what he stood for.

He didn't want to make the same mistakes with Eddie. Apart from the fucking gorgeous wrapping that was his body, in his heart, Will knew Eddie was a good man. Beautiful both inside and out. Will wanted to know everything about him.

The kiss to his shoulder and the weight of his arm as Eddie curled himself around Will's body had contentment unfurling through him like the petals of a flower opening under the sun's rays. "Good night, Will."

* * * * *

Will woke in the middle of the night, a loud crash sounding outside the door followed by a slurred, "Sorry, sorry." Will shook his head. The number one rule for staff parties was don't get so hammered you couldn't work the next day. Unless whoever it was had a few good hours to get sober and over the hangover that would no doubt follow, they were going to be struggling.

Eddie didn't stir, his arm still slung over Will's waist. He rolled to face him and smiled at what he saw. The eyeliner Eddie always wore had been cleaned, and his dark lashes splayed in perfect arcs along his cheeks. His plump lips, no longer shiny from the lip gloss, begged Will to kiss them. Will did, but not on them. Pressing his lips gently to Eddie's cheek, his touch whisper-soft, Will slowly pushed him to his back and moved his mouth to Eddie's throat as he straddled his hips. Still dressed in his tiny black boxer briefs, Eddie was sexy as hell in Will's bed.

Will moved his mouth to Eddie's nipple, licking and sucking as best as he could with his injured lip on the pebbled peak, and as he did, Eddie's hands came up and tangled in Will's hair holding him in place. He stilled when Eddie moaned, but Will's whispered name on his lips spurred him on. Barely there touches and teasing licks and nips had Eddie gasping and shifting around in his sleep. He was a heavy sleeper, something that Will planned to use to his advantage. He shifted down Eddie's legs, and the desperate moan he let loose had Will's hole clenching, begging to be filled by the shaft that was standing proudly erect beneath Eddie's underwear.

Curling his fingers under the waistband, Will tugged the front down, exposing the man before him. Eddie was beautiful. Long and thick, uncut. His thatch of dark pubes was neatly trimmed, his balls almost hairless. Leaning in close,

Will breathed him in, loving his spicy scent mixed with the faint hint of the fruity body wash he used. Will nipped at Eddie's hip bone before following the small indentations of his cum gutters with his tongue. Eddie wasn't ripped and absolutely wasn't as built as Will, but his slim, strong physique made him all the more stunningly beautiful to Will.

And his cock? God damn, that thing made Will's mouth water. As if it knew his eyes were on it, Eddie's dick flexed, hardening even further, the foreskin pulling completely back. A pearl of clear pre-cum beaded at his slit, and Will licked it away, savouring his salty taste. Eddie hissed and bowed up off the bed, his legs scrambling for purchase as Will circled his fingers around the base and licked him like a lollipop. It was the best he could do with his still-swollen lip.

"Oh, fuck. Fuck," the man beneath him breathed. Will swirled his tongue around the mushroom head of Eddie's dick and stroked him before licking a path down to his balls. Burying his nose in the soft skin, Will nuzzled. Eddie ran his fingers through Will's hair and touched his thumb to his cheek. "Will," he whispered, making him look up. The affection in his gaze, the longing, and warmth had Will's heart beating faster.

Will moved up his body and wrapped Eddie in his arms, gently pressing their lips together. Eddie ran his fingertips down Will's side, his touch light. Will shivered and Eddie moaned.

"I love how responsive you are," Eddie murmured against his lips. "And that mouth, it should be illegal; it feels so good." Will kissed him again, pressing his weight onto

Eddie, and they both moaned. Their cocks aligned, the rigid lengths trapped between their bodies. Eddie hooked his ankle over Will's calf, and he thrust, grinding against him. Will wanted to share that next step with him, to take him to the edge and feel him surrender in his arms. Will shifted, starting to move off him, but Eddie tightened his grip.

"Stay right there," he whispered, then tried to reach out for Will's nightstand. "Shit," he complained when he realized he was too far away. Will chuckled and leaned over, fetching the box of condoms he'd picked up from Ezio and the lube. Will bit down on the wrapper, readying to tear it open, but Eddie grasped his wrist.

"Not yet. Let's take it slow. We'll work our way up to that." Will hummed his agreement and shifted his weight back onto Eddie before he kissed him until they were drunk. Will couldn't get enough of touching Eddie, of his smooth skin sliding under his fingertips as Will caressed him. "Lift your hips a little, handsome," Eddie breathed in Will's ear before getting frisky with his lobe and moving further south to suck on the skin under it. It was one of Will's strongest erogenous zones—Eddie touched him there, and he was putty in his hands. But Eddie didn't just touch Will; he owned him.

Will tried to do what Eddie had asked, but his dick was a slave to the press of their bodies and the slow grind they had going on. "Let me make you feel good too, Will."

Will's breath caught as Eddie played with the top of his crack. He lifted his arse, straining to get closer to him when Eddie's cool, slick hand closed around their shafts. Will cried out from the shock and muttered, "Evil bastard." But his complaints didn't last long. When Eddie started stroking their lengths, his fist gripping them tightly, Will's eyes rolled back and he arched into Eddie's touch, pumping his hips in a slow grind. Eddie kissed him again, his tongue slipping into Will's mouth, tasting and tormenting Will in the sweetest way while he worked them over and sent Will spinning towards an orgasm he wasn't sure he would ever recover from.

"Oh fuck," Will gasped as Eddie twisted his hand over the head of Will's cock. He was right there on the edge, balls drawn up tightly and his dick throbbing. One more push of Eddie's hand down Will's length, and he cried out, cum shooting from Will's cock onto Eddie's chest in long, hard pulses. The heat of his gaze was on Will. The way Eddie watched as Will's mind spun and ecstasy pounded his body left Will gasping for air and dizzy. Eddie kept going, kept moving his tight fist over them until Eddie arched under him, and he came hard, grunting with every throb of his dick.

Will collapsed on top of the man who'd captured his attention so completely, mashing the evidence of their orgasms together. He kissed Eddie's salty skin, the sweat on it already cooling in the circulated air of the stateroom. Turning his face, Will pressed their lips together, their kiss lazy as they came down from their high.

"I like waking up with you," Eddie murmured. "And not just for the orgasm." Will hummed and kissed him again, rolling them to the side, so his head was pillowed on Will's arm.

Barely a moment later, Will's watch alarm buzzed, rousing Will and making Eddie jump. "What the bloody hell was that?"

Will stretched and his neck cracked. He assessed the damage—his head wasn't hurting anymore, but the hangover from the migraine settled like a haze over him. "That's my alarm. I need to get up. My shift starts soon."

"What time do you finish?"

"Split shift today. I have a four-hour break, but then I'm working through the night, so I'm at the helm to dock us in Sydney. Then Felice takes over and gets us ready to depart again."

"That is so freaking sexy hearing you say that," Eddie murmured, shifting to lean his chin on his steepled hands, propped up on Will's chest. "Use my room to get ready in; it's closer. I'll get us some breakfast."

Will looked up and down the corridor as he let himself into Eddie's suite. He wasn't ashamed to be going in there, but it did feel strange walking into another person's private space. Looking around, Will could see Eddie had made the room his own—books were stacked up on one of the shelves, and a tablet sat on the nightstand. He had photos pinned to the walls—probably his family and friends. As much as he wanted to, Will didn't stop to look at them, instead slipping into the bathroom and stripping down. Being naked in Eddie's space, even without him there, was oddly intimate. His body wash, shampoo, and conditioner sat on the shelf in the shower, and Will placed his next to them, taking a mental snapshot of the bottles as the water warmed. He rushed through his shower and oiled his beard before dressing and dashing back to his suite.

He let himself back into the room to find Eddie curled up with his pillow, fast asleep. Tea and breakfast sat on the desk, waiting for Will. He ate quietly, trying not to wake up Eddie, his iPad staring at him. Will owed both his parents a video call, but he'd been putting it off. His mum was oddly perceptive—she'd know he was crazy for someone the moment he thought of Eddie and the goofy smile appeared—and his dad could read him like an open book. They would know he'd met someone the moment they spoke, but as excited as he was about the potential for their relationship, he and Eddie weren't exactly at the "meet the parents" stage. It was a little like the HR Director finding out. That hadn't turned out how he'd planned either, but there was no going back now.

Will resolved to make time to talk to them during the split in his shift later that day.

* * * * *

The early dinner service on the first night of the cruise was beginning, and both the buffet and the dining hall would be filling up. After that, people would either head for the show, the casino, or the pool deck to watch the twilight movie. Will's shift was only getting started, having taken over from Felice after she had guided the ship out of the headlands forming the entry to Sydney Harbour. High cliffs rose out of the water on either side of them, and the imposing naval bases marked the last signs of land for a full day and two nights' sailing.

It was one of the few times during the year that the cruise did exactly the same route back-to-back, but the crew loved it. The islands in the South Pacific were paradise, and Will was looking forward to having a day off. The trade-off for the double shift he had to pull to make it happen was worth it. Felice's favourite place on earth was Mare. She loved the island and its people and always wanted to spend as much time onshore as possible. They were able to arrange their schedules so that Will worked when they were docked at Mare, and Felice would reciprocate when they arrived in Lifou.

If only Will could coordinate the same day off with Eddie, made infinitely more difficult when Eddie didn't set his own schedule.

The rest of his shift passed in a blur. Coffee kept him alert enough to do his job, but by the end of the day, Will was more than ready to hand over to Felice. She looked as fresh as a daisy when she stepped up to the console he'd been staring at for hours. The hangover from the migraine was still niggling at the back of his brain, and he needed sleep to banish it.

"All quiet on the home front," Will mumbled to her, rubbing his eyes as he stepped away from the monitors.

He didn't even have the energy for a shower. Will had eaten the dinner served up to him on the bridge the night before and two of his three meals that day, and all he wanted to do at that moment was fall into bed.

Naked, Will fell, face first, onto the sheets and drew Eddie's pillow to him again. He couldn't help but think about the conversation he'd had with his mum during the break between his shifts.

"Will! Hi, baby," she said when he'd dialled her. His mum was big and buxom and had a personality to match. He loved her spark. She cocked her head and furrowed her brow. "Is that bruising on your lip? Did you cut it?"

"Yeah, but it's not too bad. Just a small cut." He fingered the scab on his lip and shrugged. "No big deal."

His ma pursed her lips but took the hint to change the subject. "How are things on the high seas?"

"Very calm at the moment. The ship is barely swaying." He paused, then smiled like the love-sick fool he was. He couldn't help it when he thought of Eddie, and that's what his mum really wanted to know—whether he was enjoying himself and still loving every second of commanding this beautiful ship. "It's good, Mum. Really good. I met someone."

Her features lit up, a smile spreading across her face. Clapping her hands excitedly, she laughed and said in a rush, "You've met someone! Tell me everything. Who is he? How did you meet? Is he cute? Is he good in bed?" She frowned. "Is he a passenger?"

Will laughed at that. "No, he's not a passenger. I rarely even get to see passengers, and you know that it's prohibited. Anyway, he's staff, but this is his first assignment, so we only met at the beginning of the last cruise." Will furrowed his brows. "Feels like a lot longer than that though."

"In a good way?" his ma asked, cautious now.

"Yeah, the best." He smiled, knowing he looked like a complete sap. "We clicked straight away. He's funny and gorgeous and really sweet, but sassy too. I feel like even though we're still learning about each other, he gets me."

"So you're dating? How did that go down with the staff and crew?"

"Overall okay, but there was a problem with one of the other entertainers." Will unconsciously touched the healing cut under his lip and reversed his earlier decision to play things down. He'd sworn to be honest to himself and to those around him. Starting to downplay Gerard's actions would only come between them. "Had a bit of a scuffle with him, but no one else has given us any grief, and he's off the ship now. We left him in Sydney."

Her eyes widened and she sucked in a breath. "Oh, baby, don't let him be bullied because of who you are. Haul those bastards over the coals." Will smiled; his mum was already protective of Eddie. When he didn't say anything, she asked, "What?"

"You never once stuck up for Stefan. You said right from day one that you didn't like him. But now you're telling me to discipline people if they're picking on Eddie."

"That's his name? Eddie?" When Will nodded, she smiled but then let out a sad little sigh. "You aren't the same person you were when you met Stefan, Will. You've grown a lot since then and know yourself so much better. I like Eddie already because Stefan never made you smile like you are now. You've got the look of someone who is totally and hopelessly smitten." She wiggled her eyebrows playfully and added, "Either that or its post-orgasm satisfaction. Oh, is he there with you? Can I meet him?"

Will shook his head. "He isn't here." He'd stretched out then and clutched the pillow Eddie had slept with. It still smelt of him, and Will inhaled deeply as he huddled it close. His mum had a knowing smile on her face, and Will couldn't help his blush. There was a piece of lint on the linen that needed brushing away. Repeatedly. Looking away from the camera, he smoothed down the pillowcase but couldn't help his grin. His mother had a "no boundaries" kind of approach to sex, and he knew she'd catch onto his action. "So anyway, let's talk about something else."

"Why, Willy? Is he that good?" She was the devil dressed in sheep's clothing, his mother. Becoming comically serious, with wide eyes and her mouth formed in an O, she asked, "Or is he bad? If you need some tips, you can talk to Brett. He's straight, obviously, but he and I smoke up the sheets."

"No, Ma, he doesn't need any tips from the man who is sleeping with my mother. And I don't either." Will held his hand up to halt her interruption. "Thanks anyway, but no."

"Happy to help, Will," Brett yelled from the background as his mother cackled. He was as bad as Will's mum, and Will wondered why karma was biting him on the arse.

"Thanks, Brett. S'all good though." Will laughed, shaking his head.

"We want to meet him, Will," his mum added quietly. "Face-to-face, in the flesh. When you're ready, we want you to come home and let us get to know him properly. And don't you dare do anything rash like last time."

"I know I've apologized to you for that." He blew out a breath, ashamed of how self-centred he was back then. "But I am sorry for leaving you out of something as important as my wedding. I was pissed with you for calling me out on it, even though I totally deserved it. But then you helped me pick up the pieces and supported me unconditionally when it all turned to shit. I was so selfish, but I promise you, Ma, it'll be different this time around."

His mum put a hand over her heart, and tears sprang to her eyes. When she took a shaky breath, he knew he'd hit close to home for her. "Will, baby, you look after your man, okay? I want him to come home with you so I can make sure he loves you like you deserve."

"I will, Ma," he whispered. "Love you."

"You take care, baby. Keep all those people safe. Love you too." His mum touched her fingers to her lips and held her hand out as if to pass Will the kiss through the screen. He did the same before cutting the connection.

* * * * *

Days had passed, and he and Eddie were, once again, like ships in the night, barely having seen each other. The day's stopover at Mare had gone smoothly, everyone off and back on-board safely. Blue bottle jellyfish had swarmed the island's main swimming beach, so Ezio had been busy for most of the day treating stings, passing on messages to the helm for warnings to be given to guests. He was keeping an eye on one severe reaction, but Will was assured that the patient was stable and in no need of further emergency medical attention.

He stood on the bridge as they sailed away from the tiny island community, the sun setting before them. It was idyllic there, pristine white sand, swaying palm trees, and only the sound of the ocean washing up against the calm beaches.

He took a sip from the coffee cup and grimaced as the cold liquid hit his tongue. Will turned to listen to one of his staff reporting on the reef they were skirting the edge of on the way to deeper water at the same time as he stepped over to the drinks cart and set the cup and saucer down.

He heard the clatter behind him and turned to see the cup slip off the edge of the saucer and crash down in slow motion. He jumped back only to crash into another staff member and watched as coffee spilled across his jacket and in a line down his pant leg. "Damn it," he swore, reaching for a napkin neatly folded on the trolley containing their evening meal.

Taking off his jacket, he tossed it to the side and dried off his pants as best he could while seeing to the safe journey of the Dreamcatcher out of shallower waters and into the cruise ship channels.

Will yawned and got a whiff of himself. He'd pulled some long shifts in the last few days. He needed a shower—stat—and his five hours of free time the next day away from the ship. All he had to do was get them to Lifou. Then he could spend the day lying blissed out on the beach or floating in the ocean. If Eddie was with him, it would be heaven. If not, he'd figure out a way to spend some time with him too.

He noticed the key card that had been pushed under the door as soon as he opened it during his thirty-minute break later that night. There was a note stuck to it too.

Hey, handsome
I've missed you. Heard a rumour that you always try to spend the day at Lifou. Good thing I've pulled done some overtime since Gerard got fired, and I'm owed a few hours. Would love some company ashore if you can.
The hot dancer who wants to see you naked in his shower tonight.

Will laughed at the note, snagged the key, and collected a new uniform. He was at Eddie's door in two minutes, swiping the card against the lock. He stepped inside and closed the door quietly behind him, unsure whether Eddie would have finished for the night and be asleep or whether his schedule was as off as Will's.

Will received a happy surprise when he stepped past the entrance to the bathroom into the room. Eddie lay fast asleep on his stomach, his naked arse looking like perfect round peaches ready to devour. Will wanted to bite into each of the globes and take Eddie to heaven with his mouth.

But he didn't have time.

The devil on his shoulder taunted Will. Tease him. Taste him. It didn't take much persuasion before Will caved, stripped, and crawled on the bed with Eddie, straddling his legs and licking a trail up his firm hamstring with its light dusting of hair, over his arse to the small of his back. Will hardened even more when Eddie moaned and lifted his hips, presenting his arse to Will in his sleep. Will slid his hand between Eddie's legs to fondle his balls, the warm skin soft to the touch, and licked his arse cheek.

"Beautiful, do you like arse play?" Will rasped as his thumb circled Eddie's hole, and Will's fingers brushed his balls. "'Cause, God, I wanna eat you out." Will's alarm rang again, signalling fifteen minutes before his shift restarted. "Fuck," he muttered.

"Hold that thought," Eddie murmured, rolling over and presenting Will with his gorgeous cock. Eddie stared at him from under heavily lidded eyes, sleep rumpled and sexy, and Will responded with base desire—his balls climbing up to sit snugly against his shaft and another drop of pre-cum leaking from his slit. Eddie's cock, rigid and veined, begged Will to suck it. To join them together. His hole clenched, and a shudder ran through Will under Eddie's watchful gaze.

Eddie began stroking himself idly as Will stared at him, taking in every inch of his lithe frame. His mouth watered at the sight, and Will couldn't help but touch himself, closing his fist around his throbbing dick and jacking his shaft slowly. Need rolled through Will, but the desire flowing thick and hot between them held a note of affection too. Lust fuelled him. Close wasn't close enough. He needed to touch and taste him. Leaning down, Will licked Eddie's balls, sucking one into the hot cavern of his mouth as he moaned long and low.

"You want this, don't you?" Eddie teased in a scratchy voice, his own cravings obvious. "You want my tight arse clenching around your cock as we fuck nice and slow. Or do you want to come while I'm buried in you? You want me to be buried balls deep in you?" Will's breath caught as Eddie tugged him to lie on top of him and kissed Will before he licked his finger and slipped it between his spread legs. Eddie's touch on Will's ring was all it took. He moaned and shuddered, crying out when Eddie took the head of Will's cock in hand and pressed a spit-lubed finger harder against his hole. Eddie didn't penetrate him, but the picture he'd created with his dirty words and his touch was enough to send Will over the edge embarrassingly fast. He spilled his seed on Eddie's chest and quaked as his orgasm swept through him.

Eddie's knuckles brushed Will's shaft as he jacked himself to completion. Eddie cried out his release and shot against Will's abs. Will's dick pulsed at the sight. His orgasm made a valiant attempt to renew itself.

Will collapsed onto Eddie, pushing them both back down onto the sheets, and he laughed breathlessly.

"When I said hold that thought, I was trying to be good. But seeing you there hovering over me all naked and sexy made every good intention fly straight out the window. You make it so hard to behave." He ran spunk-coated fingertips over Will's back, and all Will could do was hum against Eddie's neck, his boneless body craving more of his touch. "Your alarm went off. Was that your start time?"

"No, fifteen-minute warning. I needed to have a shower and get changed. Spilled coffee all over myself."

"Up. Shower," he ordered, slapping Will playfully on the arse. Will's cock twitched; he loved the spark of sensation as warmth bloomed on his arse. Eddie groaned when he saw the movement. "Seriously, up. Or we'll be going for round two, and you'll miss the second half of your shift."

Will rolled off him and sat up, instantly missing the feel of Eddie against him. He was pressed up against Will's back barely a second later, nudging him off the bed and into his tiny shower. "How did you know about Lifou being my favourite place?" Will asked as Eddie slid the curtain shut, separating them, and he turned the spray on.

"A little birdie might have mentioned it." Will stuck his head out from behind the shower screen, but Eddie motioned zipping his lips closed, locking them, and tossing away the key. "But you might not get to come there with me if you aren't out of the shower, dressed, and up to the bridge within two minutes. You're really late."

Will scrubbed himself down as quickly as he could, rinsed, and turned off the shower, making barely a half-arsed effort to dry before tugging his clean uniform on. Leaving the buttons of his white shirt undone, Will pulled on his shoes and dashed out the door. Three steps out, he realized what he'd done and spun to find Eddie standing at his door stark naked, one hand on his hip and the other holding out Will's hat. But that wasn't the only thing he'd rushed out without doing, and Will was glad that once he had his hat perched on his head, Eddie pointed to his lips. He was barely repressing a smirk, and Will was struck dumb by how gorgeous he was. Running his fingertips down Eddie's stubbled cheek, he murmured, "I'll see you at ten."

He pressed his lips to Eddie's, but a quick kiss wasn't enough. Once he'd gotten a taste, he did it again, this time kissing him slower, longer, before Eddie pushed him away.

"Off with you. Just bring your sexiest swimwear and a towel." Eddie paused thoughtfully. "Or maybe just a towel if you know a deserted beach somewhere. I'll handle everything else, handsome."

Will grinned and jogged down the hall, buttoning his shirt at the same time.

He made it to the bridge two minutes late, his hat skewed, and apparently, his shirt buttoned incorrectly. As soon as he burst through the door, everyone stopped what they were doing, took one look at him, and sniggered. "Not one word, any of you." Will pointed around the room and aimed for intimidating, which was hard considering his laughter. Turning toward the computer screens lining the controls, he tossed his hat aside and re-buttoned his shirt, tucking it in properly.

"O, Captain! My Captain!" Felice announced theatrically, posing like she was in a Shakespearean play. "Oh, how good you look after getting lucky." She preened, incredibly pleased with herself. Lower than her earlier comment, she added, "And please tell me at least one of us is getting lucky."

"How long have you been waiting to use that line?" Will shook his head, checking over the electronic charts and trying not to laugh again. They were about to enter the lesser protected waters between the island chains where the bigger swell could toss the ship around a bit. For the comfort of all the passengers, it was important they were all focused on the job ahead of them. But Will was never one to squash levity on the bridge—they were in paradise on a cruise ship. They had to at least have some fun.

"About five years now." She nudged Will with her elbow and pointed to the screen showing the depth change as they passed over the continental shelf.

SIXTEEN

Eddie

Eddie barely had any time before his short shift started, but he desperately wanted to organize something that Will, a man who could literally have anything he wanted on board, would enjoy. He was feeling the pressure. Pacing up and down the short length of his stateroom, he tried to push through his mind blank. How could he make their date on Lifou a special one?

He'd looked at what was on the island, and the most spectacular things—the church and a bay where people could snorkel in the marine reserve—would be teeming with tourists. He really wanted some time away from everyone. Somewhere where they could just have some alone time together. The island looked to be idyllic and laid back, and he wanted to gift a few perfect hours for Will to do nothing except be.

Eddie grinned. He had it.

* * * * *

With a smile in place, Eddie scanned identification cards for the queued disembarking passengers and exchanged a few kind words with the passengers. The crowds were already thinning, most of the passengers getting on the tenders within an hour of mooring in the deep channel just off the island's coast. He couldn't wait to head over there himself. The azure water and white sand called to him, begging him to jump and make a swim for it.

The staff member taking over for Eddie after his shift ended arrived, and Eddie slipped into the staff-only area, making his way quickly across the ship. He ducked into his suite to pick up the things he needed before dashing off to collect the basket of goodies he'd organized.

Will met him right on ten o'clock. The captain walked down the corridor towards him, looking all stupidly sexy in a pair of long swim trunks, a tank top, and flip-flops, a pair of wraparound sunglasses hanging from his loose shirt, and a ball cap on, Eddie was transfixed. The grin that lit up Will's face was mesmerizing, and Eddie found himself mirroring it until Will swept him into his arms and dipped him low. Giggling like a teenager, Eddie kicked up a leg and threw his arms around Will's shoulders, kissing him like they'd been apart for months. It started out playful but quickly turned long and slow, incredibly sexy and a little desperate too. Eddie's shy boy was becoming bolder, showing him what he wanted, and Eddie loved that side of him. He smiled against Will's lips. "Happy to see me, handsome?"

"No, just needed some lip gloss," he teased, straightening up then leaning in to kiss Eddie again. Taking him by the hand, Will tugged him towards the elevators. "Come on, I need some sun and sand." They walked together to the disembarkation point, enjoying the quiet corridors followed by the short queue of people. In plain clothes, they blended in, no one blinking an eyelid at them until they got to the front of the line.

"Good morning, Captain. Enjoy your day onshore," one of the crew members said, looking Eddie up and down and apparently finding him lacking.

"We will, thank you," Will replied bluntly, his displeasure at the other man's reaction obvious. Chastised, the man handed back their ID cards and smiled politely at them. Once they got out of earshot, Will pulled him close, adding, "I'm sorry. I hate that they look at you differently because you're with me. If it's too much—"

"If it's too much, I'll tell them to grow the fuck up and butt the hell out of my life, Will. We've already been through enough. There's no way in hell I'm walking away from you because someone else has their nose out of joint. I thought you realized I'm not that man."

Will smiled, a blush staining his cheeks, and he kissed Eddie's knuckles softly. He didn't need Will to thank him to see just how much Eddie's loyalty meant to him.

"Ma told me I should protect you from anyone being an arse to you," he said sheepishly when they were seated in a corner of the tender boat. There were people around them, but they paid them no attention, talking to each other in hushed tones.

"You told your mother about me?" Eddie squeaked, nerves assailing him. What happened if his mum didn't like Eddie? He knew how much Will valued his family and how important it was to him that their relationship be completely different to the one he'd had with Stefan—the bastard—but bloody hell! Every irrational fear ran through his mind, and yet his heart whispered that he'd wanted to move things forward too. He'd made things more official as well and had taken a step that was important to him. And just like that, he was smiling again. His smile spread even more broadly when Will nodded.

Eddie squeezed his hand and tried to tamper down his nervous excitement. "I know she already knows, but I made things a little more official too." Eddie paused, adding, "That's how I knew that you had time off today."

"Who?" Will furrowed his eyebrows and then grinned. "Emira. The HR Director," Will clarified, smoothing his thumb over the palm of Eddie's hand.

"Yeah." Eddie looked at him, hoping Will was okay with him having spoken to her in an official capacity without Will's knowledge. Any concern he had dissipated when Will's smile turned boyishly shy. He was adorable, and Eddie wanted to kiss him. That was the wonderful thing about Will being out of uniform—Eddie could, so he did.

"Thank you." Will ran his fingertips down Eddie's face in the way he loved. He was quickly coming to crave Will's touch. His affections. "For waiting for me and still moving us forward."

"I'm not pressuring you—"

"I know. This is good. We're good. We are good, aren't we? Do I need to do anything?"

"We're good. I asked the director whether we needed to do anything. She said that given you're not my immediate supervisor, there's no additional protocols that need to be put in place."

He nodded, smiling, but before Will said anything, his gaze cut to the window over his other shoulder. They'd pulled up to the jetty, and the tender was being lashed to the pylons so they could get off. Will picked up the basket Eddie had set between his feet and waved off his protests.

Eddie followed him out, and as soon as he stood on the pier, he understood why Will was enamoured with the island. It was exactly as he'd pictured the South Pacific. Swaying palm trees and water so clear that he could see the fish and turtles swimming below them and every piece of coral and seagrass on the sandy bottom. Buildings made of weathered logs and palm-frond roofs lined the hill away from the beach. A larger open-air pergola-like structure stood in the middle of the village, with a lawn surrounding it. Flowers blossomed on bushes lining the paths, and fruit dangled heavily from the branches of others. The smell of barbequed meat and fish surrounded them, and Eddie's mouth watered. He'd be stopping there on the way back from their swim.

"There's lots to see on the island. What would you like to do?"

"Your favourite thing," Eddie replied, hoping like hell he didn't want to go for a swim at the same beach that every other passenger from the ship was swimming at. Even though it was busy, everyone had their own space along what looked like a mile-long stretch of sand, but there was no privacy, and Eddie was dearly hoping for that. "But I would love a swim."

"Follow me." His heart sank when Will led them to the beach, but Eddie bit his tongue. He wanted the day to be special for Will, and if swimming at the main beach was his favourite spot, then that's where they'd go.

They walked down the steep descent onto the sandy foreshore, and Eddie kicked off his flip-flops before pulling his hat out of the bag.

They traversed the full length of the beach, walking along the waterline on the hard-packed sand. Children played at the water's edge, their parents snapping photos and chasing after them, laughing. People young and old snorkelled in the shallow reefs along the beach and swam while others stretched out on towels in and out of the sun. The atmosphere was relaxed, and Eddie basked in it, his body needing a few hours to soak up the oasis of calm after a couple of weeks of crazy schedules, run-ins with a person he'd rather forget, and non-stop performances. He was living the dream, but it was damn good to unwind. It was also the perfect opportunity to spend time with Will. If only the beach wasn't quite as busy.

At the end of the long stretch of sand, there was a steep, narrow, rock-strewn path disappearing between dense vegetation and tall palm trees. Will didn't hesitate to push aside the low-hanging branches and motion for Eddie to go first. The noise level dipped immediately when Will let the branch go, and it slipped back into place. A bird's song had Eddie smiling and looking around in wonder at the pocket of rainforest they'd entered. The ground was no longer sandy but covered in leaf litter, and the air seemed thicker. The brush of the palms and flowering vines against Eddie's skin were soft, their perfume making the shadowed walk along the narrow path a degustation for all the senses.

Breaking through to the other side took less than a minute, but it was like emerging a world away. The only indication there were a thousand-odd guests only footsteps away on the tiny island was the cruise ship floating peacefully in the deep waters off the island.

A small cove stood before Eddie, with the same white sand and perfect clear water as the other beach. Except that this one was deserted and blissfully quiet. The almost vertical bluff running down to the sand ensured there was only one easy entrance and exit for their secluded getaway, and the trees behind them shielded them from prying eyes. The afternoon would see the little cove in shadow, but at that time of the morning, brilliant sunlight lit the beach, drying the sand and making the water sparkle like diamonds. The tide lapped against the shoreline, the tiny waves barely ebbing and flowing. The rustle of the trees behind them in the soft breeze was music to the caress of the wind against

Eddie's skin. He closed his eyes and breathed deep when Will's arm slipped around his waist, sighing happily.

"It's perfect here. Like an oasis."

"This beach is underwater when the tide is at its highest. We've only got a few hours here before we'll have to shift back over to the other side," Will explained. "But it's worth it."

"It doesn't matter. It's heaven." Eddie breathed again, letting relaxation wash over him as the salt breeze filled his lungs.

"I'm glad you like it." Will was behind him then, his big body pressed against Eddie's as he wrapped his arms around him. He kissed down Eddie's throat and tugged his tee out of the way so Will could nibble along his shoulder, and Eddie's knees almost buckled. Will's touch lit a fire of need in him that he could quite easily cave to. Damn, he wanted that. He wanted to give himself to Will.

But he wanted to wait and give Will the respect he deserved. The love he deserved, and if he didn't move away, he'd be on his knees within moments. So, forcing himself away, Eddie laid out the towels and patted the one next to him, kneeling down and wiggling in the sand to get comfortable.

He stripped off his tee and turned to see Will staring at him. The man above him licked his lips, looking hungry. As if given half a chance, he'd devour him. Damn, Eddie wanted that too.

Eddie sucked in a breath when Will peeled off the loose singlet he wore and dropped it on the sand without hesitation. Stalking towards him, Will ignored the towel and knelt before him, reaching out to clasp Eddie's nape and drag his body close. Their lips crashed together, and Will took his mouth in a needy kiss. Their tongues tangled, and Will squeezed the hand on Eddie's arse, aligning their bodies from nose to knees.

They broke apart long moments later, Eddie sucking in a breath as his world spun in dizzying circles. "What's up, handsome?" Eddie's tease came out huskier than usual, the rasp pronounced. Will shook his head as if forcing himself back into the present and ran his fingers down Eddie's pale chest.

"Sunscreen or you'll burn, and it won't matter what part of me is up." Will grasped the bottle Eddie dug out from the basket and lathered his skin, taking care to cover every inch of Eddie's shoulders, arms, hands, and chest. When he reached Eddie's belly, Will motioned for him to lie down, and Eddie did, pillowing his head in his crossed hands. Will straddled his hips, smoothing the cream over the flat planes of Eddie's stomach before shuffling down.

He popped the button on Eddie's cute cut-off jean shorts and met Eddie's gaze as he flicked up the pull tab on the zip and slowly tugged it down. With both hands on his hips, Will lifted Eddie's arse and smoothed the shorts down his legs. While Will was kneeling up, Eddie took the chance to kick off his shorts and run his hands up Will's thick legs pulling his hips closer. Only then did Will break their gaze, trailing his eyes down Eddie's body and warming him with every part he took in.

Will sucked in a breath when he reached Eddie's micro-swimwear and Eddie's cock flexed. He needed friction, unable to help the thrust of his hips. Will squeezed Eddie's hips with his legs and fell forward, hovering above him on outstretched arms. "Do that again," he rasped, and Eddie couldn't have stopped if he tried.

Will dropped his hips, bringing their cocks into contact, and Eddie bucked again, his dick fighting to break free of the tiny scrap of material covering him. Will kissed him then like a man possessed. Like a man who knew what he wanted and wasn't tiptoeing around his desires. Eddie loved his shy side, but this commanding and demanding man was hot.

"Roll over," Will urged, with a line of kisses down Eddie's throat to his collarbone and a flick of his tongue over it. Eddie did when Will lifted his arse. He moaned when Will gripped his hip and ground down, sliding the length of his shaft between Eddie's cheeks. Eddie shuddered and tilted his hips up, encouraging Will to do it again. The puff of breath on his nape drove him wild. Eddie reached up to grip Will's face, and Will went to him, kissing him as he rolled his hips and took what he needed from Eddie's body.

"Need you," Eddie whispered. Will responded by shifting his hand under Eddie and gripping his cock, massaging it over his swimwear. The head of his dick poked up, exposing itself and sliding against the soft towel separating him from the sand. Lost in Will, Eddie cried out as the man above him squeezed him tighter. Eddie moaned in frustration when Will froze, breathing hard and shuddering. It was as if he was fighting himself, trying to hold off the need to come.

Eddie understood, the overwhelming need firing through Eddie quicker than ever before.

Will pulled back, putting some distance between their bodies, and Eddie shifted, needing him to come back. "Not yet," Will murmured in his ear, licking his throat. "Hikers above might see, and when I make you mine, no one but me will be looking."

Eddie moaned, loving the hint of possession in Will's tone. His cock pulsed, and when Will squeezed him hard, he could feel the smile against his skin. He pulled back, leaving Eddie aching, and squirted more sunscreen onto his hands before rubbing over Eddie's heated skin.

Will shuffled down and licked the curve of Eddie's arse at the top of the tiny floral-print shorts he'd chosen in Sydney before getting on the ship. His handsome captain's hands followed, rubbing the sunblock into his skin. Will's beard prickled against his arse as he nuzzled his face into Eddie's rounded globes and teased him with swipes of his tongue along the bottom of the swim shorts.

"These things are sexy as fuck, you know that?" Will rasped as he scooted down and spread the sunscreen over Eddie's legs. When Will nudged him to roll over again, Eddie held his breath, praying that Will would straddle him again. He wasn't disappointed.

Will's strong legs, thick from hours in the gym, gripped Eddie's smaller hips tight, and Will teased him, not resting his full weight on Eddie's aching cock. Snatching the sunscreen away from Will, Eddie squeezed a generous portion in his hands and reached up to rub down Will's skin. In the bright light of day, Eddie could see the grey hairs in the smattering of chest hair he had. When Eddie ran his thumbs over Will's nipples, they hardened at his touch, Will's abs quivering as Eddie splayed his hands over them and around his waist, rubbing in the cream.

Pulling Will down onto him, Eddie thrust up at the same time and watched, enraptured, as Will's back bowed, and he choked out a cry. God damn, this man was sexy. Eddie couldn't wait for the moment that they did this for real.

He wanted to be buried in him or be stretched by Will— he didn't much care at this point. All he knew was that he wanted the picture Will painted so badly that he was going cross-eyed with lust.

Eddie reached around, gripping Will's muscular arse, and thrust up again, making Will cry out a second time. He could watch that reaction all day; it was that fucking sexy. He couldn't get enough of Will, couldn't touch enough of him at once. With their tongues tangling, their breaths mingling, Eddie moaned into his mouth, desperate to get closer. He slipped his hands under the waistband of Will's bright blue shorts and grasped his ass, gripping the firm globes in his hands.

Eddie wanted to touch him so bad, wanted to make Will a slave to lust like he was, to delve deep inside his hole and stretch him for his cock.

But Eddie hesitated.

This was supposed to be a date, their time in the sea and sun to enjoy and relax. Hell, he loved sex, but as Will said— not there, not then. Will deserved so much more than a quick fuck on the beach. Eddie wanted to worship him, to taste every dip and curve of Will's body. To send him into orbit with his tongue and fingers.

Eddie pulled his hands free and trailed them up to Will's chest, curling his fingers into the hairs there. Will broke their kiss, breathing hard as his hips twitched, base desire still controlling his movements.

"Swim," Eddie murmured, unable to utter anything more coherent.

Will shifted, nudging Eddie's knees apart with his own, and reached down to wrap Eddie's legs around his waist. Eddie held onto his muscled man like a spider monkey as his world tilted, and Will lifted him effortlessly until he was standing, carrying him to the water like he weighed nothing. Eddie loved his strength, his gentle touch as Will handled him reverently, even when a moment earlier their simulated fucking was dirty and raw.

Will sank down slowly, the cold water enveloping them as Will went to his knees in the shallows. The cold water was a shock to his system, but his captain's warmth overrode the desire to get straight back out. Kissing him gently, Will tipped them to the side, and they went under, their mouths never separating. Only when Eddie's lungs were burning, his body screaming for oxygen, did he nudge Will, who lifted them out of the water. Eyes dark with desire, Will crushed him against his body, and Eddie moaned, their lips finding each other again.

Their kiss changed, and Eddie was hit with a wave of affection. Will was beautiful. Water dripped from his hair and slid down his face, his beard glittering with the tiny droplets on it. Eddie cupped his face and brushed his thumbs over Will's cheeks before kissing him softly again.

Will smiled against his lips, and the butterflies took up residence in Eddie's heart, taking flight and making him giddy. It wasn't just lust between them. It was something far deeper. Looking into his rich, chocolate brown eyes, Eddie saw the same warmth, the same affection reflected back at him and fell even harder. Will was magnificent— every inch of him. But it wasn't just his mussed-up, blond, sexy surfer hair, the greys at his temple, or his big body. It was his heart, his brilliant mind, the caring and shy man who Eddie wanted to call his own.

The thought of forever whispered in his mind. It should have terrified him, but it didn't. Eddie couldn't explain it. He knew he was falling for Will. How couldn't he? But they'd still only had a few dates. They were still getting to know each other. Eddie couldn't deny their connection, both physical and mental. He loved spending time with the man as much as he loved touching and tasting Will. He knew it would only be a matter of time before three little words that he'd never uttered to another soul outside of his family were spilling from his lips.

One day, he coached himself.

It was far too early to be professing his undying love for Will, no matter what he saw in the other man's eyes. But knowing that Will was right there, too, made Eddie fall even harder.

They floated like that for what could have been hours, wrapped in each other's arms as they kissed slowly right there in the South Pacific on their tiny slice of paradise.

When Eddie had auditioned for the cruise company, he'd hoped to have the experience of a lifetime, dancing his way around the world. Never in his wildest dreams did he believe it could lead him to Will. He sighed happily and speared his fingers through Will's hair, tugging gently on the strands as he kissed him harder.

"Beautiful," Will murmured against his lips, his tone changing from the warm teasing as they'd whispered together into something huskier. He opened his eyes, and Eddie saw the blazing need in their depths, the same desire reflected in his heart in Will's. He wanted this, wanted to take the next step. When he tilted his head toward the ship, Eddie nodded immediately. He wanted whatever Will was prepared to give. Still in his arms, Will carried him to shore. Capturing his mouth again, Eddie kissed him harder, longer, his tongue stroking against Will's in a sensual dance. It was a goodbye of sorts—one more passionate kiss before they had to straighten themselves for the trek through the public part of the beach.

The walk back to the tender and trip to the ship was a sweet form of torture—a never-ending form of foreplay. The air between them crackled and sparked with anticipation, arcing between their only point of contact—their linked pinkies.

Desire flooded Eddie. He wanted Will like he'd never wanted anyone before. His mind swirled with fantasies of

Will's hot and sweaty body against his own as they slaked their lust. But it was the tenderness in the way Will held his hand and placed his other at the small of Eddie's back when he'd stepped up onto the tender that made Eddie's heart flip-flop. Will motioned for him to go first when the boat docked against the ship, and Eddie led the way through the embarkation checkpoint and into the crew-only area.

Finding himself standing between their staterooms, Eddie paused. Shower or bed? Looking at the time, he realized there was no rush. He could take his time with Will and make every moment together special. He began to lead them to his room, but Will hesitated.

"Want to try out my brand-new shower?"

Eddie grinned and changed direction, stripping off his wet towel before the door had even clicked closed behind them. Will followed, dropping it in the doorway. Dressed only in their swimming shorts, Eddie sucked in a breath and trailed his fingertips down Will's face, his beard salty from the ocean water.

He stepped away from his fantasy man, and turned on the shower, adjusting the water temperature before hooking his fingers into the waistband of Will's shorts. "You ready for this, handsome?"

He nodded, and Eddie leaned in and kissed his collarbone and chest as he tugged the offending material down, letting it pool on the floor. Eddie's breath caught when Will was revealed in all his glory. He was tall and strong, muscled all over, but not super ripped like he was 'roided up. A smattering of greying chest hair dusted his pecs, and he had a flat belly with cum gutters that Eddie wanted to lick, which pointed down to a thatch of trimmed pubes framing a beautiful cock—erect, long, and thick. Eddie wanted to fall to his knees and blow Will's mind.

Eddie resisted—barely—instead stripping off his own shorts without fanfare and dragging Will under the warm spray. Eddie took his time, lathering Will's hair and skin with the shampoo and body wash in Will's shower. He'd left the same brand in Eddie's shower. It was a hell of a thrill when he'd seen it, knowing Will was comfortable enough to keep it there.

Will's skin was silky smooth against the palms of Eddie's hands, his soft moans as he rubbed Will down, ramping up his own excitement. Eddie washed down Will's legs, falling to his knees as he did. Eddie in looking up at his man, at his beautiful face, his lids low and pupils blown with lust. When Will's tongue snaked out to wet his bottom lip like he was hungry, he turned Eddie inside out. Eddie didn't just want him anymore; he needed him. Will was his oxygen, the blood pumping through his veins. Like they had a mind of their own, his hands moved to Will's arse, cupping his solid cheeks in his hands as Eddie toyed with and teased his crack.

"Please," Will whispered, tilting his hips and begging Eddie to go further. He couldn't resist Will even if he wanted to. Kissing up his leg and across his hip towards his cock, Eddie breathed him in before licking up the length of his veiny shaft and swirling his tongue over Will's crown. The salty tang of Will's pre-cum burst onto his tongue, and

Eddie relished the flavour with a hum. A shudder passed through both of them when Eddie swallowed him down, working Will's shaft until his balls were snug against his body and his cock was dripping pre-cum.

"Eddie, no," Will gasped. The urgency in his tone stopped him in his tracks. "I'm gonna come." Will wrapped his fingers around his sac and pulled down, visibly trying to stave off his orgasm. His shallow breaths made his chest rise and fall rapidly. "I want you."

He was up off the floor in an instant, rinsing what was left of the ocean's salt off himself with a sluice of the warm water over his body. Tumbling out of the shower, Eddie waited for Will to turn off the tap and handed him a fluffy towel. He scrubbed it over his hair, drying the blond strands before wrapping it around his waist and stepping out of the cubicle. Standing on his little mat, Eddie did the same, and when they were done, he clasped Will's hand and... hesitated.

Will didn't, kicking open the bathroom door and tugging Eddie into the main part of his suite. They weren't even fully through the door before Eddie was on him. Will's mouth, sweet and yielding, only made Eddie hungrier. He wanted to devour the man, to lick and nip at every inch of his skin. To make Will his. To give himself over completely to him. He wanted Will to feel the way his heart was beating out a frenetic rhythm for him.

Walking them backwards, Will led them to the bed, and when his knees hit the mattress, Eddie paused and smiled, loving Will being in that position again. His captain's shy smile had him tugging off their towels and tossing them aside, leaving them naked together.

Will sat down and kissed Eddie's hip, but he knew he'd lose his head if Will touched his cock. Eddie pushed him back playfully, and Will scooted up the mattress, making room for him. Aligning their bodies, Eddie's smaller one lying on top of Will's solid bulk, between his spread legs, was like coming home. Eddie fell into Will's warm gaze. The heat of Will's body and the soft hairs on his legs rubbing against Eddie's cocooned him. Eddie licked his bottom lip before he pressed his mouth to Will's. He sucked on his tongue, and Will cried out, his hips jacking up, seeking out friction against his cock.

"Want you," his man breathed.

"What do you prefer, Will? How do you want me?" Eddie licked his throat, feeling Will's breath catch.

"Need you inside me," he rasped.

Eddie nearly swallowed his tongue. Lightning struck him, and electricity lit him up. He'd seen hints that Will liked to bottom, but never in a million years did he think that Will would want Eddie inside him that first time. Eddie had never much enjoyed bottoming, but stereotypes being stereotypes and Eddie's preference for older men often had him negotiating a verse arrangement. But Will lying there before him all sexy and tousled, waiting for him and wanting Eddie to top him ramped up his desire a hundred-fold. Eddie moaned and couldn't help but stroke himself, Will watching the motion intently.

"That okay?"

When Eddie found his voice, he nodded, rasping, "Good. Bottoming's good."

Will opened his legs wider in invitation, lifting his foot up off the bed. Eddie didn't need more of a hint. Moving down Will's body, Eddie kissed him, nipping the taut skin stretched over firm muscle, licking the grooves between his abs and down his cum gutter to his pubes. Will sucked in a sharp breath when Eddie nuzzled his sac, his balls already drawn up tight again. He could do this for hours; tasting Will was intoxicating. Licking down the soft skin under his testicles, Eddie rimmed him, circling his hole once, twice, before flattening the pad of his tongue and swiping right across him. His taste wasn't entirely masked by the soap, and Eddie was grateful for that as he worked his tongue over Will's tight muscle, softening it for his fingers to enter him.

"You're so tight. How long has it been?"

"Years. Not since I was married." Eddie didn't want to give Will any doubts about bottoming for him again because one time with Will would never be enough.

"You use toys?"

Will moaned, and a shudder passed through him before he nodded. His eyes were closed, his neck corded. Ragged breaths made his chest rise and fall rapidly. Will was a sight for sore eyes—the sexiest creature Eddie had ever seen. Eddie's mouth watered at the sight of Will's open legs, and his cock lying heavy on his hip, pre-cum leaking from its slit. When a drop of the clear liquid fell, smearing over Will's belly as his cock flexed, Eddie couldn't resist any longer. He shifted, lapping up the pre-cum and rubbing his fingers over the ring of muscle framed by Will's arse.

Eddie pulled open the drawer and, shifting around underwear, found the lube and a thick dildo with a suction cup on its base. He drew it out and walked his fingertips up Will's leg, waiting for the other man to open his eyes a crack. Eddie licked it, sucking on the crown of the dildo while Will watched him with heavily lidded eyes. Eddie's dick leaked, thinking about how sexy it would be to watch Will fuck himself on the dildo until it was buried to the hilt. He deep throated the dildo showing Will just what he wanted to see.

"Oh fuck," Will gasped, wrapping his fingers around his shaft.

"I want to watch you use this one day. I want to see you swallow every inch of it into your arse as I sink into your mouth. Want to watch you get yourself off so I can do it again to you straight after. We'll see how many orgasms we can wring out of you one after the other."

Will's hips snapped up and his dick pulsed. "Fuck, I'm going to come."

"Not without my dick in your tight little hole." Eddie tossed aside the dildo and drizzled clear slick on his fingers. He took one last taste of Will before kneeling and introducing his finger to Will's puckered hole. Will lay before him, legs up in the air and all flushed and gorgeous. He held the covers in a white-knuckled grip, his eyes closed and mouth open, breathing hard. A sheen of sweat had broken out over his skin, and Eddie wanted to lick it off him. He had the insane urge to take a photo to remember this moment and the blissed-out frustration painted on Will's face forever.

With his legs curled into his chest and Will's hard cock saluting the air, a drip of pre-cum fell from his slit, landing on his belly. Eddie pressed against him but resisted pushing further into Will, even though he was bearing down, begging Eddie to slide his fingers into him. Eddie wanted Will crazy for him. He kept up the taunting, the featherlight touches, and the sensual tease until Will mewled and thrust his hips, trying to impale himself on Eddie's fingers. When the veins on Will's cock throbbed, his shaft flexing with need, Eddie used his middle finger to penetrate him slowly. Will's breath left him in a rush, a shudder passing through him before he moaned.

Eddie didn't wait long before he gave him a second finger, letting him feel the burn of the stretch. Will was riding his digits, and Eddie was harder than an iron rod. Will's choked gasps and moans, as well as the schlick, schlick, schlick of Eddie's fingers inside him, drove him wild. Eddie was going to come before he managed to get inside Will if he didn't get his wayward cock under control. But having his captain there, knowing they were taking that step, was huge.

"Eddie," he gasped. "I'm ready." He opened his eyes, and his darkened gaze bore into Eddie's, beseeching him to understand what he needed. Eddie did, and there, kneeling between his beautiful man's legs, he promised himself that he'd always give Will everything he needed. Whatever it was, whatever it took, Eddie would do it for him.

He sheathed himself in the condom he'd pulled from the paper bag stuffed in Will's drawer and slathered his shaft in lube. It'd be a hell of a slippery ride, but that was half the fun. Hovering above him, Eddie took Will's lips with his and kissed him slowly as he moved into place. Without breaking their kiss, he lined himself up and hooked Will's calf over his hip, opening him as much as possible. He pressed forward, the tight ring of Will's arse stretching to accommodate Eddie's girth and enveloping him in nirvana. Will was slick and hot, silky smooth, and wrapped around Eddie like a glove. Sensation raced up and down Eddie's spine, making every nerve ending sing a concerto worthy of the London Symphony Orchestra. Staring into Will's eyes, something sparked between them, and Eddie held himself still, never wanting to break their connection. Finally, the puff of air against his overheated skin came as Will exhaled the breath he'd been holding. When his other leg came up, wrapping tight around Eddie's hips and forcing him deeper, they moaned together.

"God damn, handsome. You feel so good." Eddie rested his forehead against Will's shoulder, nuzzling into his throat as he pushed in deeper still, not stopping until his hips were flush against Will's skin—buried to the hilt. Will's arms came around Eddie's shoulders, his fingers spearing through Eddie's short hair. He tilted his head, giving Eddie room to nibble on his throat. Eddie hooked his hands under Will's shoulders anchoring them together, and ever so slowly, he pulled almost all the way out.

Eddie rolled his hips, moving leisurely enough that he could savour Will's channel clasping tight around him. The moans he made were so fucking sensual, so sexy that Eddie had to capture them and keep them close within him. Eddie kissed him, their tongues stroking as he pumped his hips. There was no wild slapping of flesh together, no crazy squeaking bedframes, but the heat between them sizzled. Eddie slaked his need on the beautiful man before him. Hands exploring and mouths caressing, they revelled in the sensation and steadily climbed to the precipice.

One day Eddie knew they'd be so damn crazy with lust that they'd lose their shit and attack each other. He would find a few surfaces to bend Will over for a quickie, especially in a ship with lots of darkened spaces, and they'd fuck with the sole purpose of getting off, but today wasn't that day.

Eddie pulled back and looked him in the eyes. Their bodies were pressed together, with Will wrapped around Eddie for a change. Every inch of him Eddie could touch, he did, but it still wasn't enough. When Eddie brushed the pad of his thumb over Will's lower lip, he kissed it, sending a spike of lust through him. Those lips were divine. So incredibly sensual. Eddie thought Will was wickedly hot on his knees, his lips wrapped around the base of Eddie's cock. It had sent him into overdrive those few times it'd happened, Eddie needing to pull the sexy man off, or he would have gone off like a bottle rocket when what he really wanted was a ride to the moon. But now... now Eddie was orbiting the sun.

When Will clenched those muscles tight around Eddie's girth, he moaned while Will grinned mischievously. Eddie muttered, "Tease." He nipped Will's lip, biting down, then sucked on it until it popped out of his mouth. Will's eyes rolled back in his head. Eddie punched his hips forward, pressing his point home and hitting Will's prostate dead centre if the shudder that rocked his body was anything to go by. Will's muscles vibrated under his touch, and when Eddie shifted to take his cock in hand, the man under him cried out.

"Oh fuck, yes. There," Will gasped. "Do it again." Keeping the same position and not daring to adjust his weight to balance on one hand, Eddie rolled his hips again, pushing deep into him. The cords in Will's neck strained, his breaths came out in stutters, and every muscle in his body tightened. He was magnificent, so fucking beautiful as he let go and came.

Will's orgasm hit him in waves and pulsed through his body and around Eddie's cock. The slick grasp of his channel tightened further, and Eddie hurtled to the edge and into sweet oblivion. He never wanted to find his way out of that magnificent place. Will's cock pulsed, painting stripes of cum between them as he moaned incoherently. Still riding out his orgasm, his eyes barely open and his plump lips slick from Eddie's kiss, a drop of sweat beaded at his temple, and Eddie licked it away. Will ran his hand down Eddie's body, and Eddie shivered. When Will grasped him around the waist, his legs still locked tight around Eddie's hips, Eddie was lost.

Will kissed him as Eddie cried out, capturing the echo of his orgasm as it washed over Eddie like the tide—

unstoppable and all-powerful. Eddie flexed his hips, reigniting the buzz of the chemical reaction firing through him, then did it again until all he knew was Will.

He didn't know when he slumped down onto Will, but the play of his fingertips along Eddie's spine and his now softening cock slipping out of Will's channel told him he needed to move, if only to toss away the condom. Eddie shifted, but it was Will who took matters into his hands and slipped the rubber off Eddie's shaft, knotted it, and tossed it in the general direction of the bathroom without lifting Eddie off him.

"I should clean you up," Eddie murmured.

Will wrapped his arms around Eddie again and replied, "There's no rush." He raised his head and looked at Will, taking in his beautiful face and that post-orgasmic glow that he was rocking. The man at his side looked thoroughly blissed out, and it was damn fine on him. Eddie wanted to bang on his chest in triumph. He wanted Will to wear that expression forever. When he smiled at Eddie, his fingers reaching up to brush against his face, Eddie's breath came out in a rush, and his heart flip-flopped.

"God, you're so beautiful," Eddie whispered, the awe in his voice obvious. "So damn sexy. Every inch of you. But when you smile, you take my breath away."

A flush stole over Will's cheeks and down his throat, and Eddie couldn't help but trail his fingertips to the hollow there. When he met Will's gaze again, Will became serious. "Me too," he whispered before tugging Eddie closer and letting out a happy sigh. He didn't know whether Will's reply was in response to his comment or the emotions that he mustn't have been good at hiding when they were riding so close to the surface, but either way, it didn't matter. He knew. Will understood what he was trying to tell him.

SEVENTEEN

Will

I t was the final performance of the cruise, and Will had timed his schedule to be able to attend the drinks after the finale. Walking out of the lift, he found some of the performers already mingling among the guests. Eddie was surrounded by the largest group, who were all toasting him. He grinned and curtseyed, lifting the skirt of the dark grey plunging V-neck mini dress he wore. Paired with thigh-high heeled boots and fishnet stockings, he looked incredible. Will swallowed hard. Pale pink lipstick finished off his outfit, and Will was torn between seeing how far down his dick that lipstick would mark him or lifting that dress and bending over the nearest couch so Eddie could fuck him into next week.

Will stood on the sidelines, watching and admiring him from afar when Seamus sidled up next to him. "Congratulations, Captain. I'm happy for you two."

"Thanks, Seamus. I appreciate that." Will shook his hand, and Seamus gave him a friendly clap on the back.

People milled around them, and he spoke to the guests who reminisced about their cruise, all the while keeping Eddie in his side vision and waiting for a chance to excuse himself to join his man.

"How long have you been captain?" a lady asked him, but Will was distracted by the coughing from behind. The last thing he needed was to get sick, so he tried to step away but couldn't go far without walking off mid-conversation. The lady he was speaking to touched his arm, drawing Will's attention back to her, making him realize he hadn't answered her.

"About five years. Sorry, if you'll excuse me." Will excused himself to look for, and avoid, whoever it was that was sick. Instead, he saw Eddie and did a double-take. It was less than five minutes since he'd had his eyes on his man, and Eddie looked completely different.

And not in a good way.

His cheeks and throat, plus part of his chest, were an angry red as if he'd broken out in an instant rash, and he was scratching his throat, making it worse. The rest of his face was deathly pale, his lips almost grey. He reached out for the wall, bracing himself on it as he swayed on the spot and gasped for breath.

Will strode over to him, barging in on the conversation a guest was trying to hold with him. "I'm sorry, excuse me," he politely interrupted, not really caring if the person he was speaking to was offended. Will pressed his hand to Eddie's forehead, but he wasn't hot. Will listened to Eddie's greeting, but he was struggling, wheezing. Terror pierced through Will, panic rushing him. Something was very wrong. But what? Will grasped his wrist and checked his pulse to find it racing. "Eddie, look at me," he demanded softly. When he did, Will's heart rate shot through the roof. His pupils were blown, fear written on his face as he panted, his breathing laboured. His lips were turning blue before Will's eyes.

"Epi," he wheezed. Will flipped his wrist over, looking again at the leather band he wore, and klaxons wailed in Will's mind. It was a medical alert bracelet—he'd told Will about his allergy to nuts and how severe it was. Will had known they could kill him, but Eddie was always so careful about what he ate. He even went as far as checking whether the people he was with had eaten any. Will had sworn off them the moment he'd found out about Eddie's anaphylaxis.

But someone—potentially any of the guests he'd been talking to—clearly didn't know Eddie. They must have gotten close enough to him that it had triggered a reaction.

Every worst-case scenario ran through Will's mind, and the knowledge that he couldn't do anything to help, except call a doctor, killed him. He was powerless to stop the reaction, completely incapable of taking Eddie's pain away.

For a moment, he knew exactly how Eddie had felt a few weeks earlier when he'd been by his side, and Gerard had thrown a punch. Except this time, it could be deadly.

Will couldn't let Eddie see him freaking out, though. He needed Will calm more than at any other time before. So, he pushed aside his own fears and tried desperately to stay rational.

Searching the foyer for another staff member, his gaze landed on Seamus, and Will shouted out to him. The panic in his voice was obvious, and thankfully the other performer came running. "I need you to get Eddie's EpiPen from his locker." Eddie was flagging, his breathing becoming shallower with each inhale. Picking him up and tucking him against his chest, Will turned to the guests hovering close, and as Seamus dashed off, he called out frantically, "I need a doctor."

A lady stepped forward. "I'll ring for the on-board GP."

"It's anaphylaxis. Tell him I need him here now." Panic was rising like the incoming tide inside Will, dragging him under and drowning him, but he fought to present a calm façade on the outside.

The lady scampered away, and with Eddie in his arms, Will rushed over to the long, padded bench lining the nearby portal windows and laid him down, kneeling at his side. His struggle for breath was getting worse, and he was getting weaker. Will rolled him onto his side, tilting his head back to open his airway, but each cough on the exhale was shallower. Will had no idea what to do other than hold his hand and brush his hair back off his forehead, whispering that he'd be okay.

He prayed he would be.

He had to be.

Hurry, Ezio. Please.

Seamus came running, pushing his way back through the crowd of people who'd gathered around them, and dropped the injector onto Will's outstretched palm. "Eddie, I'm giving you your EpiPen." He wished that he'd asked for instructions on how to use it, but neither of them had thought he'd ever need it. Apparently, Eddie's being careful wasn't enough. Will's hands shook as he scanned the instructions, his fear all-consuming. Fumbling, he pulled off the safety release and nearly dropped it, cursing as he tried to position the pen correctly on Eddie's outer thigh as he lay awkwardly on the seat. Pushing it down hard, the needle pierced through his skin, and Will counted out the dose in his head—one one-thousand, two one-thousand, three one-thousand—before pulling it away.

Grasping his hand again, Will waited, hoping and praying that Eddie would improve. Time stretched out interminably. What was probably only a minute could have been a millennia, but eventually, he heard Eddie's breathing settle a little, his gasping not so pronounced. Will watched him carefully, cataloguing every detail. He hated seeing Eddie so ill, but the impact of the medicine was almost immediate. The colour slowly returned to his lips, and he focused on Will and smiled, reaching out to touch his face.

Seeing him come back had Will crumpling against him. When Eddie buried his face into his chest, Will blinked back the tears that were threatening to track down his cheeks, and he trembled with the shock of it all. He wanted to wrap Eddie up in his arms, to protect him from being hurt again, but what happened if he relapsed? Could that even happen? He needed an emergency ward. Shit, can the doc treat him? Can I get the coast guard out here in time if we need to? Will held his hand and ran his fingers through Eddie's hair as he unsuccessfully tried to calm himself down, the adrenaline still coursing through him.

"I'm okay, handsome," Eddie rasped.

"Don't you ever die on me. Got it?" Will whispered.

"I won't." He huffed out a laugh as the throngs of people moved aside, clearing a path for Ezio, who wheeled the gurney up to them. Eddie sat up, leaning heavily against Will, who hugged him tightly, resting his forehead against Eddie's.

"I'm sorry. You're the one who's sick, and I'm blubbering like a baby."

"It's okay." He kissed Will, and Ezio tutted them.

"Eddie, I need you up here." Ezio patted the sheet-covered padding and continued, "You know you shouldn't be kissing anyone until we've identified the source of the reac—"

"It wasn't me," Will interrupted, glancing back at Dr Dimitriades and imploring him to understand. "I haven't touched nuts since I found out he's allergic. Everything I've eaten is nut-free." Eddie tried to move off the seat, but Will stopped him, scooping him into his arms instead and placing him gently on the sheet.

"My hero." Eddie winked, lying back and taking a long, slow breath before coughing again.

"This is oxygen to help you breathe, Eddie. Just relax, and when we're back in the infirmary, I'll give you some other medicine to open up your airways." Ezio hooked a face mask over Eddie's face and squeezed his shoulder.

"I'm coming too," Will said, and led the way through the people crowded around them, pulling the gurney towards the lifts while Ezio steered from behind. The doctor was speaking with Eddie the whole time, checking him over and making sure he stayed conscious. He was trying to figure out what caused the reaction.

* * * * *

Eddie had his eyes closed, and his breathing was evening out after the various medicines he'd been given. Will sat next to his bed in the infirmary and waited, his hands cradling his head and his eyes closed. He was at war with himself. He couldn't leave Eddie when he needed him most, but he had a responsibility to the ship too. If Will didn't get some sleep before his shift started in the early morning hours, he'd be risking everyone's lives on board and a ship worth hundreds of millions of dollars. Changeover day was always crazy, and Will needed to be at the top of his game.

As if reading his thoughts, Eddie murmured in a voice that was still raspy, "Can you lie next to me, handsome?" Will cracked open his eyes to see him patting the bed next to him, closest to where Will was sitting.

"I… yes." Will didn't care whether Ezio had a problem with him being up there with him. Eddie wanted Will to hold him, so that's where he'd be. It was never a chore, and having him in his arms might let the hammering of Will's heart slow. He kicked off his shoes, shrugged out of his jacket, and climbed up next to Eddie. "How do you want me?" he asked quietly, more concerned about Eddie's comfort than his own.

"On your side?"

He rolled over, and Will fitted in behind him so they were spooning. Connected from head to toe, with Will's hand low on his abs, he snuggled in close and breathed Eddie in. Even with the antiseptic smell of Eddie's hospital gown and the harsh soap from the sponge bath Will had given him earlier, his natural sweet musk surrounded Will. Eddie sighed and nuzzled in closer to him, and Will smiled for the first time in hours, pressing kisses along his nape. He couldn't believe what a close call he'd had. Eddie's allergic reaction was the scariest thing Will had ever experienced. Holding the man who meant so much to him in his arms, knowing he was safe, was everything.

Will closed his eyes and drifted, jumping when Dr Dimitriades walked in and huffed. "I can't leave you two alone for a minute, can I? Captain, you may run this ship, but you're in my domain now—"

"I want him here," Eddie murmured sleepily.

"And I can still overrule your opinion, Doc." Will smirked at his colleague over his shoulder. Even though Will could technically do it, he'd always held Ezio in the utmost of respect, and the other man knew his medical opinions were always considered. With Ezio being one of the best doctors he'd ever come across, Will followed his advice. They were friends too, Ezio having stayed at his house more than once for breaks between their contracts. But this time, Will was happy to pull rank. "If it makes you feel better, I'm a light sleeper, and if any of the beeping changes, I'll wake up and get off."

"We need to swap positions for that," Eddie whispered so only Will could hear him. He couldn't help his snort of laughter, and even burying his face in Eddie's hair didn't hide it.

"Fine," Dr Dimitriades sighed loudly. "You know best."

That had Will sitting up. "Seriously, Doc, is he at risk if I lie here with him? If he is, I'll get off the bed."

"No, you're okay, Captain. Stay there." He shook out a light blanket and laid it across the end of the bed so Will could easily pull it up over them. "He's under observation, so I need to check his vitals regularly, and he'll need to be on oxygen until his levels are okay again, but otherwise, with the medicine he's had, he's a low risk for another re-action. Lie down again and get some sleep."

Ezio dimmed the lights and pulled the door closed behind him, leaving them alone. Eddie sighed, and his body went lax. "I was scared, handsome. It's been years since I had an attack that bad."

"I was too," Will whispered. "I didn't really know what to do."

"You were perfect." He laced their fingers together and pressed closer again, trembling in Will's arms. Reaching down, he pulled the blanket over them, making sure Eddie was covered properly.

"You still cold, beautiful? I can get another blanket if you need it."

"No, just need your arms around me. Wish I could feel your skin against mine." With every word he uttered, Eddie's speech slowed, getting quieter. He was falling asleep fast. Will didn't respond, holding him tighter instead, grateful he still had the ability to do it.

Will didn't know what time it was when he'd fallen asleep, but when his watch buzzed, waking him up, it didn't feel like anywhere near enough. He was still exhausted. Eyes burning and his mouth as dry as the Sahara, Will shifted and edged his way off the narrow bed, trying not to disturb Eddie. The curtain between the two beds in the room was drawn closed. Another patient must have come in during the night, and he hadn't even heard them.

Will straightened himself as best he could and picked up his discarded jacket and hat before kissing a still sleeping Eddie on his forehead. He looked so peaceful, but he was still too pale. Love surged through Will, and he smiled softly, never expecting to experience it again. He brushed the backs of his fingers down Eddie's cheek, grateful that he no longer needed the oxygen mask.

Will still didn't want to leave, but ultimately, his wants didn't matter. He had a responsibility to bring the ship into dock. A shower, coffee, and a jog up to the bridge were in his immediate future when all he wanted was to stay with his man. At least Ezio would be able to keep him updated on Eddie's condition. With that thought, Will resisted the temptation to touch him again and slipped out the door, closing it softly behind him.

He stopped dead in his tracks. Blinking, Will looked, then rubbed his eyes and looked again. It wasn't his imagination. Ezio had his arms wrapped around a man, holding him close as they kissed deeply. Running his fingertips up and down the other man's spine, Ezio was tender with him, but the heat between them was at inferno levels. Shirtless and gorgeous, the man was built like a damn bodybuilder, a deep tan tinting his skin. Who is he?

The man's big hands gripped Ezio's white lab coat, pulling the doctor tight against his body. Every inch of them was pressed together. When they pulled back, they kept their faces close, turned into one another as they spoke in hushed tones. Even in Will's dazed, overtired state, he could tell that there was something more between them. An intimate connection. The shock of it had him blurting, "Oh shit, sorry." Ezio stumbled backwards and looked at him wide-eyed, his horror at being caught obvious.

"C-Cap... Captain—" the doctor stuttered, wide-eyed with shock. Will held his hand up. The other man huffed and stalked past him, shaking his head before slipping inside the room where Will had come from. The click of the door as it closed echoed through the silence that descended in the small consultation room.

Will looked at his friend and sighed when Ezio opened his mouth again to speak. "Ezio, can we talk? I'm not awake enough to deal with it now, but come and see me after we've docked."

"Yeah," he rasped, then cleared his throat, nodded, and spoke again. "Yes, Captain." Shoulders slumped, and lips turned down in a frown, Ezio clearly wasn't happy.

"Ezio." Will closed a hand over his shoulder and smiled, squeezing gently. He was trying to show his support. It was a big deal when someone was outed, and Will wanted to let him know that he'd never communicate what he saw with anyone. "It's all good."

"Thank you." The doc paused and added. "I'll ring through your coffee order, so it's delivered straight to you."

EIGHTEEN

Will

There was a knock on the office door, and he called out, "Come in." Will looked up to see Ezio closing the door behind him. He stretched his neck, leaning back on the chair before putting the documents he'd been reviewing away. He had already spoken with the doc a few times that morning asking for updates on Eddie. Thankfully, he was okay and had been discharged from his care. Eddie had been in to see him an hour earlier. The relief at seeing Eddie almost back to normal had nearly buckled his knees. Will had held him close, never wanting to let go.

Then he'd forbidden Eddie to do another meet and greet again.

It hadn't gone down well.

Every protective instinct in Will screamed at him when Eddie slid into the seat, and Will got a closer look at the dark circles under his eyes and the sallow tone to his skin. It was irrational and probably illegal too, but he found himself fighting the desire to lock his man away and keep him safe and healthy. He'd asked Eddie to sit that night's performance out too.

Eddie had pursed his lips and cocked his head to the side, his sass showing through even in his less-than-full-health state. Instead of agreeing to Will's demands and slightly nicer request, Eddie had schooled him on the pressures faced by entertainers on the ship. He understood that the other performers were relying on him and the reality that they were already a performer down thanks to Gerard's replacement not arriving until the next cruise, ten days away. Will understood dedication and passion. He also understood the obligation and commitment to each other that every staff and crew member developed while working on the ship. Then Eddie had politely told him to pull his head out of his arse and butt out of his career.

He respected Eddie even more after that.

"Afternoon, Captain." Ezio's words jolted him back to the present, and Will shook off the memory of Eddie's lips against his as he'd apologized. Repeatedly. With kisses.

"We can dispense with formalities, Ezio. This chat is purely off the record."

"Okay." He nodded, and Will motioned to the couches for them to sit at, moving over to them.

"About this morning… I wanted to apologize for walking in on you. It's not a private room per se, but you weren't exactly standing in the corridor either. You were entitled to expect that no one would interrupt you."

A ghost of a smile tilted Ezio's lips, but the sadness in them remained. "Thanks, William. I appreciate the sentiment, but you really don't need to apologize. You're right. I should have been more discreet."

Will held up his hand to stop Ezio from continuing. "That's not what I meant. I'm still struggling with last night; my brain doesn't seem to be working. I was trying to say that I won't share anything about you and the man you were with."

"It's all good, and I'm glad that Eddie is okay. He seems like a great guy."

"He is." Heat washed over Will's face, and his smile turned goofy. When Ezio grinned back, Will looked away, pressing his hands to his cheeks to ward off the blush he knew was staining his skin red. "Okay, well, that was it. I just wanted to reassure you that I won't be starting rumours. We've never spoken about whether you're out at work, so I wanted to reassure you that no one will hear it from me if you prefer to keep your sexuality to yourself."

"He's a passenger," Ezio blurted and squeezed his eyes closed, gritting his teeth.

"Oh," Will stumbled, rendered speechless for a moment. "Wh…." He didn't even know where to start. Will knew there were ethical issues with doctors dating patients, but it hadn't appeared that the man was there for treatment. Was he visiting someone? Will remembered the curtain between the beds. The man had pushed through the door to the treatment room. Who had been on the other side of the curtain? Was it his child? Elderly parent? Will didn't even want to know about the quagmire of ethical issues that Ezio was possibly skirting the line of, but there was one rule he was in clear breach of. "Ezio, you can't date passengers. You know this. Every staff and crew member has it written into their contract. You can't have any relationship with them other than a professional one. What I saw was… not professional."

"I know." He sighed and scrubbed his forehead. "I know. I don't even know how it happened. One minute I went for a walk on deck to get some sun. The next he was there, and I was… hooked. He's everything I ever wanted in a partner."

Will pressed his fingers into his temples, a headache quickly building. This was the part of the job he hated. "I know I said that this conversation was off the record, but Ezio, I can't ignore this. I don't want to do anything, but I don't have a choice."

"I know." Ezio nodded. "I get it. I've broken the rules, Captain. More than once."

Will sat up straight. He thought he knew Ezio; this revelation wasn't what he expected to hear. "More than once with the same passenger or on more than one occasion with different passengers?"

The horror on Ezio's face said it all. "No. God no. One passenger only. And he was very definitely consenting."

"Who was he visiting in the infirmary?"

"His daughter. She was dehydrated and fainted. I had her on an IV drip overnight to make sure she was okay in case they had a long trip home today."

"So you met her father before she became your patient?"

Ezio paled. "Yes. But, Captain, I conducted myself ethically. I—"

"I'm not suggesting you engaged in anything unethical, but I needed to ask the question. This is a liability issue for the ship and for yourself. You could get into a world of hurt professionally if what went down ever gets back to the medical association, or even head office."

Ezio nodded. "Yeah." He sighed again. "When do you want me to finish up?"

"I'm not firing you, Ezio, because if I do, it needs to go on record, and I won't do that to a friend. Can you resign? You can finish up at the end of your contract." Will had asked him a question, but it was purely rhetorical. If Ezio didn't resign, he would need to ensure head office didn't renew his contract. Will pinched the bridge of his nose. "As captain, I need to tell you to keep your dick in your pants with the passengers until then. If it happens again…"

He nodded again, tight-lipped. "It won't. Thank you," he whispered after a moment. "I'll submit the letter directly to Emira later today." Ezio stood and held his hand out to Will, who took it and pulled him in for a hug. He clapped Ezio on the back and asked, "Did you get his number?"

Ezio shook his head sadly. "I didn't want to overstep the boundaries by asking for it."

Will's mouth popped open in surprise, and a laugh broke free. "Um—"

"Yeah, I know. Stupid now that I think about it."

"Sorry, mate. About everything." Will walked him to the door and rested his hand on the knob.

"You've done me a solid, William. I appreciate it. It was my mistake that put me in this situation to begin with. But even though I've lost my job over it, I can't count him as that."

"I get it." Will nodded and opened the door for Ezio, watching him walk away with a sadness that wasn't entirely selfish. The doctor was damn good at his job, and they worked well together. His departure would be a loss for the Dreamcatcher. But his friend had just lost everything, and that hurt Will more.

NINETEEN

Eddie

THREE MONTHS LATER

E ddie stepped off the MV Dreamcatcher onto the dock at Sydney Harbour, Dr Dimitriades walking next to him. They'd developed a friendship after Eddie had his anaphylactic attack. Will had finished his assignment two weeks earlier and was already on leave. So Eddie, with a couple of weeks left on his contract, found himself alone. He and Ezio had spent time together, both of them counting down the hours before their assignment ended.

Ezio had trusted Eddie with news of his pending departure—he'd wanted to keep it quiet—and Eddie had done his best to make Ezio's last couple of weeks special. They'd gone to visit as many of the tourist sites on the islands as he could wrangle time off for and spent their nights playing cards.

He was sad to see Ezio leaving, knowing he wouldn't be back, but it wouldn't be long until they saw each other again. Will had invited Ezio to housesit for him while he and Eddie travelled together. Ezio hadn't yet decided where he wanted to settle down, so it was a win-win for all of them.

They followed the stream of disembarking passengers into the terminal, Eddie's duffel hitched over his shoulder. The last time he'd been there was three months earlier, but in his time at sea, everything had changed. He was a different man, with a different outlook on life, and he couldn't wait for what was ahead.

First up on his list was a flight to the Gold Coast to meet Will's family. Then they were travelling together, spending the next few weeks road-tripping up the coast to the Whitsundays and island hopping around the Great Barrier Reef. Eddie couldn't wait to go snorkelling among the coral and walk the pure white sand at Whitehaven Beach. He'd always fancied visiting Australia, and he was finally getting the chance. It was a dream come true, but even that paled in comparison to the best thing that had happened to him since joining the Dreamcatcher. It was the man who would be waiting for him at Gold Coast Airport when Eddie arrived there in a few hours' time.

He was excited about what the next month would bring, if not a little nervous. He and Will had been in constant contact since Will had gone on leave, and he'd had a quick conversation with Will's mum, but he was nervous about being introduced to them. It seemed awfully formal, but Eddie understood why it was important to them all. Will was determined to do the right thing by his family, and Eddie wanted to support him in any way he could, even if it did feel a little like he was going to the gallows. He had to keep telling himself that they'd be okay. Whatever happened didn't matter. He could pretend that it was easy to persuade himself when he knew the reward was seeing Will again.

Anticipation bubbled within him, and he could barely hold back his grin at the next few weeks. Two weeks had never felt so long. But they weren't going to be apart for much longer. Lugging his bag, he followed closely behind Ezio as he dodged passengers milling around and headed for customs. As a departing staff member, he was grateful that he didn't have to wait in a long queue to exit. Eddie was hoping to make good time to the airport; avoiding rush hour would make the trip so much easier. So even though he was early, he still had to get a move on.

Arriving at the doors, he and Ezio parted ways, hugging briefly before Ezio headed towards the cab rank, and Eddie walked to the train station at Circular Quay.

He hit the boardwalk and saw the buses and tour companies lined up waiting for disembarking passengers. Eddie strode past them, enjoying the morning sunshine and ocean breezes on his face. Closing his eyes and tilting his face to the skies, he smiled and started walking a little faster to get to his destination. But his gaze stuttered.

His vision snagged on an unexpected sight.

Will.

Standing there, dressed casually in tan chinos and a white short-sleeved shirt, sunglasses, and a pair of well-worn Vans, he was dashing. The tailored button-down framed his broad shoulders and thick arms beautifully, the open collar highlighting the tease of chest hair peeking above it. He was so damn handsome that he took Eddie's breath away.

When he spotted Eddie, the smile that lit his face was warm and full of affection. His greying blond hair blew freely, not fixed in place with the product he wore during his shifts to keep his look professional. The relaxed vibe he had going on only made him look sexier.

Eddie failed miserably at keeping his excited squeal at bay as he launched himself into Will's arms. Catching him, Will laughed and kissed Eddie hard, holding him tight while Eddie wound his arms and legs around Will's muscled body. "Hel-lo, handsome," Eddie murmured between kisses, his voice sounding like a breathless giggle. "You meeting some-one special, or are you here alone?"

Eddie loved the blush that stained Will's cheeks. His shy man was as adorable as he was hot. "I'm waiting for some-one exactly like you."

Will hugged him tighter, and Eddie laughed, happiness lighting up every part of his soul. He loved having Will's arms around him, something he'd craved endlessly during his last fortnight on board without him.

"God, I've missed you," Will murmured against his throat as Eddie held him tightly. He kissed a line softly up to

Eddie's cheek. "I couldn't wait for you to get to the Goldie, so I came here."

"Missed you too." Turning his head when Will went to press another kiss to Eddie's cheek, Will's lips met his, and he smiled. It was like their first kiss all over again—just a chaste brush of their lips together—until Eddie opened to him and Will dived in.

"So, I might have changed your flight," Will confessed. "We're not leaving until tomorrow afternoon. I can't wait a few hours to get my hands on you."

"Oh, yeah?" Eddie's voice turned husky, and his dick let out a happy twitch. He'd missed Will to no end, and the thought of getting to touch and taste him again sent Eddie's desire rocketing into overdrive. Spearing his fingers through Will's hair, Eddie ground against him and kissed him, sucking on Will's tongue when he responded. "It's a little early for check-in, isn't it?" Eddie asked, disappointment colouring his tone.

Will grumbled and nodded. "We could hop off the train a stop or two early and walk to the hotel via Hyde Park. Stop for a coffee?"

Eddie smiled and nodded, excited to see more of Sydney. Will let Eddie down slowly, keeping their bodies as close as possible for as long as he could, before taking Eddie's heavy duffel and shouldering it along with the bag sitting at Will's feet that Eddie hadn't noticed.

Hand in hand, they made the short trip to the station and within minutes were stepping onto the cobblestone avenue that marked the entrance into the park. The bustle of the city didn't intrude into the calm of the gardens. It was like being transported into a different world under the tree-lined canopy. Manicured lawns stretched to either side of them and gardens filled with flowers drew Eddie's eye. Will led them up the path and into an open quad. Before them was a bronze fountain and beyond that, a grand cathedral. Walkers passed them, some with pets, some in suits and walking shoes, getting their morning exercise in before a day in the office. Will was the only one carrying luggage, but no one really paid them any attention.

There was something Eddie wanted to raise with Will, a topic he wanted to talk about that he'd taken for granted. He thought they'd be on the same page, both having indirectly spoken about it before, but Eddie was still nervous. "Let's sit." Eddie motioned to the fountain and the flat stone hexagonal-shaped wall that surrounded it.

Will furrowed his brow. "Everything okay?"

"Yes. Yeah, I... I wanted to talk to you about something. About us."

"Sure. Anything." Will withdrew his hand from Eddie's and hesitated before slowly placing Eddie's duffel and the satchel he carried on the ground between his legs. When he sat, he clasped his hands together, resting his elbows on his knees. Will looked to Eddie, but his expression was inscrutable.

Eddie's palms were sweating and he wiped them down his pants. "We've never actually spoken about being exclusive—"

Will paled. "I thought it was obvious—"

"And you thought right. As far as I'm concerned, we are exclusive and have been since day one. I'd never cheat on you, Will. I'm not Stefan and I'm not Henri. I want to make this official—dot all the i's and cross all the t's. When I meet your parents tomorrow, I want to be called your boyfriend."

"You are." Will smiled, the joy lighting up his features like the sun emerging on a cloudy day. He turned sidewards on the ledge, hooking an ankle under his knee and reaching for Eddie's hands.

"Good, and we're serious. Like long-term serious."

Will's smile grew, and he caressed Eddie's hands with his thumbs. "Yes, I'd like that. I want long-term too." Will leaned in and kissed him, a slow press of his lips and a gentle swipe of his tongue against Eddie's. "Are you nervous about meeting Ma and Dad, beautiful?"

"You have no idea." Eddie huffed and shook his head, as much in a self-deprecating move as to clear his fried brain cells after the sweet but steamy kiss Will had laid on him. "But it's not the only reason why I wanted to speak to you. Now that we're back on dry land and we can... I thought..." Eddie sucked in a breath and looked down at the ground, concentrating hard on the terracotta flagstone pavers below his feet. "What would you say to getting tested?"

Will hooked a finger under Eddie's chin and lifted his gaze. His expression was filled with warmth. Affection radiated from him. His smile was shy and a blush stained his cheeks. The people around them faded away and all Eddie could concentrate on was the handsome man before him. The sunlight highlighted the blond in his greying hair, and his chocolate brown eyes shone. Will leaned in and kissed him, another press of his lips to Eddie's, but this time he didn't pull back.

"Yes. I want that. I want permanent and exclusive and I want it with you." Will shifted closer, nibbling a path along Eddie's jaw and to his ear. Whispering, so only Eddie could hear his response, Will said, "I want to make love to you with nothing between us. No barriers, nothing except me and you."

"Yeah? You want that?" Eddie asked hopefully.

Will cupped Eddie's nape and stroked his thumb along Eddie's cheek as he dropped soft kisses on Eddie's throat. "You have no idea how many times I've imagined you sliding into me bare."

Eddie's breath hitched and he willed his cock not to stand to attention. It was no use though—Eddie had zero control over his body when Will was sucking on the sensitive patch of skin below his ear. Eddie cleared his throat. "Let's go then. Let's do it right now."

He bit back a moan when Will hummed and pulled back, eyes glazed with desire and lips wet. Sucking in a breath, Eddie stood, taking Will's satchel and holding it in front of him while Will subtly adjusted himself and propped Eddie's duffel on his lap as he looked up locations for testing clinics. He showed Eddie the search results. There was a walk-in clinic walking distance from them and they'd have the results within hours. It was right on opening too.

* * * * *

Three hours later, armed with negative test results and finally gripping a hotel key, Will led him into the lift. The hotel was swanky, an old building loaded with style and class right on Oxford Street. But Eddie wouldn't have seen the view even if they were surrounded by glass. He only had eyes for Will. They weren't touching each other—they weren't even alone in the small compartment—but it didn't matter. Undressing him with his gaze, Eddie watched as Will subtly shifted the bag to cover more of his front and adjusted himself, blushing when the elderly lady smiled at him.

Finally stopping at their floor, Eddie led the way to their room for the night, adding a swish to his hips that had Will sucking in a breath behind him. Flashing the card against the lock, Eddie didn't even have a chance to depress the handle before Will pressed up against him, pinning him to the door. His shaft lodged between Eddie's cheeks, and Eddie dropped his head back on Will's shoulder, breathing him in. A wall of muscle surrounded him, and Eddie was so very tempted to rub himself all over Will, getting them off right there in the corridor. But he wanted more. Needed to be skin on skin with his man with no barriers between them.

"Need you," Will rasped, punching his hips forward.

Eddie fumbled the card and pushed open the door, sending them tumbling into the room. Will caught him, stopping Eddie from landing face first on the floor, and unceremoniously dropped their bags where they fell.

Eddie couldn't wait. Not even for another moment. Dragging Will by the shirt, he pushed him onto the floor and tried to strip his man naked. He struggled to get him out of his clothes, wishing he'd undressed him before clambering onto Will's lap.

Soon enough, Will's shirt was unbuttoned, and his chinos pushed halfway down his legs, and Eddie had torn his clothes off. He kissed every inch of smooth skin and hairy chest he could reach, smearing his pale pink lipstick all over Will's muscled torso. Heated skin pressed against his own and Eddie breathed him in. The contrast between the cool timber of the floor underneath his knees and the heat of Will's body was heady—hard and unyielding against firm and yet pliable muscle. Eddie paused for a moment, overcome with the need to take in the man below him. He looked down at Will sure his expression would reveal to his captain exactly what his heart had told him weeks earlier. "I missed you, handsome. So much."

"Me too, beautiful." Will's kiss was tender but full of need. Skin to skin, they rocked together, kissing and touching. Electric shocks ran down the length of Eddie's spine as he dragged his dick against Will's. Pushing up on straightened arms, Eddie thrust his hips fluidly as Will slipped a hand between their bodies and closed his fist around their cocks.

Eddie's eyes rolled back as sensation overwhelmed him. His hips bucked, seeking a release his body was programmed to chase. Powerless to stop, he repeated the move again and again, his thrusts jerky and his breathing choppy. Below him, Will strained, his muscles drawn tight as he lifted his hips, jerked them off, and pinned Eddie against him all at once. Mouth open and eyes at half mast, with his pupils blown, Will was sexy as fuck. Seeing him using Eddie's body to chase his orgasm was pushing Eddie to the brink.

"Fuck, I'm there." Will cried out as he thrust his hips upward again, freezing in place as he moaned long and low.

The first warm splash of Will's cum on Eddie's chest had him shuddering, the extra lube as Will sped up his movements sending the tingling at the base of Eddie's spine erupting outward in waves. His balls drew up tight and Eddie hurtled over the edge. He couldn't stop even if he wanted to, his body demanding that he keep moving. Keep chasing ecstasy. He caved to its demands and rolled his hips once more, his mind whiting out and sensation rocking through his body like an out-of-control forest fire.

His arms gelatinous, Eddie slumped forward onto Will's chest, his man wrapping Eddie up in his embrace. A sheen of sweat coated Will's skin, and he ran his hands over the damp curls on his chest. Eddie nuzzled him, never wanting to let go. As his mind came back to him and his breathing slowed, Eddie's knees twinged, and it occurred to him how uncomfortable Will must be. "Need to get you up off the floor, handsome."

"Mmhmm." Will nodded, his eyes still closed. Eddie licked his nipple, tasting some of their release, and he moaned.

"I need to get you off the floor, or I'm gonna do this again, and you're not going to be able to move."

Will rolled them, pinning Eddie to the floor, the cold an even starker contrast to the heat radiating off his sexy captain than it was before. He grasped Eddie's hands, intertwining their fingers together, and lifted them above his head, using his forearms to pin Eddie down. Surrounded by Will's bulkier frame, Eddie could have been intimidated, but the look of absolute adoration Will wore when he looked down at him made Eddie's heart flip. He finally understood why symphonies performed in those grand love stories. Will leaned down and kissed him, soft and slow, until Eddie wound his legs around him, locking the length of their bodies together again. Arching up into Will, he pulled back and tilted his head. Will took the hint and sucked and bit his way down his throat. When their lips met again, the kiss was dirty. Their tongues tangling and hips thrusting, Eddie moaned, and before he knew what was happening, Will was lifting him, awkwardly hitching up his pants and leading them to the bathroom.

Eddie laughed and held on tighter as Will tried to deposit him on the granite counter in the bathroom. When his arse hit the surface, the shock of the cold had him sucking in a breath, but it didn't last long. Will stripped the rest of the way off and turned on the shower, dragging him under the warm stream in only a few moments.

"I made plans for dinner." Will dropped a kiss on Eddie's nape as he shampooed his hair.

"Yeah?"

"Mmhmm. Was kinda hoping we could go to a club afterwards too. I want to dance with you."

Eddie leaned his head back against Will's solid chest and smiled. "I'd like that."

"You think you can wear a dress? Maybe those fishnets you've worn before?" Will nuzzled him, ghosting his hands down Eddie's sides and pulling his arse back against Will's semi. "I'd really like to see them on you again."

Eddie nodded, shifting Will's hand to his thickening shaft. He stroked him slowly, once then twice, then Will let go, and Eddie groaned. He pulled back and spun Eddie around. Looking him in the eye, he asked, "Can you come three times in one day?"

Eddie sucked in a breath and nodded as Will fell to his knees.

TWENTY

Will

The club was dark, save for the strobes on the dance floor and coloured lights painting the plush seating areas with a dim glow. The DJ in the booth was rocking out to the mix blasting through the speakers, and Will, with his arms wrapped around Eddie, danced. Will inched his hand higher on Eddie's leg, slipping up underneath the hem of his mini. He couldn't help palming the globe of his arse, naked save for the G-string and fishnets he wore. He'd watched Eddie get ready, slipping on the lingerie and stepping into the stockings, walking around in the four-inch stiletto-heeled boots Eddie wore until Will was wiping drool from his chin. The boots brought them closer to the same height—perfect for pressing their bodies together and writhing on the dancefloor. Eddie was taking full advantage, palming Will's erection as Eddie rubbed his own on Will's thick leg while straddling him.

Will broke their kiss and sucked in a lung full of air filled with musk and sex. It only ramped his desire up more, and Will licked the sweat from Eddie's throat. Nuzzling Eddie's ear, he spoke, just loud enough that Eddie could hear. "I want to make you come again. This time inside me. With nothing between us."

Eddie's eyes widened in surprise before his lids lowered, and he licked his lips. He looked like he'd swallowed his tongue, but there was an undeniable urgency in his tone. He was just as turned on as Will by the thought of nothing being between them. "Yes."

Hand in hand, they rushed out of the club. He would have jogged to the hotel if it weren't for Eddie wearing heels that he could break an ankle in. But Eddie wasn't having a bar of Will's slow walk. He tugged on his hand, picking up the pace as he weaved between the crowds lining Oxford Street. They were on Sydney's famous Mardi Gras route, filled with rainbow flags and LGBTIQA+ friendly businesses. Will instinctively felt safe there, knowing Eddie wouldn't be harassed in a dress. When he'd pulled out the same one he'd worn on the night of his anaphylactic attack, Will smiled. That night hadn't ended as planned, but it could have been a whole lot worse, and he was looking forward to creating new memories. The night stretching out before them was infinitely better already, and it had only just begun. Will's arse was already tender in anticipation of Eddie taking him. He'd asked earlier if Eddie could come three times, and Eddie had whispered back, "Four, five, and six times too, especially bare in you."

Kicking the door to their hotel room closed, Eddie stalked him. Prowled forward with each step, and Will's mouth dried. He walked backwards in the dim light penetrating the white gauzy curtains from outside. It was as if they were in a bubble. A secret, intimate hideaway made for just the two of them. In some ways, it was. As open as Will was with his sexuality, and even his relationship status with Eddie, this was something Will wanted to keep close to him. Just between them. Making the leap to committed boyfriends was a natural evolution in their relationship that was probably overdue even though they'd only been together for a few months. Even though they'd waited to have sex, their relationship had travelled at light speed, getting serious quickly. Losing the protection seemed like a big step, but Will didn't hesitate. He trusted Eddie implicitly, and he wanted everything with him.

The backs of Will's knees hit the bed, and Eddie smoothed a hand down his chest. "Are you ready for this, handsome? I can use a condom if you'd still prefer."

"No, nothing between us. I want to share it all with you. Every part of me."

"Me too." Eddie kissed him, a slow melding of their mouths as he pressed their bodies together. Will was hard. Aching. He ran his hand down Eddie's front, feeling his lean frame under his palms, and reached his dick, straining against the confines of the tiny scrap of silky material Will had watched him tuck his cock into before slipping on the fishnets. He knew his underwear barely contained Eddie, and it only made Will want him more.

Will pressed his palm against Eddie's rigid shaft and Eddie moaned. Will stroked him through the dress before slipping a hand under it and trailing it up between his legs. The heat scalded him, and Will's breath caught. Desire coursed through him. He needed Eddie. Needed to feel Eddie's cock stretching his channel as he pushed into him and sent him to heaven.

Eddie unbuttoned Will's shirt slowly, slipping it off his shoulders and forcing his hands away so he could toss it aside. The rasp of his belt, leather sliding against metal, made Will shiver, knowing that one less piece of clothing would stand between them once his pants came off.

He toed out of his shoes and kicked out of the pants pooling around his ankles when Eddie let them fall. Dressed only in a pair of tight Calvin Kleins, Will's breath caught when Eddie palmed his cock for the first time since they'd walked back in. His eyes closed of their own accord, and he moaned quietly as Eddie worked his hand over the soft material of Will's underwear.

Will dropped to his knees and slowly pushed Eddie's dress up, revealing long toned legs draped in black fishnet stockings. Pale skin against dark criss-crosses. He nuzzled the soft skin at the apex of his thighs and licked a line from satin-covered balls to the tip of Eddie's cock, poking up above the skimpy underwear. Will did it again and was met with a drop of pre-cum and Eddie's breathy moan, his name on his lover's lips.

Will watched with hooded eyes as Eddie's cock flexed and leaked again before he lapped it up eagerly and framed Eddie's package with cupped hands. Massaging him, Will watched Eddie's nostrils flare, and his chest rise with the sharp inhale of breath. Will shifted, a burst of sensation rippling through him. He was done waiting. He needed Eddie as much as his man wanted him. Will gripped the fishnets, pushing his thumbs through the squares, and tore them, freeing the prize he needed so desperately. Tugging the scrap of material down, Will hooked the G-string under Eddie's cock and balls and sucked him deep.

Eddie's cry had him upping his ministrations until his lover's hands speared into his hair and tugged hard. "Stop," he begged. "Need to come in you, not in your throat."

Will pulled off with a pop, a fine silken-like thread of pre-cum linking Eddie's cock to his lip and Eddie, fingered it, slipping two fingers into Will's mouth. Will sucked and wet them, needing something—anything—to distract him from his need.

"Strip," Eddie rasped. "I want you completely naked on your hands and knees." Will slowly rose to his feet, stripping out of his remaining clothes as quickly as his fumbling fingers would allow. Eddie reverently ran a hand down his chest, leaning in to lick his nipple and nuzzle the thatch of greying hair. Will had once felt self-conscious about the greys, but Eddie worshipped his hair, letting him know exactly how much he loved it.

He lifted the hem of Eddie's dress up and over his head, leaving his lover in a pair of thigh-high boots, torn fishnets, and an erect cock that he needed inside him. Eddie lifted his leg, resting one booted foot on the bed, and gripped his cock, sliding his fist up and down as he watched Will watch him. Biting his bottom lip and fondling his balls, Eddie was debauchery personified, and Will couldn't wait to let Eddie have his way with him. Spinning, he climbed on the bed, spreading his knees and bending over, presenting his arse to Eddie.

The sharp intake of breath had Will wiggling his hips. When Eddie's finger circled the black plug stretching his pucker, he moaned. "When did you put this in, handsome? Before our shower, or after?"

"After. It's had me on edge all fucking night."

"This is a lovely surprise." Eddie's voice was hoarse, rough with desire. His warm breath ghosted over Will's skin and he shivered. Eddie licked him, getting frisky with the sensitive skin of Will's stretched ring and all Will could concentrate on was the heated electricity coursing through him. His moans were incoherent, need and desire spoken at a breathy pitch and a deeper guttural groan. Eddie splayed his hands, one over his hip to hold him steady while the other fingered the plug. The orgasm curled low in Will's gut. Will was seeing double. The constant press against his prostate while they'd been sitting down, then its shifting when they'd been dancing, was overwhelming. His cock leaked a steady stream onto the bed as Eddie licked and stroked him, ten times slower than Will needed. Frustration clawed in his gut. Will mewled and Eddie paused.

"Will, look at us. Look how decadent you look spread out for me." Will turned his head to the side, seeing them in the mirrored door of the wardrobe. Eddie stood behind him, one leg still up on the bed in a shiny black boot, his cock pointing towards Will's hole. Eddie's chest heaved, and a fine sheen of sweat coated his skin. Eddie was burning up just as much as he was.

Will knelt before him, knees spread and an arch in his back that, if it was in porn, would have been downright sexy. His eyes were wild, his hair an un-styled mess. Seeing his white-knuckled grip on the snowy covers made Will un-clench and try to smooth them out.

"No. Stay right there, handsome. I want you to watch as I eat you out, then make love to you just like this. I want you to see everything I'm doing to you, and I want to see your reactions." Eddie ran a blunt nail down his spine, and Will saw the shiver run through him. Eddie's smile turned wicked as he shifted to the plug. Will cried out as Eddie pressed gently against the plug and wiggled it in Will's chan-nel. When his eyes fell closed, Eddie tut-tutted him and licked around his entrance, pulling on the plug until his hole was stretched around the widest part of the toy, only a little narrower than Eddie's fat cock.

His gaze met Eddie's in the mirror, and they held, a red flush staining Will's cheeks from the attention. "I love that blush." Eddie smiled at him and licked the part where the toy met his hole. Gently easing it out until he felt too empty, Eddie watched him and slowly pushed forward, fucking him with the toy. Stretching him and hitting his prostate dead on every time. Will's orgasm was inevitable, rising up like the tide under the moon's control. But Eddie watched him closely, backing off every time Will gave him some telltale cue, giving him enough of a break that Will came down from the precipice.

Eddie bent over more, sticking his arse out to lick at Will's cock and balls, sliding the toy in and out even slower.

"Eddie," Will begged, unashamed of the need pulsating through him. "Please."

A smile as bright as the sun emerging from a solar eclipse greeted him, and Eddie licked down Will's cock, over his balls and right when he would have gone around the toy, he tugged it free of him and tossed it on the bed, jamming his tongue into Will's trembling hole. Will shouted, his pucker clenching around Eddie's tongue, trying to hold him there. Eddie soothed him, running his hands up and down the backs of his legs and over his arse. Soon he pulled free and shifted, licking up Will's spine until his groin was pressed against Will's arse.

Will shifted, trying to position Eddie where he needed him. Trying to impale himself on the younger man's cock. But Eddie held him tight, stopping him from getting the angle right. He closed his hand around Will's throat, not squeezing or even really gripping him, but it had the desired effect. Will surrendered to him, knowing that Eddie would look after him. He melted into the mattress, and Eddie hummed. "Open your eyes, Will. Watch me come inside you."

Will did, unable to tear his eyes away as Eddie straightened, gripped his cock and stroked, rubbing the tip against his stretched hole and spreading the lube he'd squirted inside himself.

The curve of Eddie's arse in those sexy as fuck tights and boots sent Will wild. He moaned when the pressure against his hole increased and his lover's thick cock breached him, stretching his ring. Watching them join together was the most sensuous, porn-worthy thing he'd ever witnessed. Will wished he had a camera, but the image of Eddie bottoming out in him without anything between them would be burned in his memory forever, especially when Eddie bit down on his lip and squeezed his eyes closed as Will clenched around him.

Slowly he moved, rolling his hips and deepening his penetration before pulling back and slamming forward again. Will shouted out, scrambling to brace himself, but Eddie didn't give him a chance. Pistoning his hips, driving hard and fast into Will, Eddie gave him everything he needed, and Will shouted out his release without even having touched his cock. Eddie slowed his movements but didn't pull out, giving Will a chance to come back into his body. Still impaled on Eddie's rigid cock, the gentle flexes of his dick made every sensitive nerve ending light up again. Will was still hard, still needy, and he gasped when Eddie pulled back and pressed into him again, deeper and slower. "Oh fuck," he breathed, wonder in his voice.

"Let's see how many times we can make that happen." Eddie shifted, and Will reached back, gripping the leg that Eddie was still balancing with on the bed and squeezed.

Eddie managed to wring another two prostate orgasms out of Will's sensitive channel before he pressed deep and moaned his release, every lean muscle twitching. Will felt every splash of hot cum inside him. His walls gripped Eddie's cock and milked him as Will's seed spilled from him, too, onto the pristine linen below. Exhausted, Will slumped forward, landing in a wet patch, but he couldn't move even if he wanted to.

Eddie tumbled forward, dislodging himself from Will and making both of them groan. He instinctively clenched, wanting to keep Eddie's cum deep within him. "Eddie," Will moaned. "I need...."

Eddie propped himself on his elbow and leaned into Will. "Anything."

"Want to keep you. Inside me." He flushed, his cheeks heating as the request tumbled out of his mouth, and he buried his face in the pillow underneath him.

"You want my cum to stay inside of you?" Eddie whispered, running a hand down his flank to his arse. Will nodded tentatively, and Eddie moaned, shivering beside him. His heat blanketed Will momentarily, their sweaty bodies sliding together as Eddie moved over him. He nudged Will's knee, and Will shifted, spreading his legs and moaning as Eddie rubbed the plug against his hole. "I'm gonna come inside you again tonight, Will." Those words... Will moaned and tilted his hips back, wanting to feel the stretch again. Working the toy into him, Eddie was gentle, shifting Will's arm until he could see his face clearly and watch every reaction. When it was seated in Will, he sighed and Eddie hummed.

"I missed you," Will said, just as Eddie blurted, "I love you."

Will's eyes widened, and he shifted to face his man. With a shaking hand, he ran his thumb over Eddie's cheek and stared at him open-mouthed. His brain short-circuited, the beautiful man before him rendering him speechless, but Will's heart took over, and he pulled Eddie towards him and kissed him slowly. His man opened to him, and Will touched their tongues together, gently caressing every part of him. When he finally found his voice again, Will nuzzled Eddie's cheek and smiled. "I love you too."

They didn't need to turn out the lights—they hadn't even switched them on. The light from the city was enough for them to see everything they needed. Will helped Eddie out of his boots, the tattered remains of his fishnets, and the underwear that had slipped most of the way down his arse in their session and pulled back the covers. Curling into each other, they slept, and when Will woke Eddie hard and wanting in the dark before dawn, Eddie pressed him onto his back and crawled between his legs, sliding into him and making slow love together.

TWENTY-ONE

Will

NINE MONTHS LATER

Will blew out a breath. Nerves jangled around through his system like acrobats on high wires, and for all the swoops and dips his stomach was doing, he might as well have been up there with them. He wanted to be sick, and it was getting worse as he watched people stream into the theatre for the final performance of the cruise.

Why are there so many people on board?

Eddie had been a performer on the ship for a year, and this cruise—the one around the South Pacific—had become special to them. They visited their beach every time they docked at Lifou, and when they'd been on leave, their travels together had continued. They'd seen some of Australia—road-tripping it up and down the east coast and into the red centre to see Uluru. He'd met Eddie's family in the UK and criss-crossed Britain to get a taste of thousands of years of history, gone hiking and mountain bike riding in New Zealand, and sailed around the Hawaiian Islands. In twelve months, Will's life had been flipped on its head, and he loved every minute of it.

This moment was one that deserved celebrating, and he was either insane and about to screw up magnificently, or he'd pull off the grand romantic gesture that Eddie deserved. Will wasn't sure which, and that terrified him. He hadn't been able to eat for two days, not since he'd feigned casual and asked Felice whether it was romantic or corny to go big on a first-anniversary celebration. He and Eddie would have a private celebration that night just the two of them, but Will took any opportunity to spend more time together.

Felice had worn a knowing smile when she'd dialled Katya, demanded an urgent meeting, then planned the most public and potentially disastrous gesture possible on a ship. Will had become their pawn. It was as if they were a tornado, and he'd been sucked into their vortex to be taken along for the ride. He just hoped that when he landed, it didn't bruise his arse too badly.

Apparently, they had faith in his abilities—Felice had heard Will's singing at the bridge more than once. He knew he wasn't great, or even good. He barely passed for okay, but what the hell, he was entitled to embarrass the shit out of himself; it was his fucking ship.

So, there he was, sitting in his nominated seat. It was the one closest to the aisle in the front row of the theatre. Wearing his dress whites, he stood out like a sore thumb, but he ignored the looks and the whispers and waited for the show to start. Eddie knew he was going—he always reserved that seat for Will—but he had no idea what was planned.

Will couldn't wait for the surprise.

They were going out with a bang. Eddie and Andrea were the lead dancers in the story, starting out as teenagers—the cheerleader and the metal head. Teen heartbreak, college romances gone awry, and a friendship that kept them going back to each other until they finally realized they were meant for one another. The show opened with Brittney's "Oops!...I Did It Again." The dance was angsty and fun and set the tone for the rest of the concert. Over-the-top costumes, sets, and lighting with special effects to match the spectacular dances, the passengers were always blown away.

A spotlight clicked on, lighting the microphone standing to the side of the stage. The audience hushed.

Katya, dressed in a long, red velvet dress, floated elegantly through the heavy black drapes and to the microphone, speaking into it. "Ladies and gentlemen, please take your seats. On behalf of all the staff and crew of the MV Dreamcatcher, we welcome you to our final performance of the cruise. Something incredibly special is happening tonight that has never been seen before. You are the privileged few who will bear witness to it. So, without further ado, please welcome the MV Dreamcatcher entertainers."

The audience clapped and cheered, but the stage remained dark.

Then an explosion of light and colour and noise, and Will was right back in high school walking the corridors with lockers lining each side and plaid uniforms. He watched as Eddie, playing the nerd, swooned after Andrea as she winked and wiggled her arse. Morphing into Wheatus's "Teenage Dirtbag," Eddie—dressed in 1990s grunge—took over, dancing the lead.

* * * * *

Ninety minutes later, a bead of sweat ran down Will's back between his shoulder blades as he wrung his hands and tried to breathe. The elephant sitting on his chest made it difficult.

The lights blacked out on the stage, and Will took his cue, standing up and climbing the steps to the stage. He fixed his hat on his head and nodded to the stagehands dressed all in black as they shifted the new set into place— a fair and a cute little Beetle that Eddie and Andrea would ride off into the sunset in a la Grease.

Will looked out among what he knew was a sea of faces hidden by the glare of the spotlight shining down on him. It made doing this a little easier. He blew out a breath and shook out his hands, closing his eyes and giving himself a pep talk.

He touched his hat, making sure it was still firmly in place, and waited for the first strains of the acoustic guitar. It was an entirely different song to what was normally performed, and Will hoped he wouldn't screw up the show too badly because of it. It was too late now, but both Katya and Andrea had waved off his concerns. Eddie would know to swap out the dance for another one they'd performed before.

A bewildered Eddie stepped out onto the stage, and on the opposite side, Andrea did too. He paused momentarily and looked at Will, a stunned expression on his face, and Will smiled.

Ever the professional, Eddie kicked into gear and moved towards Andrea. Taking a deep breath, Will closed his eyes and sang a song about wise men believing that only the foolish rush into love.

He sang to Eddie and Eddie alone, even though there were hundreds of people in the audience. With every note, every word, he got a little more comfortable. A little more confident. It helped that he couldn't really see the guests. Instead, he watched Eddie dance with Andrea, lifting her and twirling her around the stage in a ballet number that was completely different to the dance that normally closed out the show.

They were beautiful together, so elegant. It looked effortless.

Before Will knew it, he was about to sing the last few lines of the song. Turning to the audience, he motioned for them to sing as well, and they took the cue, a huge choir of fans joining him.

After the music cut out, Will sang the final line one last time and looked to Eddie, who was dipping Andrea. Will knew he was supposed to kiss her in that final scene as cables rolled the VW offstage, but he didn't. He hugged her instead, and that little gesture made Will ridiculously happy.

Will blew out a breath and turned to the crowd, who clapped wildly, whistling and cheering uproariously. He grinned and motioned to where Eddie and Andrea had exited the stage, clapping as he waited for the music to start again so the entertainers could come out for the final time, bowing and celebrating the end of another successful cruise.

It didn't happen.

Will stood there awkwardly, waiting. Instead of the scheduled music and pre-recorded voiceover, Eddie stepped out holding a microphone.

The crowd hushed instantly.

The theatre full of people faded away when Eddie's emerald green eyes locked on his. It never failed to send a familiar zing through him. Will smiled, his face heating as he suddenly felt shy in front of his man.

Eddie grinned at him, his smile happy, which sent butterflies flittering around Will's belly. Then his gorgeous man began singing. Eddie's voice was like melted caramel, warm and rich as it surrounded Will, while Eddie sang, repeating the same line Will had just performed from Elvis's famous hit.

Joy, euphoria, and something a whole lot sweeter rushed through Will. His heart flip-flopped, and those butterflies did loop the loops. Eddie stepped into his arms, and Will hugged him close, loving their bodies being pressed together. The cheering of the crowd faded into the distance when Eddie tilted his face up to Will's and smiled, the move taking his breath away. Their lips met in a soft kiss, and Eddie opened to him instantly. Sweeping into Eddie's mouth, Will was rewarded when their tongues met gently. Keeping it as chaste as a make-out session could be, he pulled back and rested his forehead against Eddie's, breathing in his cologne and that uniquely Eddie scent he adored.

"I love you," Will whispered.

"Me too. I love you too." Eddie pressed another kiss to his lips, pulled back and smiled at him then motioned for the side of the stage.

Will hesitated a moment and looked out to the expectant crowd. They were waiting for a proposal, but Will... well, he wasn't ready to give it to them. Time slowed and his heart pounded, racing instead of its steady thump, thump, thump. A split-second decision. Should he, or shouldn't he? Yes? He loved Eddie, more than anyone else in the world. He was his soulmate, the other half of his heart. But this didn't represent them. They were happy, deliriously so. Why would he go messing with things now?

Thump, thump, thump, a rapid beat.

It was now or never.

He looked to Eddie again and the warmth and love shining in his eyes nearly made Will's legs buckle. Beautiful inside and out. His brave, wonderful man. He wanted him by his side forever, to be the one to love Eddie. Maybe Will was being overly cautious. Maybe he was being reckless, but his decision was made. The answer was no. Proposing wasn't the right thing for them.

Will gave Eddie a quick nod, and Eddie winked, his smirk sassy as usual. Into the microphone, so that the whole crowd could hear, Eddie announced, "Captain William Preston." The audience clapped and cheered, and Will's heart settled, slowing its pounding. The tightness in his chest unclenched and he sucked in a breath. Had he been holding it the entire time? Lightheaded, Will pressed a kiss to his man's temple and breathed him in, before walking to the side of the stage hand in hand.

Music started in the background, loud and lively, and the entertainers ran out onto the stage, the announcer introducing them for a final time so they could take their bows. Will shifted, letting Eddie back into the limelight when his name was called. Eddie bowed and held his hand out, motioning for Will to join him. He did, entwining their hands and not letting go even as the curtain closed, and they exited the stage to go to the change rooms.

"Give me five, handsome." Eddie reached up and kissed his cheek before walking backwards into the change room, not letting go until the last possible moment.

It wasn't long before Eddie reappeared wearing the hot pink heels Will loved, silky black skinny pants rolled up above his ankles, and a pale pink scoop-necked blouse that was super soft to the touch. Will wanted to run his hands all over him and then touch every part of Eddie without the fabric in the way.

"I thought we might go for a drink," Eddie explained when Will stared at him for a little too long. Who could blame him? Eddie was gorgeous.

"Anything you want."

Eddie smiled and led him to the lifts, but instead of going down a level to the staff bar, he pressed the button for the top floor. Will knew instantly where they were going, and he smiled, loving the sweet gesture. They pushed through the door out to the executive deck they'd frequented many times since their first date. When the ship got too much—the people, the pace—they disappeared here for much-needed moments of quiet time together.

But instead of the simple layout of deckchairs on green Astroturf and a single string of fairy lights strung over the pergola-like structure, the deck had been transformed. Coloured lanterns hanging at different levels from the canopy of white-painted steel girders swayed gently in the breeze. A picnic rug was laid out on the floor, basket and all, with a chilling bottle of something sitting to the side. Thick cushions were piled up around the rug, making the small space look like a nest they could burrow into. A sheet had been pinned up, blocking the view of the deck from the helm. Will swiped his card against the lock, securing the door and preventing any unannounced visitors from intruding into their private moment.

Will wrapped his arms around Eddie and kissed him like he'd wanted to do all night, breaking apart only to suck in a much-needed breath of air.

"Let's have a drink."

Will followed him to the blanket, and they sat, Eddie motioning for Will to sit between his outstretched legs. But Will knelt before his man instead. "In a second." He pressed a kiss to his beautiful dancer's temple before grasping Eddie's hand and reaching into his pocket with the other. Will's fingers closed around the warmed gold and he gripped it, sucking in a breath. This time, his heart was steady. His palms weren't sweaty, and he was lightheaded for an entirely different reason, but having a moment alone with his man did it to him every time. "Eddie," he implored as he lifted his lover's left hand to his lips. When Eddie saw the ring and his eyes widened, Will smiled and pressed on. "I chickened out of doing this on stage. Not because I didn't want to, but because it wasn't us. Being up there on the stage is your thing, and you're fabulous at it. I love every minute I get to watch you. But it's not the two of us. This, here? This is us. Lifou is us."

Eddie smiled and shifted, moving to his knees too. He wrapped an arm around Will's waist and leaned in close, seeking a connection that Will was only too happy to give in to. They kissed, slow and sweet before Will pulled back and nudged Eddie's nose with his.

"You'll side-track me." Will smiled at his man but became serious again soon. "You make me happier than any man has a right to be. You've taught me what love really means and I'm head over heels in love with you."

Will slipped the simple square-edged band on Eddie's finger, a perfect fit. "I don't know whether this is a proposal, or a promise. Maybe more of a pledge. I don't need the vows or to be on stage. I just need you. What do you say? Me and you, together forever?"

Eddie bit down on his lip and smiled, his eyes shining with unshed tears and Will's heart somersaulted. "Yes, my handsome captain," he whispered, nodding quickly and reaching up to cup Will's cheek. Against his lips, Eddie whispered, "Always and forever."

Will wrapped him in a hug, needing to be closer to his man. He joined their lips, tasting and teasing Eddie's tongue with his own. Right there on the deck of his ship, holding his man and promising to love him for eternity, was heaven.

When they finally broke apart what could have been minutes or hours later, Eddie sat and patted the cushion between his legs. Will moved, sitting in the spot Eddie wanted him. He only waited for Will to still before Eddie wrapped his arms and legs around him, pulling him closer. Will slipped off the heels Eddie wore, massaging his feet between sips of the chilled champagne. At the groan leaving Eddie's mouth, Will reached up to capture his lips.

"Can't believe a year has passed since we first did this," Eddie whispered against Will's lips. "Best year of my life."

"Mine too. I can't wait to spend forever with you."

Eddie's hand went to Will's heart, and a smile lit up his face as he sighed happily.

"Happy anniversary, Eddie."

"You too, handsome." Eddie shifted then, straddling Will's legs and cupping his face as Will laid back on the pillows. He kissed Eddie again, smiling against his lips. The man atop him had chased away the loneliness residing inside Will. He'd wiped away the cobwebs in his heart with his laughter and love and had made Will adventurous again. Eddie lit up Will's entire being with the brilliance of the sun, bringing happiness back into his life where Will hadn't realized it was missing.

Their life together was fast and crazy. Every day was a roller-coaster ride, which ended when they fell into bed together, exhausted. But Will was up for embracing the thrill or screaming as loud as he could on the ride as long as Eddie was by his side.

They kissed, and Will slid his hands up under Eddie's shirt, expecting to touch smooth skin, instead finding another layer of soft material. Eddie pulled back and sensually inched his blouse up his belly, then over his head, letting it dangle in his fingertips. With every slow movement, pale skin against fine baby pink lace was revealed. Will licked his lips and groaned. There Eddie was, straddling him, his erection tenting in his silky black pants while a lace bodysuit clung to his leanly muscled body. Will walked his fingertips up Eddie's belly to the taut nipples peeking through the fine weave, then up over his shoulders and down his back. He followed the plunging backline, the lace disappearing into Eddie's pants, and Will's breath hitched.

His semi had thickened, hardening at the sight of the beautiful man before him. The man who Will knew loved him as much as he adored Eddie. "So fucking sexy."

Will pulled him down again, lining up their hard cocks, and kissed him as Eddie rocked. But soon it wasn't enough. As their clothes were peeled away and tossed haphazardly to the side of their cocoon made of blankets and pillows right there on the deck of the MV Dreamcatcher, Will knew fate worked in wonderful ways. When Eddie sank into him—lace bodysuit still firmly in place—and moved slowly inside Will, making love to him, Will knew that every winding path he'd followed, each decision, twist of luck, hard road and heartbreak, and every happy accident had worked together to bring him to this point. To bring him to Eddie.

Will gripped Eddie's arse, framed beautifully by the line of the lacy G-string plunging between his taut cheeks, and urged him to keep moving, gasping as sensation flooded him.

Later, when they lay in each other's arms, wrapped only in the blanket Eddie had spread over them, Will touched the ring on Eddie's finger and looked up to the sky. Among the million stars overhead, one flickered, winking at him. Eddie gasped and pointed, a shooting star streaking across the skyline. "Make a wish," he encouraged excitedly.

"I don't need to."

"Of course you do." Eddie playfully pinched Will's side.

"Star light, star bright—"

Eddie closed his hand over Will's mouth and lifted onto one elbow, sputtering out an indignant laugh. "Don't say it aloud!"

Will laced his fingers with Eddie's and rested their hands on his chest. "It doesn't matter whether you hear it or not, because you know what I'll wish for. You just gave it to me. Us. Together, forever. Just like this. A future where we live and love exactly like we've done over the last year."

"Oh, Will. I love you. I always will." Eddie kissed him then, and Will rolled, covering Eddie's body with his bigger one. He whispered the words back to him and kissed a line up his throat. They made love long into the night, watching the dawn of the sun light up the sky. When the twin cliffs marking the entrance to Sydney Harbour greeted them, they dressed and padded down to their stateroom hand in hand, greeting the day exactly as they would for the rest of their lives. Together.

They'd navigated choppy seas and chartered a course into waters where they could hitch their sails together and drift smoothly into paradise. The wind could take them anywhere; it didn't matter to Will. Whatever this voyage of life had in store for them was simply another adventure—one that Will would love, because all that mattered was the knowledge Eddie would be by his side. Always.

The end

Thank you so much for reading Will and Eddie's story. I hope you fell for them as hard as I did. If you loved them, please leave a review.

Leaving a review—doesn't matter whether it's long or short—not only helps readers choose their next book but helps indie authors like me get the word out.

Thank you

Ann xx

ABOUT ANN GRECH

By day Ann Grech lives in the corporate world and can be found sitting behind a desk typing away at reports and papers or lecturing to a room full of students. She graduated with a PhD in 2016 and is now an over-qualified nerd. Glasses, briefcase, high heels and a pencil skirt, she's got the librarian look nailed too. If only they knew! She swears like a sailor, so that's got to be a hint. The other one was "the look" from her tattoo artist when she told him that she wanted her kids initials "B" and "J" tattooed on her foot. It took a second to register that it might be a bad idea.

She's never entirely fit in and loves escaping into a book—whether it's reading or writing one. But she's found her tribe now and loves her MM book world family. She dislikes cooking, but loves eating, can't figure out technology, but is addicted to it, and her guilty pleasure is Byron Bay Cookies. Oh and shoes. And lingerie. And maybe handbags too. Well, if we're being honest, we'd probably have to add her library too given the state of her credit card every month (what can she say, she's a bookworm at heart)!

In 2019 she was an Award-Winning Finalist in the Fiction: LGBTQ category of the 2019 Best Book Awards sponsored by American Book Fest for her story In Safe Arms.

She also publishes her raunchier short stories under her pen name, Olive Hiscock.

Ann loves chatting to people online, so if you'd like to keep up with what she's got going on:

Join her newsletter (you'll get two free books!):
https://landing.mailerlite.com/webforms/landing/d8
m4r2
Like her on Facebook:
https://www.facebook.com/pages/Ann-
Grech/458420227655212
Join her reader group:
https://www.facebook.com/groups/1871698189780
535/
Follow her on Twitter and Instagram:
@anngrechauthor
Follow her on Goodreads:
https://www.goodreads.com/author/show/7536397.
Ann_Grech
Follow her on BookBub:
https://www.bookbub.com/authors/ann-grech

She'd love to hear from you directly, too. Please feel free to e-mail her at **ann@anngrech.com** or check out her website **www.anngrech.com** for updates.

ANN GRECH'S BOOKS

RULE OF THREE

Three Hearts (MMF)
Yes, Captain (MM)
Triple Beat (MMF – coming 2021)

UNEXPECTED

Whiteout (MM)
White Noise (MM)
Whitewash (MM)

MY TRUTH

All He Needs (MMM)
In Safe Arms (MM)

PEARCE STATION DUET

Outback Treasure I (MM)
Outback Treasure II (MM)

SPINOFF FROM PEARCE STATION

Three of Us (MMF)

STANDALONES

Home For Christmas (MM)
The Gift (FMMM - free for newsletter subscribers):
https://bookhip.com/QPNLBF
Take Two (MM — free for newsletter subscribers):
https://dl.bookfunnel.com/dzltn5qzyt

M/F TITLES

One night in Daytona
Ink'd